MW01138644

DEDICATION

This one is for my Godsons Lars Sorenson, Trever Sebring, Preston Wallace, Gabe Hirsch and Keaton Sebring who were the inspiration for this book. Always remember no matter how big you get, I can still whip all of you though maybe now it would just have to be one at a time. With a month off between.

Special thanks to Betty Stein, Sheryl and Dave Krieg, Richard McIntyre, Rich and Lisa Griffis, Mike and Laura Stuckey and Angel Knuth.

Almost every name of there characters in this book comes from the generosity of friends who donated to my campaign when I took part in the 2011 Muscular Dystrophy Association's Lock-Up. Either they or their children have their names scattered throughout the book. Thank you to all!

I'd also like to thank my Big Brothers/Big Sisters Lunch Buddy Max Curry who luckily talks a little bit more than the character named for him in this book. So does this year's Lunch Buddy, Logan Carter. Somehow, both have learned to become huge cheaters at Uno. It's a fantastic program I would encourage everyone to consider participating in. You can't beat the rewards for 90 minutes a week.

MORE BOOKS
BY BLAKE SEBRING

Tales of the Komets

Legends of the Komets

Live from Radio Rinkside with Bob Chase

The Biggest Mistake I Never Made with Lloy Ball

The Lake Effect

Homecoming Game

Fort Wayne Sports History

Lethal Ghost

On to the Show (coming in 2018)

Available at blakesebring.com

CHAPTER 1
JUNE, THE PRESENT

"Time out! Time out, Ref!" I yell.

I didn't want to use our last time out, but five seconds are all that remain on the clock so I have no choice. My team trails 8-6, and we are down to our final snap on our opponents' 25-yard line. Normally in this situation, the coach sends out the field goal unit, but our kicker can't kick the ball 5 yards. That might be because he's only 8 years old.

This is the wind-up day of the UC-Camarillo Thunderbolts football camp and after four days of drills and teaching and encouraging (mostly it's like herding cats, actually), we're down to the final play of the day's last scrimmage. The two-a-day sessions ended with our awards ceremony this morning, and then the kids play games in the afternoon with one of the college players as a teammate in seven-on-seven contests.

They love these games because it makes them feel like they are part of our team. Plus, they can show off what they have learned all week to Mom and Dad sitting in the stands. It can be a chore for the varsity players, but you forget that pretty quickly when looking at the kids' faces. Everybody is smiling and happy and excited like it's the last day of school before Christmas. It's easy to suck energy from the munchkins.

Plus, these kids are the only people who can talk more than me.

Since I'm the Thunderbolts' senior quarterback, I'm everybody's favorite player and I've already played in five of these games today and have a 4-1 record. My opponent this time is "Big Dummy" Jordan Eichorn, UC-Camarillo's starting linebacker who can run like Michael Vick, hit like Dwight Freeney but is as smart as a puppy. Eichorn has so far dominated the scrimmage, forgetting we are supposed to let the kids be the stars. He probably figures the kids on his side are happy because they are winning.

The point is, the kids are supposed to be the ones dominating, and we are supposed to play a supporting role.

"It's hopeless, Lars," center Kenny Wiegmann says to me on his way back to our huddle after "Big Dummy" knocks down my pass.

"No, it's not, Kenny, because I've got a trick or two left. It's never over until the clock runs out. You wanna hear my trick? Then everybody huddle up."

All the players look at me, a few reaching up to grab their facemasks and shove them up so they can move the helmet back and see me. Finding the correct size helmets for 8-year-olds is pretty tricky. Even though I'm kneeling down, some of them are still looking up at me.

"Any of you guys hear of 'the cheese touch' play?" I ask.

"You mean like from 'Diary of a Wimpy Kid?' " Hunter Sosenheimer says. He's one of three brothers on my team and loves playing sports even more than video games. Yes, he's that one kid in this generation. He even reads books. Someday he'll be my boss.

Wearing pads, all the kids look the same, but luckily, their names are written on masking tape across their helmets so I can tell who's who.

"That's right, Hunter. We only use this in the most dire situations, though. Like touching the cheese, it's a last-ditch, miracle play that can end in disaster."

"Like a Hail Mary?" Cole Foreman asks.

"It's better than one of those, Cole, but everyone has to trust me and do exactly what I tell you to, OK? Can you do that?"

Everybody nods, and again, five kids move to shove their facemasks back up.

"OK, here's what we're gonna do. Kenny, how far can you snap the ball?"

"I dunno. Pretty far, I guess. How far do you need?"

"I'm going to line up like a punter so you have to snap it to me pretty deep. Hunter, you, Kedrick and Drake have been arguing like brothers all week..."

"Yeah, and Kedrick keeps getting us in trouble for it," Drake interrupts.

"Which is why this is going to work, and this time you won't get in trouble for it. Here's what we're going to do..."

After I finish explaining the play, we clap to come out of the huddle, I turn to the one referee – who just happens to be my buddy Max Curry – and tell him no matter what, don't blow the whistle until the play is really dead.

" 'Don't touch the cheese' is your strategy? Really?" Max says. "Lars, that hasn't worked the first four times you've tried it. It didn't work when we were 8 and we used to call it 'The Flubber play.' "

Before we started the second grade, Max's family moved to my hometown of Talbott, Indiana, and we became neighbors and quickly friends. Maybe it was because I talked a lot and Max never said much. Actually, I never really gave him much of a chance. Now he's my favorite wide receiver with the Thunderbolts and my roommate so I still don't give him much chance to talk.

"Shut up, Max," I say with a grin, "I'm working here. If this works, you cook dinner."

When everyone is lined up on both sides of the ball, I set up Hunter and Drake beside each other 3 yards behind the line of scrimmage on left end. Then I start my cadence.

"One Mississippi, SpongeBob is yellow, two Mississippi, Huckleberry Hound, Carmen Sandiego!"

Of course, the guys on the defensive side think this is hilarious, especially when I start waving my arms like the world's worst dancer, which there is little doubt I am. My favorite dance move is The Sprinkler where you put your right hand by your ear and then sporadically wave your elbow around in a halting motion like a sprinkler going off. At least everybody laughs at it intentionally instead of unintentionally at my usual dance moves.

I'm finally done stalling and yell "Hut two!" and Kenny's snap comes looping at my face with only a little bit of wobble.

That's when Hunter and Drake start yelling at each other as only brothers can. As they move toward each other and it looks like they are about to throw punches, on the other side of the line Isabelle Miller drops down to one knee on right end like she has slipped. Standing next to her is Kedrick Sosenheimer who turns to look at his brothers arguing in the backfield.

"C'mon, guys, this is getting old," Kedrick yells at his brothers. All week he's tried to play peacemaker with no luck. Someday he'll be Secretary of State.

"Butthead started it!" Hunter yells, but Drake immediately yells back, "I'm not a butthead, and I didn't start it! You did!"

Can you tell these guys are experts at this? It's a wonder their parents haven't thrown them into military school. Just as Kedrick approaches his brothers to step in, Hunter pulls back his right arm like he's going

4

to swing at Drake. I stop my dropback, visibly relax and flip the ball to my left hand and hold the ball toward the ground and stand up straight – just like the play has been blown dead for an offsides call.

As everyone else is looking at the Sosenheimer boys, Isabelle gets up slowly and starts skipping down the field. Everyone on the defense is standing up, hands on hips as if they think the play is over – as they are supposed to. I hold the ball in my left hand and look like I am trotting forward to interject myself into the situation and stop the Sosenheimer boys from really going at it.

"Hey you guys, stop fighting," I bellow. "Big Dummy" even falls for it, standing up out of his linebacker stance to start walking toward the line of scrimmage to break up the fight – just as Isabelle skips by him. "Guys, stop it!" he yells loud enough to be heard above the noise.

The whole situation with the brothers looks and sounds much more serious than it is. Because of his red face and killer glare, you'd swear Drake is about to snap and really throw a punch! For his part, Hunter just stands right there jawing at him, sticking his chin out as if he's daring Drake to let fly.

That's the whole plan. No one on this field knows I can also throw with my left hand. It's something I used to mess around with in practice during high school, but I have never thrown a left-handed pass in a game before. Maybe it's a leftover from my basketball days when I always worked on my off-hand dribbling and shooting, but it's also something that my best friend Max and I often goofed around with growing up. We'd play catch that way in the back yard when we got bored. We could always come up with a new game by making up rules for existing contests.

Now Isabelle is the key to the entire play. She's one of only five girls in the camp and the smallest player on the field, but her daddy is a booster so what the heck? These are 8-year olds and we are just having fun anyway. Though nobody knows that because she's a girl and all the boys pretty much ignored her all week, Isabelle is one of the best athletes on the field. Despite her size, she can run like the wind and she's one of the smartest kids around.

Once "Big Dummy" turns his head, she skips right by on his blindside and then takes off sprinting for the end zone. Even if someone turns their head to see her, there's no way they could catch up with her in time because she has a 15-yard head start – and again, she's really fast. As soon as I get to the Sosenheimers, I stop, lean back and flip the ball left-handed toward Isabelle who is wide open in the middle of the end zone. She's almost too wide open because I'm a little afraid of under- or over-throwing her. It's not the prettiest pass I've ever thrown, kind of a wobbling shot put actually, but it floats all the way there easily. Just like we taught her all week, Isabelle catches the ball in her stomach and gathers both arms below the ball.

Touchdown! And ballgame! We win 12-8.

She's not the only one who is surprised.

"Hey, wait a minute!" "Big Dummy" roars when he's finally able to close his mouth and turn back toward me. "That's cheating!"

"How?" I say back with a huge grin on my face. "What was illegal? Were we offsides? Just because you fell for it doesn't mean it's cheating."

Max, the referee, blows his whistle and signals touchdown so the game is over. By then, all the players on our team are running down to Isabelle where I pick her up and swing her around in a big hug.

"You did it!" I yell. "I knew you could do it. Nice job!"

Just like their pro heroes on TV, everyone is jumping onto me to form a puppy pile, slapping Isabelle on the head. Only problem is they never show the guy who ends up on the bottom of the pile getting the worst of it, and that's where I am, discovering that 8-year olds have very sharp knees and elbows. Plus, I have to kind of hold up the whole load so we don't crush Isabelle who is laying on the ground giggling.

Even the Sosenheimer boys' faces show big smiles, and maybe they are the happiest players out of all of the kids because they realize for once they aren't in trouble.

``You guys see how much fun you can have when you work together instead of fighting?" I say after climbing out from under the pile and tapping each of them on the helmet.

They just nod and then reach up to push their facemasks up over their grins.

CHAPTER 2
JUNE, THE PRESENT AND FIVE YEARS AGO

After telling the kids goodbye and giving out quite a few hugs, I hit the showers and then walk to my econ class. Because the fall is so busy with practices, travel and games, I try to take at least three classes each summer to cut into my workload during the season. I'm on schedule to graduate in May with a business degree. I always tell my dad I can't wait to only work 40 hours a week and I'm ready for a vacation. He just laughs and says, "Son, this is your vacation. Wait until you get a real job where you can't take a break between classes, there are no Christmas breaks and no spring breaks."

Maybe, but in some ways it has to be easier than this because I feel like I already have two full-time jobs, being a student and competing as an athlete.

As I walk into my apartment and sigh when I feel the air conditioning, Max looks up from the TV and points toward the answering machine's flickering red light.

"Is that Mikala?" I ask. She's my girlfriend of seven years.

"No, lover boy, that's Coach," he says. "He wants to meet."

"What did you do?"

"Me? Figured I was going to have to bail you out – as usual."

Max and I are such good friends we know neither of us is in trouble, but we also don't know what Coach Schebig wants, either, which is odd. He's the reason we came to UC-Camarillo and we're his two captains so we usually know what's going on ahead of time.

"I called his secretary, and she said we're meeting with him at 10 a.m.," Max said. "Mrs. Nation said she doesn't know what it's about, either, but he's been in a good mood so she doesn't think we're in trouble."

Usually, no matter how bad the situation, I can talk us out of trouble. That's the way it's worked our whole lives. I say it's a gift, but Max says it just allows me to push situations a little further after getting us into the spots in the first place. It's all perspective, I say, and so far we haven't gotten into any permanent trouble.

My talking was kind of a problem with my teachers early in life, but that's also why my parents got me started in sports. They got tired of having to listen to me all the time.

On a baseball team, I was the best in the world at chanting, "Hey batter!" I even did it for my own team a few times. I had to be the quarterback in football because there was no way I could stay quiet in a huddle. My grandma says I started babbling as a baby and just never stopped, while my father once suggested they hook a pump up to my jaw to provide a generator with some extra juice. The worst times of my year were my dentist appointments because I couldn't talk as much as I wanted to.

Max and I just seemed to kind of stick together in grade school and by the time we started playing junior high sports, we were lucky enough to be able to think alike which gave us a big advantage. Maybe we spent too much time together but we were always doing something. We made the varsity football team as freshmen and as sophomores I was the starting quarterback and he was my favorite receiver. By the time we were juniors, the team had a record number of players because we bugged everybody to come out. By then, no one could stop us as we won back-to-back state titles in the second-smallest division. We always wanted to play the big boys to see how we'd do but it was never an option.

Max kept running crossing patterns and I'd hit him in stride so he could take off. No cornerback could cover him, and we got rid of the ball so fast, no defensive lineman could get to me in time. As soon as defenses tried to stack the middle, Max would just turn north and I'd hit him on a fly pattern. That also opened things up for our teammates. Because most opposing coaches concentrated on running the ball, their defensives usually had no idea how to stop a passing game. Our fullback, Jim Huk, scored 20 touchdowns our senior t year because whenever we'd get the ball close, he would bulldoze into the end zone.

We set a few state records, including most completions and touchdowns by a quarterback and receiver combination. By the time we were seniors, our games were all played in front of huge crowds because everyone wanted to see if we were for real. Our numbers were a bit ridiculous, almost like video game scores, especially as we matured and played against younger teams.

We had a lot of fun. Because Max and I watched so much video together, we always seemed to see the same things at the same time in the defense. It just became an instinct. We didn't even have to check off or use an audible system because we just knew.

We also played basketball and baseball, winning regional titles, but we lacked the depth on our teams to win more state titles. Those sports were what we did for fun because we both loved football and wanted futures there. We finished up with all kinds of records and a 37-1 mark over our last three seasons on the gridiron. We were the team captains, mostly because Max was the one person on the field who could shut me up. We were also the hardest-working players on any team we played for.

The biggest question we faced all senior year was where we were going to play in college, which was a little bit of a problem. Everybody in town was pulling for us to go to some big school together, and we both had good grades, but there were other intangibles we didn't have. Max is super-fast, but he's only 5-foot-9 and 175 pounds. I have tons of passing records but I'm 6-0, 185 pounds. Maybe because we were shorter than most of them, that made it easy for college coaches to overlook us. We were also from a small town and a small conference. In other words, we were not exactly major college Midwest Conference material. Everyone in the college game figured we'd get buried behind bigger players or we'd waste a scholarship by never getting to play.

But we thought we deserved the chance, though even a strong showing in the state coaches association all-star game didn't get much interest. Maybe we were naïve, but Max and I aren't stupid so we never expected to use college as a stepping stone to the NFL, and we simply wanted to see if we could compete on the big-time college level. We weren't cocky or unrealistic, but we were stubborn in a good way. We'd had a handful of offers to NAIA or Division III schools, but we had a bigger school in mind, one we'd always dreamed of playing for.

We had grown up rooting for Indiana Western University and legendary coach Mike Burgess, listening to their games on radio while we recorded them on the TV. We also went to two or three games a year with our dads. IWU wasn't the second or even the third-most popular school in the state, but the Sagamores were our favorites and we were loyal, maybe because we always saw them as the underdogs.

After the all-star game that June, we met with coach Burgess, and he was definitely honest with us, maybe too honest.

``Boys, I don't think you can make it here," he said. ``I'm sorry, but I'd rather be straight with you up front than have you come back here in three years complaining that I'd lied to you or led you on by promising you this or that. I think you'd be better off going somewhere else to play in a smaller division where you could start earlier in your careers and have a good time playing as well as learning."

He was basically saying this was big-boy football and we weren't big enough boys. The one big thing we both possessed, though, was bullheadedness. We were just a little too stubborn to take that as his final answer.

"But, Coach, here's how we see it...'"

The only reason we got a meeting with Coach Burgess was because he knew us. Max and I had been attending Indiana Western's football camps since we were in the fifth grade. When we reached high school, our team used to take part in IWU team camps, setting up our offensive and defensive systems there early each summer before we switched to position camps. We even worked as coaches the summer before our senior year, helping out the little kids after our camps were done for the day. We knew the Indiana Western campus as well as we knew our own backyards, and our high school coach, Anthony Snuff, was on a first-name basis with Coach Burgess. Because we had been to all the camps, we also knew every recruit the Sagamores had coming in on a first-name basis. We knew what they could do, and we thought we knew what we could do.

"We're not asking for a scholarship, Coach," I said. "All we're asking for is the chance to walk-on. We want to see if we can stack up. We're not expecting to play right away or maybe ever, we just want to see if we can do it. We're not going to gripe about being treated unfairly. You know us better than that. If we come back here a year from now, and you say we're wasting your time, we'll shake your hand, thank you sincerely and move on with no complaints. We just want to see if it's possible. We won't cost you a scholarship."

"Boys, you have no idea how difficult this is going to be. You're too small, Lars, and you're too slow, and Max, if you were four inches taller I'd take you in a heartbeat. You two aren't stupid; you know how you stack up physically, so why do you think you can do this? Convince me."

"We don't know but we want the chance to find out," I said. "We're not rich kids who are using our dad's influence and money to force you into giving us a chance. We're not begging. We're not idiots who don't have a clue what we're in for, but we also don't want to have any regrets 20 years from now. We don't want to be the guys always wondering if we could have done it. If we see we can't compete early on, we'll step out of the way and it won't cost you anything.

"We just want the opportunity. We respect you enough to know the worst thing that could happen would be for us to waste your time, and we promise that won't happen. We'll be in such good shape and work so hard you'll be able to use us as whipping boys or examples, whatever you need. You need someone to use as an example for something you are trying to get the whole team to understand, we're your men."

Coach shook his head and said he wanted to think about it some more.

"You boys realize you'll be buried so far down the depth chart you'll never even see me, and your position coaches won't want to waste time on you because there will be others who will be playing they need to concentrate on. You'll be nobodies to everybody else on that practice field, even the trainers and the managers. You'll be practice fodder. Everyone will hate you because they'll see you as threats to their position and playing time, and nobody wants to get beat out by a walk-on.

"What am I going to do with you two?"

"Whatever you want," Max said. "That's our point."

As usual, Max always says a lot with a few words. Maybe that's one reason why he's such a good leader.

By the time we walked out of Coach Burgess's office, we felt like we'd made our case, but didn't know if it was enough to sway his decision. We'd been calm, direct and assured, stressing that Coach Burgess knew us and knew what kind of men we were as well as players.

It was still a very long few days waiting to hear from him. We tried not to get our hopes up, and the longer we had to wait, the easier that became. My folks tried to reassure us by saying Coach was probably taking his time trying to think of an excuse to keep us.

We must have done OK, because five days later he called to tell us we had the chance – one slim chance. The catch was that he would be the one to tell us early on if things weren't working. That was fair enough for us. We really had no choice but to accept it if we wanted any chance at all, and we desperately did.

So how did we eventually end up playing at UC-Camarillo? Playing at IWU turned out to be a dream come true for us – at least for a while.

CHAPTER 3
JUNE, THE PRESENT AND FOUR YEARS AGO

Still a little anxious, Max and I we walk into Coach Schebig's office at the Krieg Family Athletic Complex the next morning. For one thing, Coach is usually fishing in Montana for the whole month of June and is never in the office. Sure, sometimes one of us gets called in to talk to him, usually me for "leadership pointers," but this is only the second time in three years we've both been in his office together. The other time was when he asked us to take care of disciplining some teammates for breaking team rules. Whatever this is, something big is cooking, or as big as it gets for UC-Camarillo, an NCAA Division I-AA school of about 12,000 students.

``Curry, Preston, you guys having a good summer so far?" he says as he stands behind his desk to shake our hands. He's built like an old-time football coach, short with white hair on top, a little bit of a beer belly because he used to be an offensive lineman and stubby legs. He also wears glasses that are usually perched on the end of his nose to he can read play charts.

``Yes, sir."

``It's killing you that you don't know what's going on, isn't it?" he says with a grin. ``I'll get right to it then because I'm sure you're dying to know what's going on, especially you, Lars. Not knowing something around here must be driving you nuts."

I knew I was guilty of that, so I didn't say anything... for once.

``Well, boys, it's big. IWU called me last week..."

``Man, won't they ever give up and just listen to us?" I say with a little heat. ``Yes, we met with the NCAA and answered their questions about IWU, but we didn't implicate them in anything because we don't know anything. We were walk-ons who didn't know if anything illegal was going on. We weren't exactly high on the pecking order for rich alumni. For sure, nobody was trying to buy us off."

"Let. Me. Finish," Coach Schebig says through clenched teeth. "It's a good thing I like you, Lars, or I'd want to strangle you like everyone else."

"The line is long," Max says.

It's true. Because of the mutual respect I have for him, Coach is one of the few people who I can get along with. I'm an acquired taste, but we respect each other completely.

"This has nothing to do with the NCAA, though I hear that isn't going to go away anytime soon," Coach says. "They need a game. They were supposed to play Ohio Valley for their Homecoming game, but The Sports Network wants them to move it up to the start of the season so they can play on national TV in late-August to kickoff the season before Labor Day. With two bowl game winners from last year and potential top 10 teams for this year, it's a great payday for IWU so they can't turn that down.

"But you can't just reschedule a Homecoming date because all the alumni have already booked their flights and hotel rooms so they need a game. No one else in their conference has an open date for a road game, either, and their athletic director needs a payday. She doesn't think any of their fans would be too excited about a guaranteed win by pounding on a mid-major. Even though we're off most fans' radar, he thinks the three of us 'coming home' might generate enough media interest to build some hype for a crowd."

Wow! I knew what he had to tell us would be big, but I never expected this. After three years, I thought IWU was completely behind all of us. Maybe it never will be.

"You've got to be kidding," I say, hanging onto the chair arms to stay seated. "I can't believe Coach Jackson is OK with this. There's no way he'd want to see us again. He hates us and he'd have everything to lose by playing us."

Coach Wally Jackson, who ended up replacing Coach Burgess, is actually why all three of us ended up leaving Indiana Western and are sitting in this office, and it certainly wasn't because we all left voluntarily. There's a mutual animosity from both sides, including Coach Schebig. That's about as polite as it can be said.

"With Ohio Valley coming in with so many new starters, Indiana Western is favored to win the Midwest Conference this year, so he figures they're good enough that we're no threat," Coach Schebig says. "He thinks he can use us to fill his needs and his seats, and he just might be right. This game might sell itself. Think about it, you two are the hometown heroes who also helped end the losing streak against Lily so you're folk heroes there. People would come see you simply for the novelty of it. You were the conquering heroes, and now we're the enemy."

Neither Max or I say anything for a few moments, trying to understand everything at once. Mostly, we can't believe anyone from IWU would even consider the situation. I look at him, he looks at me.

"We are not circus freaks," Max finally says.

"Yeah, what would we get out of this other than being the oddities? We're Division I-AA, not even mid-major," I say. "I know we don't have any choice in this, but why should we consider this? I guess we should thank you for telling us ahead of time, but, really, what's the point?"

"You do have a say in it because we know you two would be the main attraction in this, and we're not going to accept unless you two are good with this. There are a few things to consider," Coach says, leaning back into his chair and starting to tap off the fingers on his left hand. "First, it would be the biggest game in Camarillo history. Second, Indiana Western is willing to give us a huge payday, which would really help the budget for next year, and cover all of our expenses on top of that. We'd also get to play on national TV for the first time because The Sports Network still wants to show the game, figuring it would have a great storyline because you are the returning heroes and all the national publicity this is sure to generate. We could use the money and the exposure around here, and it could help get you two some all-American recognition if you play well, though I know you don't care much about that.

"The other thing, and the most important to me, is it gives the rest of the guys on the team something to shoot for. It would be our eighth game of the season, so you know how dead that time of year is when everybody is tired and beat up. Everyone usually sleepwalks through practice for two or three weeks until we get closer to the playoffs. That won't be a problem with this game. We'll be razor sharp going into the playoffs.

"What do you two get? A free trip home. It's on our fall break so we could take the whole team back and spend most of the week there on IWU's bill. Your parents would love it. You could even go to Talbott's game the night before. Lars, you know Mikala would beat you around the ears if you turned this down. It would sort of be an early-Thanksgiving trip that we never get because we're always in the playoffs. It's all paid for and all we'd have to do is swallow a little pride."

It sounds perfect, but like your mother always says, if it sounds too good to be true, it always is. Somehow I feel like the pig who was invited to the luau.

Max and I just sit here. My gut reaction is "Heck, no!" Absolutely not. IWU didn't want us when they had us, and now they want us to come in and rescue them? No stinking way!

"Why should we even consider this?" I ask, trying to keep my temper under control. "I can see where Max and I could just say it's another game, and I know we have to play some big road games to help pay for the program, but Coach, how can you consider doing this? They fired you! They just knocked you off the staff like a cat lying on the back of a chair. They gave you no respect."

Coach leans forward in his chair to put his elbows on the desk and fold his hands.

"Because I'm past it," he says. "When you get to be my age, holding a grudge doesn't do anything for you except age you three times faster. I'm willing to be the bigger man about this, but the question is if you are."

"I don't believe that," I say. "I remember how hard it was for you back then. They never even gave you a chance. They didn't even hold the door for you; they just let you read in the paper you didn't have a job any more. I can't believe your wife is even letting you consider this."

"Teresa is OK with this because she supports me and knows how important this is to me. If I'm good with it, so is she.

"I understand you two have some hard feelings about this, I'm sure your first thought is to not even give this any serious consideration, but there's one other thing you aren't considering."

Max and I look at each other before Max says, "What's that?"

Coach leans forward, a twinkle in his eye and a smirk on his face before saying, ``What if we could win the game?''

CHAPTER 4
JUNE, THE PRESENT AND FOUR YEARS AGO

Now I know for sure Coach hasn't thought about this enough.

``C'mon, Coach, there's no way! They are favored to win the Midwest Conference this year! They've got 17 starters back from the team that crushed Northern California in the Tulip Bowl. Even as good as we think we can be this season, we're a Division I-AA team and we'd have no chance. We'd get slaughtered, which is exactly what they want. What if somebody gets hurt a couple of weeks before the playoffs? Why take the chance on blowing up our whole season to do a favor for them?"

``Well, there's certainly no way it can happen with an attitude like that," Coach Schebig says. ``I can't believe you guys are the underdogs who somehow found a way to beat Lily."

He has a point there.

There was a time when no one else could believe it, either, even Max and me. I guess we were just too dumb to know any better.

When we started our freshman season at IWU, we were so far down the depth charts we needed to climb a 20-foot rope just to be in danger of getting a paper cut. There were five quarterbacks ahead of me, the starter, the back-up, the emergency back-up and two highly recruited freshmen who were supposed to sit out a redshirt season. They were all at least 6-foot-3 and 200 pounds and could throw the ball 50 yards on a line about eight feet off the ground.

Max was in the same situation, except there were 10 receivers and all were just as fast as he was and had longer reach and shoulders like the bumpers on heavy-duty pick-up trucks. They would have made great power forwards on the basketball team, were the best athletes we'd ever seen in person – and they were only about average for the Midwest Conference that year.

Because we were walk-ons, on picture day we were in the group standing behind the freshmen class, and we were the entire group of walk-ons. The photographer didn't even waste time taking our picture. We wouldn't be included in the football yearbook or the game programs that were sold at the stadiums. We didn't care because we were on the team – at least for a few days.

But we had two advantages, big ones, too. Because we lived close, Max and I spent every day that summer on campus, working out, attending meetings with coaches and making sure we were in the best shape of our lives. We could do as many push-ups as anyone on the team, run longer than everyone else and maxed out in the weight room as the best at our positions. We knew we only had once shot at this, and we were not going to give Coach Burgess an excuse to send us home.

Once practice started in early August, whenever they asked for a volunteer, we stepped forward. We'd try anything. A couple of times we even sneaked in and made them tell us to get off the field. One time we ran onto the field for the kickoff return against the varsity, and Coach Burgess laughed and just left us out there. After I had nearly been destroyed by the blocking wedge, Max made the tackle on that play, but we got the job done. I got hit so hard, it's amazing my shoelaces stayed tied.

We just wanted one play to have a chance to show what we could do, but we never knew when that one play might happen.

We hustled everywhere, anticipated whistles and always gave maximum effort. We even ran to and from the water wagon. We were always standing around the coaches on the sidelines, hoping for a chance that they'd see us when they looked around for new bodies to send in.

When practice was over, Max and I would stay late to make sure the field was cleaned up. Yeah, there were managers to do some of that, but when we'd told Coach Burgess we'd do anything, we meant it. We also developed a bond with the managers and trainers who started to give us a little encouragement during practices. When no one else would say hi to us, they always said, "Nice play!" whenever we did anything right.

The other big advantage? Because Max and I have been such long-time fans, we had watched every IWU game for years, and we knew the plays and the systems as well as if not better than the starters. We just needed to learn some of the terminology. We had watched tons of video so we knew exactly what the tendencies were for the offense and the defense. We even used to turn the TV volume way up so we could hear what the quarterback was calling and we'd write it down and then see what happened on the next play. We had a library of IWU tapes going back five years in my living room which we had studied all summer.

A couple of times, we even used IWU plays in our high school games. Remember how I said Coach Snuff and Coach Burgess were on a first-name basis? Coach Snuff had a copy of Coach Burgess's playbook and we memorized every page of that thing, making up quizzes for each other to test ourselves. We had to be the best-prepared freshmen on the field, at least mentally.

Physically, no matter how much we had worked out, we still needed to adjust. We hung in there, and that's really all that can be said about the first few weeks. Every freshman was expected to live with the hazing from the upperclassmen and just stay out of the way as the real players got going. Since they were used to being the stars of their high school teams, some of the freshmen had a hard time getting used to college practices, especially when it came to keeping their mouths shut. Max and I never had that problem. Oh, I still talked constantly. I just made sure it was positive chatter.

We learned everything we could, kept working hard and moving quickly. Every time we got tackled or hit in any way, we made sure to immediately jump back up. We didn't want to get noticed for the wrong things.

I can't ever remember being as tired and sore as I was that summer, but I never showed a hint of either during practices. I'd go home between practices and nap, eat and drink something quickly and head back for more punishment, making sure we were always the first ones into the locker room. I slept great the entire month.

The one place we made our mark was in the end-of-practice wind sprints. The starters were mostly dogging it every day, putting out just enough effort to get through without getting yelled at, but Max and I sprinted hard every time, every rotation. Two days in, the seniors were cursing us, telling us to slow down and quit making them look so bad. We just kept running, even anticipating the whistle though we knew we'd finish first anyway. Three days in, everyone was trying to catch up. By the end of the week, they had given up.

Of course this drove defensive coordinator Wally Jackson nuts, but instead of yelling at everybody else to push harder, we became his tongue's favorite targets.

"How are you guys going to beat Lily when you can't even keep up with these two McLovin wannabes?" Coach Jackson screamed. He was the defensive coordinator and everybody hated him. He was so old-school, he'd drink coffee instead of water during practice on 90-degree days, and you knew he was just dying for a cigarette because his voice had a gravelly pitch to it. He didn't need to use a whistle because his bark could be heard two fields away. The older defensive players told us they hate his film sessions, saying he's merciless. He was maybe 5-10, but he could make 6-6 defensive ends cry.

Even though we were making his players work harder, he hated us more than anyone else. Every chance he got, he'd belittle us.

``Can't we get rid of these bums, Mike?'' he'd say to Coach Burgess. ``They're making everyone else look bad.''

``That's their job,'' Coach Burgess would say.

``I don't mind them working hard, but do you want these toothpicks setting the pace for the program? They're embarrassing!''

``Then get somebody else to step up and lead, Wally. Isn't that what a coach is supposed to do?''

That just made Coach Jackson even madder. Max and I never let up, from the pre-practice stretching all the way through practice. Once in a while we'd get onto the field for a snap or two, but always when someone got hurt or at the very end of practice. We really were practice fodder.

The longer we lasted, the stronger we got. After three weeks of practice, we actually were doing well enough that we fit in with our position groups. We weren't any bigger or faster, and we weren't moving up the depth charts, but we fought hard enough to earn some respect from our teammates.

We did OK, but we were still as shocked as anyone when they told us we were allowed to dress for the season-opening game.

``You've earned it,'' Coach Burgess said. ``This is the reward for the hard work you've done so far. Of course you're still not going to get to play, and I can still jerk those uniforms away from you at any time, but keep it up. I'm impressed with how tough you've been so far."

And we thought he had forgotten our names because he had never said anything to us during practices.

We were still so far down on the depth chart that we had to share numbers with older players who were actually playing, but I can't tell you what a thrill that day was. Our folks drove in for the game and got to watch us warm up and then stand on the sidelines for three-and-a-half hours. Max actually got onto the field once. When a fellow receiver suffered a knee injury in the third quarter, Max ran out to help carry him off. Afterward our folks took our pictures wearing our green, gold and black jerseys. We had photographic proof that we were part of the team, and whatever happened, they would never be able to take that away from us.

IWU won big that day, but no one seemed too excited. Even though the Sagamores were picked to finish in the lower second division of the Midwest Conference, the early-season schedule was soft enough to have the consistency of a soggy diaper. The school needed the home games to pay the bills, and the football team needed some easy wins to build confidence before the conference schedule. The school was happy, but none of the fans were too satisfied, and really, neither were the players. I never thought I'd ever be part of a team that didn't celebrate a win.

"We're supposed to win these games, Preston," starting quarterback Donny Black told me. "They're about getting us ready for the league schedule. The most important thing is that no one gets hurt."

Because the next game was on the road, Max and I didn't travel for that one, but that gave us a chance to go home to Talbott that weekend. None of our friends could believe how built up we were, and they all treated us like we were rock stars at the high school game that Friday. I was glad to see Talbott win, and the next day, along with members of our families, we watched on TV as the Sagamores got beat handily by our in-state rival to the north.

Though the season was only two weeks old, Coach Burgess was feeling pressure. He was in his 10th season at IWU, and after some early success, things had started to slide back to the way the program had been performing before he got here. When he first came in, no one in the conference was throwing the ball so his style was new, radical and fun. He was the one team every other school had to prepare for differently. A trip to the Tulip Bowl during his third season raised expectations tremendously, but most years the Sagamores struggled to finish .500, and they always lost to Lily to end the season, seven years in a row, the longest streak in school history. Though none of the team members talked about it, everyone knew he needed a big year for a contract extension or at the very least a .500 record with a win at home over Lily at the end of the season.

We could tell after the third game that wasn't going to happen, though. Lexington came in and drilled us in our last non-conference game before Wisconsin State opened the league schedule with a 20-point win. Worse than the games were the practices where some starter seemed to get hurt at least once a week. The starting quarterback broke his throwing arm, and then his back-up broke his leg the next week. The emergency back-up was a sophomore who had never taken a live snap in college, and he looked it. Instead of using Coach Burgess's air-it-out style, the offensive coordinator, Coach Schebig, had to go conservative and emphasize the running game. He had no choice because we were too inexperienced on defense to survive any turnovers.

As the losses kept coming, the weirdest things kept happening. Two receivers were declared academically ineligible and another was kicked off the squad for breaking team rules. Then our top receiver tore his hamstring against Minnesota Tech. This season was turning into a disaster. We were competitive for about a half each game, and then our opponents would wear us down in the second half and pull away.

Max and I got our chances, but not the way we wanted to. Our record was 1-6 heading into a game at Nebraska A&M when Coach Burgess named me the back-up quarterback because the two prized freshmen recruits finally admitted they didn't know the plays. Coach also didn't want to waste their red-shirt seasons by possibly playing them so late in the year in what obviously were going to be meaningless games. Truthfully, they were meaningless players who'd always had it too easy and had no idea how to work hard.

While they had been useless in practice, Max and I were driving Coach Jackson crazy with our play on the scout team. For two days each week we'd get a list of plays our upcoming opponents used and then we'd have to run them for the first-string defense. We couldn't beat the starters, but we made sure everybody on our side of the ball was having fun and giving it their best effort. We'd make up plays in the huddle and then sometimes throw long just to see what would happen. Sure, we'd run the upcoming opponents' plays for the first 10 or so, but then we'd mix things up with something new. A couple of times Max and I would make eye contact and he would take off.

``What in tarnation was that?'' Coach Jackson screamed at us one time. ``They don't run that play!''

``They might,'' I said, trying not to laugh out loud before Max got back to the huddle.

``Just run the plays we tell you to run or you're out of here!''

``Yes, sir.''

All that did was make the scout team laugh and pull together even tighter. We were like our own little squad within the team, except we were having a better year. The bright spot for Max and me was that after a few players got kicked off the team and out of school, we were placed on scholarship. We were humbled and honored, though Coach Burgess warned us it was not guaranteed for next year. No scholarship is, though. That's how new coaches are able to come in and create openings for all their new recruits. They just don't renew scholarships for existing players, and there's nothing the players can do about it.

Max actually got to play against Illinois Southern, even catching a pass on an inside screen. He dodged one tackler and was able to drive forward enough for a first down. He got to keep the ball as a souvenir.

Though we kept getting killed, I never saw the field. Coach Burgess just said if the season was lost, he wanted to get sophomore Mason Parker as much playing time as possible to develop for next year. Mason was a lefthander, about 6-foot-4, and he had some spirit. The girls all loved him. I liked him, too, and respected how hard he worked and how quickly he learned.

I was now the back-up, but I still had to run the scout team, which meant Coach Jackson's defensive players sometimes got a free shot on me. There was a bunch of younger players backing up the starters that Coach Jackson was trying to meld into a unit he called "The Green Monsters" because our colors were green, gold and black. They had nothing to lose, so they'd play dirty, hit us late and do whatever they thought would work to try intimidating us. Freshman Andrew Crow, in particular, liked driving around the end on my blind side and drilling me in the back with his helmet. With no referees in practice, there were no personal fouls, and Coach Jackson loved it, laughing whenever Crow would just stand over me and grin while I tried to roll over like a fish on a bank.

"Now c'mon, Andrew, you know he's wearing a red jersey for a reason," Coach Jackson would "scold" him.

"Sorry, Coach, I just want to play so badly and show what I can do that I forget," Crow said. "Here, let me help you up, Preston."

I was lying there thinking, "Yeah, so you can get another cheap shot in?" except I still didn't have the breath to say it. A couple of my teammates shoved Crow away.

Finally, one day I'd had enough and we pulled out a special "play" for Mr. Crow. We started an option away from his end until I pitched the ball to the running back and turned the other way. The running back then pitched the ball to Max cutting behind on a reverse. The left side of the offense line all turned and joined me in charging Crow who had his head down, thinking the play was going the other way. He never saw us coming. Even Max joined in as five of us hit him head on, leading with our helmets. Crow went down like he had been tasered.

"Nice tackle, Crow," I said as I got up. "Here, let me help you up." He just moaned.

"What's up with that!" Coach Jackson roared. "That's bush league! End of scrimmage! You guys get out of here before I kill you!"

"Sorry, Coach," I said. "We just want to play so badly and show what we can do that we kind of forgot what was happening."

Turned out Crow was fine, but he was done for that week of practice because of a slight concussion. He came back later in the year to get a little bit of playing time at the end of the season, but he didn't take any more cheap shots on me in practice. He never even said much to me.

That didn't mean the cheap shots ended, though. Another day a few weeks later, middle linebacker Duncan Welker thought he'd get cute. When our tight end Arne Sorenson went over the middle on a route, before I ever threw the ball, Welker stuck his arm out and nailed Sorenson with an elbow to the chin to knock him out. I didn't even throw the ball before I got in Coach Jackson's face.

"That's garbage, Coach, and you better take care of it before I do!" I screamed.

"What are you talking about?" he said with a grin.

"Fine, then I'll handle it," I said as they helped Sorenson from the field. "Huddle up!"

Everybody came back and nobody said a word – except me.

"That's ridiculous and we will not stand for it. If they want to play dirty and take out one of our guys, then we'll play that way, too. We are not standing for this! Period!"

I could tell the guys in our huddle were a little shook at how hot I was. I slowed down to take a deep breath.

"We're not going to do anything on this play because he'll be expecting it, but after this play everybody get back to the huddle fast."

With most of the defense bunched toward Welker, we ran the fullback up the middle on the next snap. Nothing happened, but my guys all hustled back. It was third-down and 15 yards to go on our own 20. A perfect blitz down.

"OK, maybe now they'll be a little more relaxed. Here's what I want to happen..."

I lined up two receivers on each sideline and then I sent my tailback in motion to the left. Basically the other two linebackers had to split out away from Welker to cover the tight end and tailback. That left five offensive linemen and me, a perfect target for an all-out blitz.

When I caught the snap, I saw everybody coming at me, "The Green Monsters" looking to bury me because all of my offensive linemen let them slide right by with a clear path. As soon as they were two steps away, I tossed the ball to the middle of the field like an alley oop right at Welker – and then I hit the dirt facedown before I got killed because there were five defenders standing around me.

But I wasn't the one who was getting smoked on this play.

Welker's eyes were only on the ball as he jumped to intercept it with arms extended. At the top of his jump, that's right when he got hit by everybody else on the offense that had all come running into the middle of the field. He never had a chance to protect himself as he got knocked back through the air about five yards, landing on his shoulders with his rear end teetering on a complete flip until his feet flopped back over to land straight out. Somehow, though he was probably unconscious, Welker held onto the ball.

Coach Jackson blew his whistle about 20 times in five seconds and came charging at me.

"That's it, Preston!" he barked.

"What are you talking about?" I said. "I didn't see anything."

"You can't pull that crap with my starters for goodness sakes!" he yelled.

"And they can't pull that crap with my players, either, or we will retaliate! If you won't do what you're supposed to, we'll protect ourselves. They'll never know when or who is coming at them."

"You can't talk to me that way!"

"I just did, would you like to continue this discussion with Coach Burgess? I'd be delighted because I'm not the one doing anything wrong here."

He kept scowling at me after that as he called off the rest of practice.

Though I know he never said anything to the defense, there were no more cheap shots on us. They kept talking about what they would do, but it never happened and they left me alone in the scrimmages. That was fine with me. I can talk with anybody.

I felt like the scout team had earned a little respect with our stunts from everyone except Coach Jackson. We were never going to be buddies anyway.

CHAPTER 5
FOUR YEARS AGO

The injuries and garbage kept piling up, and then the worst happened. The week before the Lily game, Athletic Director Madeleine Laird announced that Coach Burgess would not return next season. Then she surprised everyone by saying Coach Jackson would be his replacement.

Max and I knew that was the end for us because Coach Jackson would want to run the ball, and he hated us anyway. If he had his choice, and he would, every play would go between the tackles. That would help set up the defense, his pride and joy. There was no chance he'd have spots for Max and me or give us even the hint of a chance. Anyway, he'd want our scholarships.

Despite Coach Jackson's protests, the school agreed to let Coach Burgess stick around for the Lily game. Coach Jackson told everyone he thought that was the wrong way to go. Really? Here was the man who hired you and gave you a chance, a chance that was leading to your first head-coaching job, and you stab him in the back like that? That just gave every upperclassman more motivation because they loved Coach Burgess and hated Coach Jackson.

Because it was our big rival and Coach Burgess's last game, the whole team was fired up to play Lily. The Appleknockers had one of the worst nicknames in sports, but they were a quality program where winning eight games was a soft year. This year they were 10-1 and ranked No. 6 nationally and had already clinched the conference title. They were good, knew it, and their fans were quick to tell you if you had any doubts. Their fans aced like they were entitled to success. Everyone at IWU hate the Lily fans for their arrogance, but we also respected them and envied them a little.

No one gave us a chance, even our own fans. We were so beat up that most of the starting lineup was made up of sophomores and even a few freshmen. This was our last home game, but half the stadium would be filled with Lily fans, and there were still plenty of tickets available because our student body was all leaving for Thanksgiving break.

Then things somehow got worse. On the morning of the game, half the starters woke up with the flu, including the quarterback. We were already 20-point underdogs at home, but this seemed like it was just too much. Because two of our regular offensive linemen were injured and three more were sick, Coach Burgess changed his entire gameplan during the pregame meal. Instead of running the ball and trying to keep the score close, he decided we were going to throw it on almost every play.

"We really have nothing to lose, and that's how we're going to play," he said. "Mason, you've got to make the right reads and get rid of the ball quickly. Receivers, you've got to make the first guy miss and then make some plays. We're also going no-huddle, but we'll take every second between plays to let you rest. Can you do that, Mason?"

"I think so, Coach," Mason said. "I'm sick, but I'll give you what I can."

It turned out he couldn't give us much. Lily ran the opening kickoff for a touchdown, and then Parker was picked off on his second throw from scrimmage. He was looking right at the receiver the whole way, hesitated, and then threw it directly into the arms of their cornerback who ran it 30 yards for another score. After Parker walked to the sidelines, he threw up behind the bench.

Things just weren't working out.

"Lars Preston! Get over here!" Coach Schebig yelled. "Bring your helmet."

When I first heard him, I had to take a second to remember where my helmet was. While I sprinted over, Coach Schebig looked over at Coach Burgess who just nodded.

"You're going in," Coach Schebig said, putting his hand on my shoulder. "You've run the offense a hundred times so you know you can do it. Just relax and let the game come to you."

Relax? Yeah, sure. I was hyperventilating, flop sweating and could barely breathe, and all of a sudden my bladder had shrunk to the size of a peanut. An overflowing peanut at that.

"Uh, huh; uh, huh," I kept saying over and over because by then I wasn't hearing a word Coach Schebig was saying.

"Lars! Snap out of it!" he finally barked, bringing my eyes back down to his. "You've wanted this chance your whole life, right? Take a deep breath and take it! Look at it this way, if you fail miserably, no one will blame you. We're already getting killed out there, but if you can bring us back and at least make us competitive, no one will ever forget you. Just relax and have fun. Scrap the no-huddle, and I'll send in the plays."

Then he told me the first play was going to be a bomb.

"They'll never expect it after what's just happened, and I figure you're so pumped up you can throw it 80 yards."

"Uh, huh," I mumbled.

"Get in there!"

My head was so out of it, until I turned to jog to the huddle I didn't even realize Coach Jackson was throwing his hat onto the turf as he argued with Coach Burgess behind me. Everyone on the team could hear him, and I'm sure the TV cameras loved the spectacle. They always seem to love what happens on the sidelines more than on the field.

When I got to the huddle, I looked around at everyone and their faces showed they were as scared as I was. There's no way they could possibly have been, but they looked that way. Their faces all looked like they were 11 years old; they were busted and knew they were all in big trouble as soon as their father walked in the door about 10 minutes from now.

"Hi, guys!" I said, trying to muster up some energy. "Everybody OK? Everybody ready to have some fun?"

Then I realized this was basically the scout team I'd been playing with all year. Things had gotten so bad, we were the only ones left who could physically play, and none of us had ever been in a real college game before, just scrimmages where we were supposed to be the punching bags.

"Oh, great, we're getting our butts kicked and they send in Peter Cottontail," said Jerry Lyle, our center and only remaining starter.

For some reason, that was what relaxed me. Realizing I had to take control in a hurry, I snapped back, "Hey, hey, this is my huddle, so shut up!"

"All, I'm saying is..." Jerry tried again.

"No! Like I said, this is my huddle now, so zip it up!'

"But all I'm trying to say is...."'

"Time out, Ref!"

Fifteen yards away, the surprised ref just looked at me and said, "Are you sure, you just got out here?"

"I'm sure," I said, so he blew his whistle and waved his arms. "You've got one left."

By now the fans are losing what's left of their minds – and hope – and Coach Jackson is throwing his hat down on the sideline again. Those things sure are hard to break in.

After I walked over to Coach Schebig, I said, "I want Bob Brown in there for Lyle."

Now he looked like he was ready to swallow his hat.

"C'mon, Lars, Jerry's your only remaining starting offensive lineman. You're going to get killed out there," Coach Schebig said.

"I don't care. I want my guys out there. I want Big Bob. It's my huddle and I want who I want."

At that point, Coach Jackson couldn't hold it in any more, as if he'd been trying, and stepped up about two inches from my face.

"My God, Preston, you're a walk-on and now you're dictating terms? Get your butt back out there and run the darn team!"

I'd also had enough of him.

"Coach, I have one question for you – Which team are you on? Because it sure seems like you aren't exactly pulling for this one right now. Give me Big Bob and let's go!"

And with that I turned and trotted back to the huddle. About halfway out, Big Bob Brown our 325-pound scout team center caught up with me and said, "You sure about this?"

"Trust me," was all I said as we reached the huddle.

I called the play, and tried to walk to the line of scrimmage in a straight line. I didn't want anyone on the other side to see how nervous I was, but the defensive players were all chirping about fresh meat and time to pad their stats.

Because I couldn't remember what snap count I called for, but I just kept calling "Hut" until Brown snapped it. Then I dropped back right away and looked over the middle. Because Lily was an in-state rival, I figured their players all knew about the relationship I had with Max and how we grew up together. They had to be thinking I'd look to him right away out of sheer comfort – which is actually why Max was the decoy on this play, cutting inside as Jim Wallace was running right behind him until he cut upfield on a post pattern. I kept looking right at Max for about two seconds until Wallace got a stride on the Lily cornerback and I let fly with the bomb. Coach Schebig was right because they weren't expecting it, and Jim could fly. It looked like he had a chance on the play at about their 30-yard-line, but I had been too jacked up, and the ball landed about five yards past him.

"Man, that was close!" left tackle Randy Marcom said. "Almost!"

By the time everyone got back to the huddle, I was finally calmed down a little bit. Coach Schebig sent in the next play, but I ignored it. I had a hunch I wanted to try.

"Anybody want to run the same play again?" I said in the huddle, grinning as everyone's heads popped up. "This time, Max you cut upfield and head to the opposite post, and Jim, you're the decoy so you continue across the field."

"You're crazy enough that this might just work," Jim said.

"Maybe I am," I said as we broke the huddle with a clap.

This time, their two cornerbacks got tangled up over the middle and both followed Jim. That left Max one-on-one with the safety, a match-up I'll take any time. A split-second after releasing the ball, I got hit and was driven into the turf so I couldn't see what happened, but the crowd reaction let me know Max got to the ball and scored a touchdown. By the time I scraped myself off the field and shook the grass out of my facemask, everyone else on the offense was running 65 yards to pound on Max.

I was figuring Coach Schebig would be ready to kill me on the sidelines, but all he said was, "Nice audible." And then he grinned.

Coach Burgess and Coach Jackson were still arguing, until Coach Burgess finally stopped that.

"This is still MY team, Wally. You don't take over until after the game. Now back off! Go run your precious defense. Let's see how good they really are today."

They were fantastic. Despite giving up three more touchdowns, they allowed us to keep the game close. Even Crow and "The Green Monsters" made some big plays. We trailed 21-14 at halftime, but by then we all knew we had a chance. When a play broke down inside their 10-yard-line inside the final minute, I scrambled in for our other touchdown. Coming off the snap, I faked an outside pitch to our tailback B.J. Cowen who was running right behind the entire offensive line. The whole defense fell for it, and I kept the ball and ran left wide-open into the end zone.

Moord Stadium was as loud as it had ever been all season as we ran off the field for halftime.

CHAPTER 6
FOUR YEARS AGO

``Defense!" Coach Burgess yelled in the locker room at halftime. ``I'm proud of you. Keep it up. Offense, way to keep firing. Remember, we have nothing to lose, so keep going for broke. Leave it all out there so they will never forget us after this game is over! We can do this! We will do this!"

None of us were tired after that speech, and we got a huge, huge break when Max ran the second-half kickoff 95 yards for a touchdown. Tie game! He just sneaked in behind his blockers and was so small no Lily tackler could find him until after he crossed midfield, and by then it was too late. He must have changed directions four times and sort of looked like a basketball player with a crossover dribble breaking ankles. Lily's kicker was the last person with a chance at him, and Max turned him around twice before he corkscrewed to the turf.

By now, the crowd was going nuts, and suddenly Max and I were best friends with everybody else on the team. Guys who hadn't spoken to us all season were slapping us on the shoulders and helmets, yelling encouragement.

``Yeah, thanks," I said to one senior special teams player. ``Sorry, I can't remember your name."

It didn't matter because for the first time all season everybody was happy.

After our defense forced Lily to punt, I told Coach Schebig I wanted to go no-huddle again. They were on their heels, and I wanted to take full advantage by keeping them guessing. My first play was a slant pass to Wallace for 15 yards, and then Cowen raced left for another six. I noticed their middle linebacker was cheating toward Max's side before the next play, so I took one step back, faked a throw toward Max and tucked the ball to take off up the middle before the linebacker could get back into position. I got 10 yards before the safety dragged me down.

The crowd, finally our crowd, kept getting louder and more confident with each play, but they quieted down after the next play when Lily's left defensive end got around Marcom to drill me in the back. Luckily, I heard him coming and ducked just in time to avoid having my head knocked off.

"That's OK, Randy," I said as he helped me back up. "Did he come inside or outside on you?"

"He went outside, but it won't happen again," Marcom said.

"No, I want him to. Line up the exact same way, and Allen, you're going to go right through that hole with this pitch, but I'm going to flip it forward to you so you start by lining up on my right side."

We didn't have any kind of play like that in our playbook, the guys trusted me enough to try it, and it worked perfectly. After I pitched it forward to Cowen, I followed the rest of the offensive line to the right while he took off to the left. Their defensive end went wide again as Randy yelled "Ole!" and Cowen scooted right by him inside the hole. Everybody else on the Lily defense was following me as Max took out his cornerback with a chop block, and Cowen sprinted the next 30 yards to the end zone.

Sagamores 28, Appleknockers 21. We had the lead!

Not for long, though. Lily came right back on the next drive and scored in three plays to tie the game. Our defense was tired and we just didn't have the depth players left to fill in.

Then I got greedy and made a big mistake trying to get that score back all at once. I tried to hit Max with another bomb, but this time their safety didn't fall for the fake to Wallace and came over in time to pick the ball off at their 25 to end the quarter.

``My fault,'' I said as I got to the sidelines.

``That's OK, it will give them something to think about,'' Coach Schebig said. ``Keep your head up.''

This time Lily started running the ball, and we couldn't stop them. They held the ball for the next nine minutes by grinding it up the middle. Four times they shoved the ball forward and our defense back on third downs to earn a new set and keep possession. Coach Jackson finally called time out with the Appleknockers pushing inside our 30.

``C'mon, you guys can't be tired!'' he yelled at his defense. ``We've got to win this game!''

Trying to push the tempo, he called an all-out blitz on the next play, but their running backs picked up the extra men and their quarterback threw over the top to hit their tight end for a touchdown. Lily led 35-28 with six minutes left. The only good thing was that the offense was well-rested, and Coach Schebig and I managed to work out a few wrinkles. We were 80 yards away from a tie.

``What's the first thing they are going to expect you to do?'' he said.

``Throw to Max.''

``Right, so I want you to run the ball the first three plays.''

So we did. I faked a quick slant to Max, and then handed to Cowen for 7 yards behind Big Bob. Then he scooted around right end for 3 yards and a first down with five minutes left. On the third play, with everyone watching Cowen, I faked a long pitch out and then turned to run the other way on a classic bootleg. No one saw it coming and I gained another 10 yards before being shoved out of bounds.

We ran an old-fashioned option play next, and I just got rid of the ball to Cowen in time before the defensive tackle crushed me. After the play gained us 2 yards, I pulled the grass out of my ear hole. Then we ran the same play off the next snap to the left, and Cowen got 6. Third-and-2 at our own 48-yard-line with 4:15 left.

Figuring all the defensive players would be close to the line of scrimmage, I tried to get cute again, taking the snap straight back and trying to hit Wallace on a fly pattern down the sideline. The ball was there, but so was the cornerback who never fell for Cowen's fake dive over the middle and knocked the ball away at the last second. Our fans all groaned, figuring that was probably our last, best chance.

I never even looked over to see if the punt team was coming in because I wasn't letting them have the field.

"That's OK, we've got one down left," I said after pulling everyone into a huddle. "They're allowed to make a good play once in a while. Here's what we're going to do."

I moved everyone in tight to the line of scrimmage with just Cowen and I in the backfield. Then we waited at the line of scrimmage for the play clock to run down. When it hit five seconds left, I stepped forward to my left and pointed at something on that side of the defense as if to audible. Max, at left end, nodded his head as I yelled "Hut two!"

Bob snapped the ball directly past me to Cowen and we both headed for right end. Wallace took out the cornerback, and Marcom stood up the defensive end, which meant I had to get to the safety before he got to Cowen. Both of us lowered our heads at the same time, but he was taller so I had the lower center of gravity. It was a slobberknocker of a collision, but I moved him back a yard, which is all Cowen needed to run 5 yards to the first down.

``All, right! Let's go!'' Marcom yelled as everyone trotted back to the huddle.

``Yeah, baby! This is fun!'' Big Bob Brown said.

``You're right, this is fun, but settle down, we've still got a game to win,'' I said. ``Everybody keep hustling.''

A Cowen sprint around left end gained us 7 yards and position on Lily's side of the field with 3:26 left. After Coach Schebig sent in fullback Erik Haley, he pounded the ball up the middle for 3 yards, and then I hit tight end Alex Eastin over the middle for 8 more yards and another first down. We were inside three minutes left, but we were moving the ball, and they were getting worried.

They should be uptight because we were gaining confidence with each play. I hit Wallace on the sideline slant for 8 yards and then came back to the other side to hit Max for 7 more and another first down to their 22-yard-line.

This time when Haley came in, I had another idea.

``Max, and you, Wallace, are going to run crossing patterns from opposite sides so you meet in the middle at the 10-yard-line. Alex, you go to the right side, and you'll be my safety valve on this play. Erik, you're going to line up at the left, and you're going right up the middle. I'll hit you at the 5, but you've got to get in around that safety. If you have to, you're going to have to drag him. Can you do it?''

``Yeah, I think so,'' he said.

``I know you can.''

Erik Haley was 6-foot-4 and around 225 pounds, but he was a long-distance runner who had really strong legs. I was counting on his reach to get the ball and his legs to get him into the end zone.

As soon as I caught Bob's snap, I tucked the ball and took one step forward like I was going for a quarterback sneak, but after the linebackers and the safety bit on the fake I stopped and took one step back. Max and Wallace passed each other perfectly behind the draw-in linebackers, and Sorenson popped free running straight for the end zone. My pass was about a foot over his helmet when he reached up to snag it, and he got one stride in before the safety nailed him from behind. Instead of going down, Sorenson kept one foot down, took a big step forward and lunged for the end zone.

Of course, I never saw any of this as a pair of Appleknockers buried me in the backfield, but I could tell from the crowd's reaction and hearing the referee's whistle that the play had worked. All five of my offensive linemen came to me this time, picking me up to my feet and then pounding me on the back hard enough to resuscitate a choking victim.

"Hey, let up guys!" I tried to yell over the crowd noise. "We've got to go for two."

They all looked at me dumbfounded, especially when the kicking team was coming onto the field. I had one time out left so I used it with 1:25 left.

"Lars, what are you doing?" Coach Burgess asked, only slightly perturbed.

"You said all week we had nothing to lose and we were going to play to win, right? Then let's play to win! I want to go for two. They're tired, we're hot and what have we got to lose?"

He just looked at me for a few seconds, turned to look at the crowd, and then turned back and nodded. "It's your call, win it."

"Yes, sir! Besides, what are they going to do if we miss it, fire you?'"

He just grinned at that one. Everyone watching on TV at home must have thought we'd both lost our minds by then.

By the time I got back to the huddle, the entire stadium was buzzing. You know how athletes will tell you they can't hear the crowd in big moments? Don't believe it for a second. I could hear everything.

"OK, guys, here's what we're going to go with. Max, you are lining up wide left, and everybody else is tight to the line. We're running the option to Cowen going right. Max, you know what to do."

Of course there was a twist. The favorite play Max and I ran all through high school was a crossing pattern/slant over the middle. Because he was so short and so fast, no cornerback could keep up with him unless they lined up way inside of him. If they did that, Max would sprint to the corner of the end zone and I'd drill him as he slid across the goal line. The only problem on the slant inside was that I wasn't tall enough to get the ball to him unless the line created a clear passing lane. The only way to stop it was if the defensive linemen knocked the ball down. That's why we always ran the play off an option fake to get the linemen moving.

I lined up in the shotgun with Cowen behind me to my right with both Eastin and Haley both on the right end. When I caught the snap, we all headed right, but the center, left guard and left tackle all took two steps that way and then dropped to cut their men down at the thighs. Four steps in, just before I would have pitched the ball to Cowen, I stopped, jumped and rifled a pass to where Max should be and he slid across the goal line like a baseball player sliding into second. The ball hit him in the breadbasket where no one else could even hope to get it.

We had the lead!

Sagamores 36, Appleknockers 35 with 1:45 remaining.

As we ran off the field, the offense was mobbed by the rest of our screaming teammates. Suddenly the defense that had been exhausted now had lots of energy, which they would need to stop this final Lily drive. All we needed to do was stop them on one set of downs and we'd pull off the biggest upset of the season and send Coach Burgess out with one of the biggest wins in IWU history.

Except this time Coach Burgess surprised even me. Instead of kicking the ball deep to the guy who had run back the second-half kickoff for a touchdown, Coach Burgess told his kicker to try an on-sides kick. He lined up all of the other special teams players like they were preparing to sprint downfield as quickly as possible to make the tackle.

Everyone on Lily's side of the field fell for it as the ball rolled exactly 10 yards before Eastin fell on it and got buried. It took the officials two minutes to clear everybody off poor Alex, who came up with scrapes on both arms and hands, but he also somehow came up with the ball. Sagamores' possession!

It was the biggest surprise of the day, and the stadium was as loud as I've ever heard anything in my life. Maybe all the local folks who had been watching on TV had decided to come to the game during the second half because somehow the stadium was full. All I had to do was kneel down three times to run out the clock.

We had ended the losing streak, cost Lily a chance at a national title and sent Coach Burgess out with his biggest victory ever. Max and I and all of our scout team members had become part of college football history.

Despite the celebration and all the congratulations from the thousands of people who swarmed the field, in the end, we were also still history at Indiana Western.

CHAPTER 7
FOUR YEARS AGO

The post-game locker room was a delirious mess. By the time we had pushed through the celebrating home crowd that had stormed the playing surface and got everyone away safely before the goalposts came down, the locker room was even worse, packed with athletic department employees, family members of the players and coaches and dozens of media members.

I hugged Mom and Dad, my girlfriend Mikala and then Max's parents. Everyone seemed to be screaming in joy so no one could hear anything else as the sounds all bounced off the ceiling back down on us. This was the happiest I'd ever been. I should have been exhausted, but for some reason I felt like I could go out and play another game.

What finally quieted everyone down was Coach Burgess singing the school song. He couldn't make it until the end before he broke down. So did a lot of other people.

Then he came around and thanked everyone personally after that.

"I'm very proud of you two," he told Max and me, a hand on each of our shoulders. "I wish things were going to get better for you here, but I know you're tough enough to do well. If you ever need anything, just call me. Thank you."

Thank God he didn't speak any longer because I'm pretty sure I would have been bawling in a few more seconds.

It took us another 90 minutes before we could finish up the media interviews, take our gear off, shower and say goodbye to some of the other players. Despite having our families waiting for us, no one really wanted to leave the locker room. The feeling was just too good. This feeling is the reason you play sports, even though you rarely if ever get to experience it. The few times you do make all the sacrifices worth it.

After finally going to dinner with our families, I crashed hard. I was just physically and mentally whipped and so glad that we didn't have practice the next day. When I woke up the next morning, I was sore, but otherwise still feeling great. I just couldn't quit smiling.

There was no practice because the season was over, but instead, we had to pose for pictures and go through another press conference. I must have done 10 interviews for TV stations and met with four or five newspapers.

Max said even I had never talked that much before.

We were everybody's darlings that week. Max and I and several scout team members were featured on the cover of Sports Illustrated which called it ``The Upset of the Century.'' No one could believe what we third-, fourth- and fifth-stringers had pulled off, not even David Letterman when Max and I appeared on his show on Tuesday night. (Top 10 duties of walk-on scout team players: No. 7 making sure not to wash all the mouthpieces with the jock straps.) Though Max and I had never been outside the state before, we were now celebrities and a few days later had to change our cell phone numbers.

We were heroes wherever we went around campus – well, everywhere but in the football office. Coach Jackson took over immediately and established a postseason workout program that started after Christmas break. Coach Burgess moved out after two weeks, as did half the coaching staff, which were looking for new positions.

While everyone else loved us, Max and I had no illusions that we'd be playing for IWU when spring practice started. We just concentrated on our studies and waited for notice from Coach Jackson. When we didn't hear from him by Jan. 20, two weeks after the workout program started, we walked over to his office one day.

"What do you two want?" he asked.

"We just want to know what our situation is," I said. "If you
don't want us, we'd like to know now so we can start the transfer
proceedings."

"Well, we've got a little problem there. I want to know where you are
going first."

"I'm sure you would, but as long as you don't want us, it's none of
your business," I said. "And second, how can we know since no one is
allowed to talk to us as long as we're still under scholarship here? You
don't want us, and we don't want to play for you, so let us just move
on."

Except he didn't want to make anything easy for us. We got a letter in
the mail one day saying our scholarships were not being renewed. We
finally called a meeting with Athletic Director Madeleine Laird where
Coach Jackson said he had the right to run his program his way.

But Max and I had come better prepared this time.

"That's fine, we'll be ready to report to practice tomorrow then," I
said. "All we ask is a fair shot at playing time."

"There's no need for that," Coach Jackson said. "You're both going to
red-shirt this season so you don't even need to show up to practice."

"OK, if you want to play it that way, if I were you I wouldn't read the
Indianapolis Post tomorrow. Max and I have an appointment in an
hour with columnist Kevin Kilbane to talk about our situation. Don't
worry, I'm sure the media will be kind to you and won't judge your
treatment of us too harshly. Or the alumni."

They weren't expecting that. After what we did in the Lily game, the alumni would have destroyed them.

"All right, that's enough," the athletic director said. "Let's just step back a bit here and work this out. We'll put out a statement tomorrow saying the school is releasing you from your scholarships and you can transfer wherever you want. Coach Jackson, as long as you are sure you don't want them on the team any more, it's not worth the aggravation."

Coach Jackson just grumbled at that. "As long as they are gone."

"We learned a lot from that game," I said. "All we ever asked for here was a fair shot. We never expected anything more. Whether you wish us the same or not, Coach, we wish the team the best."

And with that, despite being the most popular people on campus and the best-liked players on the team at the end of the season, we walked out of the office and off the IWU football team.

"I don't care what you say, Max," I said once we walked outside the building, "that's the hottest athletic director in the conference."

"The country," he said.

The next day we held a press conference to say leaving was our decision and did not reflect against anyone in the program. Several questioners tried to lead us into saying something else, but we stuck to our version that we just felt it would be better for us to try playing somewhere else.

We tried to be the bigger men, but it wasn't easy. Coach Jackson made a couple of statements later about how he didn't think we'd be able to play in his new offensive system which he said needed stronger and faster players. "But we appreciate everything they've done for Indiana Western," he finished off.

Whatever. Though it was killing me, we kept our mouths shut and finished off the semester while trying to figure out what was next because we had no ideas.

Then in April, Coach Schebig called.

CHAPTER 8

After we got permission to transfer, we had no idea where we wanted to go, which was a problem. For one thing, almost every school had already distributed their scholarships for next year. Every small school in the Midwest made us offers, but none of them wowed us enough to take a visit. After just leading the win over Lily, they all seemed like they were offers for us to take a step back. We figured the best thing would be to get away from Indiana somewhere where we wouldn't always have to answer questions about Indiana Western.

Somewhere warm would have been nice, too.

Without being able to hang around the football office, it was a little difficult to find out what happened with the rest of the coaching staff. Coach Burgess was trying to help them find new jobs, but assistants coming from a 2-9 team were not getting too many second interviews unless they had prior connections.

The one assistant who still had some cred was Dennis Schebig who had coached three quarterbacks who later played in the NFL. He called us one spring afternoon and asked if we'd consider a free trip to California, Camarillo, specifically.

"This is my alma mater," he said. "It's also going to be my last job, but I won't retire until after you two are done if you come here."

The Thunderbolts were kind of starting from nothing. They had been 3-32 over the past three seasons and were winless last year, which led to the change in coaches. As an alumnus, Coach Schebig said he had always known what was going on at UC-Camarillo.

With no other offers to our liking, Max and I talked it over and decided we'd at least go make a visit.

Like almost everything in California, it was beautiful. Of course, going in April didn't hurt. The one thing that scared us to death was the traffic on the freeway from the airport, but Coach Schebig was driving. This kind of traffic where everyone drives 20 miles over the speed limit bumper-to-bumper was not what small-town Indiana boys were used to. I made Max sit up front and only opened my eyes every two miles or so.

"The great thing about this place is they are letting me do whatever I want," he said. "I'm going to run the same offense with a few tweaks, so we'll have some action and be fun to play for. There's also a lot of talent in the area, but I'm hoping you two can help me recruit on a little broader scale. We're not that big out here compared to the big schools, but we're still in California and some studs from the cold weather back east might consider us, especially if you two help sell the place."

Once we got to the campus, we were sold almost before we got out of the car. The weather was perfect, so were the girls, and it was simply a beautiful campus.

"I know," coach said. "Not what you expected from a small school with a losing football team. Too many distractions, right?"

We could only nod.

"But coach, I understand why you are here, but I'm still not sure why should we come here," I said.

"Wouldn't you just like to have some fun playing the game again, Lars? We're going to have one of the most radical offenses in the country, and I'll let you throw it 45 times a game. Even in November and December, the weather out here is perfect, and you'll still be able to throw it that much. Plus, we've got some backers who really want the school to do well so they are willing to put the money up that gives us a generous operating budget so we can recruit nationally and host some playoff games.

"You both know you're not going to the NFL, so why not get a great education and have some fun playing? You'll also get to play some decent teams because we've got to make some road trips early to help pay the bills. We'll play at San Francisco this year, and at Oregon Coast next year, so we'll get to show them we can play. It won't take us long to turn this around, so I'm hoping to make the national tournament in two years at the latest. I just need some leaders to take over the locker room and preach my system and that's where you two fit in. This will be my team, but you'll be my captains."

"As sophomores?" Max said.

"Sure, why not? You'll be the best players on the team and you've also got credibility because of the Lily win. The seniors coming back have never won anything and won't know any better. They just need somebody to follow.

"Look, you two know how I run things. I'm not going to jerk you around like Coach Jackson would have. I trust you and you respect me. It wouldn't take you long to adjust here, and because we're the lower division, you don't have to sit out a transfer year. You can play right away."

Those might have been his best points because we did like him and knew we'd have fun playing for him. We still wanted to check out the academic side, and I wanted to talk to Mikala and our parents. They would be making the biggest sacrifices with all this because they wouldn't be able to fly out every weekend to see us play.

The facilities were a little less than what we were used to, but they were fine, and Coach said they were also going to be the focus of a major campus renovation over the next year. The stadium was only a little bigger than a decent-size high school football field back home, but again it was about to be updated. It still had grass in the middle with goal posts at either end.

We met some of the players the second day, and they had as many questions for us as we had for them. They were still trying to figure out what Coach Schebig was like and wanted to know what we thought.

"You must respect him or you wouldn't be here for this visit," linebacker Jordan Eichorn said. "Maybe you just wanted a free trip to California. You two can certainly go to a bigger school than this, though you dudes are smaller than I expected. How'd you guys survive in the Midwest Conference?"

"Sometimes brains are more important than size, big guy," I said, keeping a straight face. He totally missed it, though. And you wonder why the nickname "Big Dummy" stuck?

Max just grinned.

It seemed to us these guys were just regular football players, though they were a little excited about the change in coaches. It had been a while since the Thunderbolts had won anything, so the talent level was a little down. Most of the players were local and didn't have many options to go anywhere else. That's another reason why they couldn't believe we were considering coming in.

"That should tell you something about Coach Schebig because he aims high," I said. "He'll want to win right away and a new talent base won't be an excuse for him or you. You guys better come to camp in shape or you'll be dead in about two days. He'll run you to death to see who really wants to play."

"That's OK," Eichorn said. "It's good to know, but it's easy to train year-round out here so we'll be ready."

When we told coach about the conversation later that night, he just chuckled. "We'll see how good they are about being in shape."

We met some of the administrators, even the school president who was this feisty little lady. Coach showed us around the apartment complex where we could live, but he didn't take us to the beach. We finally sneaked away one evening for that.

One of the biggest adjustments for both of us was going to be the weather and the fact that nobody seemed to be wearing enough clothes. It felt like we were walking onto the set of a TV show based on the beach. The girls were all beautiful; well, actually, everyone was beautiful.

"Max, I'm going to need your help if we come here because I could get into a whole lot of trouble out there," I said as we were standing on the beach.

"Uh, huh," Max said. "Usually, you don't need any extra help, either."

"I know, which is why I'm a little scared here."

"As usual, we'll look out for each other."

There were a lot of females on that beach which I'd never seen anything like in Indiana. I felt like a cartoon character whose eyes were popping out of his head.

Before flying home the next night, we told Coach we'd seriously think about this and let him know our decision within a week.

"We like what we see," I said. "I want to let it percolate a bit to make sure I'm not just rushing into a mistake."

"Take your time. It's not like I've got a ton of quarterbacks sitting around, and I've got a few scholarships left over. If you do decide to come, I want you out here in June. Before that, I want your help finding some players back there."

At least we finally had an option.

CHAPTER 9

I really thought the hardest part would be convincing Mikala. We'd been sweethearts since the Homecoming dance of our freshman year. As a volleyball player she was tall and strong and she had the most startling blue eyes I'd ever seen. She was also shy and turned me down the first two times I asked her to dance. Luckily, I am not only not shy but stupidly fearless. If you haven't figured it out yet, I also don't handle it well when I'm told I can't do something.

"C'mon, I'm going to keep asking until you say yes, so just say yes, give me one dance and then you can break my heart and forget about me," I said with a smile.

"Why can't you just leave me alone?"

"Because you're beautiful and I can't wait to see if the person on the inside is as beautiful as she is on the outside."

I mentally gave myself a high five for that one, but then for some reason she just laughed.

"How long have you been practicing that one? Everyone, be careful where you step around here."

But then she followed me to the dance floor and afterward I followed her everywhere. I always treated her like a lady, and she never broke my heart. So far, we've never dated anyone else. Even Max likes her, which I thought could have been a problem. Sometimes he talks to her more than he talks to me.

"That's because she actually lets me speak in full sentences without interrupting," he said.

Sure.

Maybe that's why they are my two best friends, because they are the two people I can be quiet with and it doesn't seem to matter. I can totally be myself. Better than anyone else, they know I'm not perfect and are quick to remind me when necessary which they seem to think is quite often.

Mikala is as deep and intelligent as she is tall. She just fits me in so many ways. I'm her biggest fan, but I don't expect her to be mine, though it's great that she is. I had no idea what I was getting into when we started going out, and now I can't imagine being without her, and I'm not ashamed to say it. She makes me a better person.

I always wondered if I would ever have what my parents have, and now I know I will for sure someday. I'll never know why she was picked for me or why she sticks with me, but I'll never take it for granted. I don't feel like I have to earn her love, but I'm thankful every day to have it.

Maybe that's why she can get me back in line with a look. She's also the one who can shut me up when I'm running off at the mouth, and usually that look is all it takes.

"Don't forget to breathe once in a while when that mouth is open," she'll say. "Oxygen to the brain helps you think about what you are saying."

Point taken. We've both grown up a lot together, and I know I'm going to marry her someday, hopefully soon.

Anyway, I figured she would be the hardest person to convince about moving to California. She was catching some heat around campus because she's on the IWU volleyball team and made the Midwest Conference all-freshman squad last year as an outside hitter. Everyone kept asking her what Max and I were going to do next, along with wanting to know why we really were leaving school.

"We get to play right away, we know the system Coach wants to run and it's a great education," I said. "Plus, it's nowhere near here so we won't have to answer questions about Indiana Western all the time. We can go out there, start fresh and be ourselves. It's a chance to go recreate ourselves and just start over with football. I think this is the right move for me.

"I think this is the right thing for me and can be the right thing for us, too. We're going to get an apartment, and I think it would be great for you to come out and stay with us sometimes. You can go down to the beach and play volleyball and train and get to know some good players out there, too. That way you'd have something to do when we're working out or whatever."

"Who are you trying to convince, me or yourself?" she said.

"What?"

"You sound like you are trying to convince yourself, and not asking me what I think."

"So what do you think?"

"I'm not sure if you yourself know what you think, so I'm not sure how I can think anything about it yet," she said. "Yes, it does sound like a good opportunity for you, but I'm not sure how good it is for us."

"But that's the most important thing to me," I said.

"No, it's not, or at least it shouldn't be," she said. "It's great that you want to know what I think, but you have to make this decision for yourself, and we'll adjust. You have to be happy with it first, because if you're not, then all you're going to do is call home all the time whining to me and then I'm not going to be happy. I've got my own life here, but our life together is something else. We have to be happy as individuals first before we can be happy as a couple. What do you want to do, and are you sure?"

"I think so."

"You should know so, so you need to go do more research until you know for sure."

Dang, she knows me too well. I talked to my parents, who basically said the same things. They would back me whatever move I decided to do.

I'm getting frustrated. How can I decide what to do if these people aren't willing to tell me what I should be doing? All my life they've been there to direct and guide me, but I'm starting to realize this time I have to pick my own direction.

It didn't help that I felt like I was making the decision for two people. I knew whatever I decided, Max would follow as well, but I also knew this was our one chance. Once we made a decision, we weren't going to get a second chance on where to go because sitting out another year for a transfer wasn't going to do us any good.

Despite making a few more unsolicited phone calls, our other option was to just stay home and play at a small school, and I'm not sure that's going to be enough for me. I guess I was really surprised there weren't any other big schools that were willing to take a chance on us. After all, they had the perfect game tape to watch. If we could do what we did against a top 10 team like Lily, why couldn't we get any sniffs from any other big teams? That didn't make any sense to me.

I finally went to see Coach Snuff, who had coached Max and me through our high school football careers.

"You have this idea that you might be better than you are," he said. "Yeah, you had that one game, but these coaches all have their holes to fill, and they all have their own ideas of what kind of players fill those holes. You two fill the holes, but there's a lot of air left over after that to plug the gaps."

"But..."

"But nothing. This is reality, son, not dreams. This is real life. They all figure Coach Jackson had the chance to look at you every day and he doesn't want you so there must be something wrong. For all anyone else knows, you guys have attitude problems and you're the ones who left IWU, right? For all you know, every one of them is calling IWU to talk to him, and confidentially, they're all asking him what he thinks. You can bet he's not sugarcoating things."

I sat there stunned for a few seconds.

"I never thought of that. I've been such an idiot."

"First thing that tipped me off that something might be going on was that nobody was calling me about you two, either. Wouldn't you think a coach who wanted you would do a little research by calling me?"

That made sense, too.

"So what should I do about Camarillo?"

"That's easy," he said, as I leaned forward anxiously. "Do what you want to. Haven't you figured it out yet that nobody is going to tell you what to do? This is one move you have to make for yourself. You have to make this decision because you are the one who has to live with it if you end up not liking it. Take responsibility for your own life. You're almost 20 now so it's time you made your own decision."

"Gee, thanks."

"You'll thank me later. End of the lesson, unless you've got anything specific you want to ask."

"I'm just not sure about going out there and starting a whole program essentially from scratch."

"Who said you were? As much as you may think this is all about you, you're not the one responsible for all of that. Coach Schebig is. And since when have you wanted everything handed to you? I taught you better than that. The No. 1 thing I always taught you was what?"

"That it didn't matter what the other team was doing, it only really it mattered what we were doing."

"Exactly. It doesn't matter that you're starting from scratch either by yourself or with that team. Life is starting from scratch every day. You better learn how to deal with it. How are you going to handle it and what are you going to do?

"Listen, Lars. I know the man you are even if you aren't sure yet. So do Mikala, your parents and Max. It's time you accepted who and what you are. Wherever you go, it's going to have some of the same problems as Camarillo and some different ones. That only constant you can worry about is that you will be there. It matters what you do and how you handle the situations. So go decide what you're going to handle. Now get out of here."

I stood up, shook his hand and headed for the door.

"And Lars…"

"Yes, sir."

"Come back and see me at Christmas whatever you decide. I've got a sophomore quarterback this year who's going to start and I'll want you to talk to him."

"Yes, sir."

I walked around town for a while to figure things out. I thought about talking to Max about things, but eventually figured out I had to make up my own mind first. Everyone said hi while I was on my walk, but thankfully, they mostly left me alone. Maybe I should have worn a sign that said, "Big decision being made here."

I walked over to Max's place and eventually ended up at Mikala's house.

"I finally know what I'm going to do," I told Mikala as we sat in her living room after her parents went to bed. We had just gotten done watching "The Big Bang Theory" which is our favorite show.

"And...?"

"Well, if you're going to drag it out of me, after much thought, deliberation and procrastination... I've decided I'm going to Camarillo. Max and I already called Coach Schebig and told him we're coming."

"About time," she said.

"Why do you say that? You say that like it was obvious. If you already had it figured out why didn't you just tell me?"

"This way's better. I knew you'd make the right call. And I got to torture you some more. This way you'll also be sure because you made the decision for yourself, not because I or someone else pushed you to it."

"I wish I was as confident as you are about all this. I still have a lot of questions, but I guess I understand now I won't get the answers until we actually get out there and start working on them."

"About time you figured that out," she said. "Now shut up, turn out the light and get over here."

"Yes, ma'am!"

See, I told you she always knew how to shut me up.

CHAPTER 10
THREE YEARS AGO

Following our decision, Max and I started our recruiting efforts, convincing a pair of receivers and a guard to come with us in the fall for their freshman seasons. Keaton Alexander was a 6-1, 165-pound receiver from Fort Wayne who had no idea how good he can be. He had all kinds of skills and athletic tools, but we needed to toughen him up a bit, along with feeding him enough to fill out his frame. Trever Andrews was a little bigger, a little faster and sometimes a little meaner. His problems were more off the field and sometimes in his lack of dedication in the classroom, but Max said he'd keep an eye on him. Either way, we had two more receivers who can run and make sure opponents will pay if they try double-covering Max too much.

Maybe our biggest signing was offensive lineman Gabe Hirsch out of northern Michigan. He's 6-2, 250 pounds and about 100 pounds of that is in his low center of gravity. In other words, he has a big butt. It means he isn't very fast, but he's nearly impossible to knock around or off his feet once he gets them set up properly. If he gets in the way and gets his hands up, he isn't going to move side-to-side or get shoved backward, and he can usually handle his man one-on-one. Our dads had played together at Valparaiso so Gabe used to come down and spend summers with us so he could go to IWU's camps. When we left IWU, he backed out of his commitment there and decided he was going with us.

We've also got some friends to come along. Bob Brown, Alex Eastin, Erik Haley and Randy Marcom also became free agents when Coach Jackson didn't renew their scholarships, and Coach Schebig quickly signed them. We suddenly have nine people to build an offense around, including six of us with big-time college experience.

Don't know why every coach always complains about recruiting because it seems pretty easy to me.

After Max and I arrived in California, the school sent out a press release, but we declined to answer any questions until the season started. Maybe because we were so far away, everybody left us alone so we spent a couple weeks moving into our apartment and getting acclimated around campus.

Getting acclimated took a while, too. Back home, we could drive anywhere in 15 minutes, maybe hitting a couple of stoplights. In California, you could go 15 minutes without moving 15 feet sometimes on the freeway. If you were running behind before you left to get someplace, it was likely time to give up and just cancel the appointment because there was no way to make up time.

Then there were these things called fish tacos. I wish they had just named them something else because I can't understand why anyone would want to disgrace a taco by putting fish in it. Everybody out here loves them, but I doubt I'll ever get used to them.

Then Max made things worse one day by asking our waitress at El Tecelote (The Owl) what brand the salsa was.

"What brand?" she asked, shaking her head. "Honey, this is no 'brand.' This is the real stuff that we make each day. You poor boys must be from out-of-state, and I'll bet you've never tasted real Mexican food."

True, the stuff here doesn't taste anything like the stuff back home. The enchiladas definitely tasted better than fish tacos, though. We also never knew you could make real salsa, and we're also not sure why you'd want to.

Other adjustments included the lack of change in seasons, which I actually kind of missed, and getting our skin used to constant sun. The time change also took a while to get used to, meaning I needed to call home before 7 p.m. local time or I'd risk waking Mom and Dad up.

On average, there are more blondes per square mile in California than there are in Sweden (though I'm not sure how many are real) and the females, especially, are very friendly people, almost too friendly at times which could be a problem if I wasn't so committed to Mikala. I also wonder how many of these people are gifted with their flawless skin and curves by God or their doctor. Almost everybody out here looks like the most beautiful cheerleaders back home.

One really cool thing about California are the missions, 21 Spanish churches built in the 1700s which are located about a solid day's walk apart. Ranging from San Diego to Sonoma, they are beautiful, stone and adobe structures surrounded by gardens. In many ways, they served the same purpose as forts in the Midwest, but are much better preserved, in part because of the climate.

Max and I decided early on we were going to visit all 21 before we graduated.

We also used the extra time that summer to get to know some of our new teammates. There were a few hard feelings when coach Schebig named us captains, but we worked through those by saying we were starting a leadership council including five seniors.

There were two months before practice officially began, but the leadership council started running workouts almost immediately. Because UC-Camarillo is an I-AA school, no one had ever tried this before. The workouts were voluntary, and our numbers were pretty low at first, maybe 30 guys on a good day. A few of the players went home for the summer, some were hanging out at the beach and the freshmen weren't on campus yet. After the first week, the players who came out didn't like Max and me very much, either, as we ran them into the ground.

"You guys have no idea what Coach Schebig expects or how he runs a practice," I said after one sprint, leaning with hands on my knees trying to catch my breath. "We do. You think we're tough... You're going to want to do this so you can be ready for Coach Schebig. You'll pay for it later if you don't."

When we started these practices, we were going four days a week, and the participation numbers weren't that good as most of the players showed up every other morning and only about half of those on time. We spent a half hour running, an hour in the weight room and then finished up with another hour working outside.

Slowly, Coach let the word out that everybody had better be listening to us. He sent out a summer workout program to the guys who weren't on campus, and it's so tough a couple of guys decided right then they weren't coming back. Suddenly, more guys finally got the message and started showing up for our workouts.

Because Max and I knew the offense, we started teaching it. The previous starting quarterback had graduated, but junior Tony Boroff thought he'd naturally be the starter. We bumped heads initially, but after a few practices, he realized he couldn't beat me out and left the team. He just quit showing up.

When the real practice started in August, Coach tried to make his mark right away during two-a-day practices. Some of the guys griped that he was just trying to weed out some players, but Max and I told them this was the way it was going to be every day. To run Coach's offense, you needed to be able to sprint 50 yards and come back ready for a no-huddle option on the next play. He started running us at the beginning of the first practice, sprint after sprint, and whistle after whistle. Five or six guys cramped up right away and a couple left because of dehydration.

``This is where we find out who wants to play and how badly,'' Coach yelled while we ran. ``How much are you willing to sacrifice? Are we going to settle for being mediocre? This is what I warned you about!''

Just after that, Big Dummy Eichorn barfed following a sprint. Luckily, only a few players quit and we had 75 on the roster.

Then one day ``Big Dummy'' used a profanity to complain that Coach was killing us.

Hearing Big Dummy's curse, everyone got real quiet and turned to look at him. He just broke one of Coach Schebig's biggest rules, maybe the biggest.

``No, just you,'' Coach said. ``You know the rule for swearing, Jordan. That's four laps. Take off.''

The one thing Coach couldn't tolerate was profanity on the football field. Everyone was so used to swearing during practice and games, no one believed it when he told us his rules. The first offense was one lap for each letter of the word. The second offense doubled it. It's amazing how much that threat cleans things up, especially when your teammates are laughing as you run the laps.

A lot of guys learned to mumble under their breath. If Coach thought that's going too far, though, he'd still make you take off for a few laps.

``Football is a game of discipline,'' Coach always said. ``If you can't control your mouth, how can you hope to control your mind and your emotions?''

There seemed to be some excitement on campus, as each day several classmates asked what we thought. I just shrugged my shoulders and said, ``Come watch us.''

Our first open-to-the-public scrimmage drew 5,000 fans, which may not sound like a lot, but it was bigger than any regular-season crowd over the last five years. We tried to keep them all entertained by throwing the ball all over the place. Though they had been practicing against us every day, the defense had no idea how to stop us, and Max caught four touchdowns because no one could keep up with him.

The crowd loved it, especially when Coach addressed them afterward.

``We're going to throw it a lot," he said. ``That's the quickest way we can compete against our schedule as we learn how I want to do things. I know you're excited, but I ask you for patience along with your support. We'll probably lose a few this season, but no matter what happens, we're going to have fun."

Everybody liked hearing that and applauded heartily. The players couldn't get too excited, though, because then he made us run sprints. This time Big Dummy managed to keep his contents to himself.

But this level of play and talent was quite a bit different from what Max and I and the other IWU cast-offs were used to. We're tried to pull everyone up to that level, but we had to be patient because they had no concept what we're talking about. Maybe the best thing we could do was continue to lead by example, but we needed them to get better in a hurry, and I was wondering how far they could improve in a short time. We would find out early in our schedule.

We started with a 30-10 win over NCAA Division II Oregon State-Salem which was almost too easy because we weren't prepared the next week when we lost at Division I San Francisco 40-25. I felt like as long as the offensive line kept the rushers away from me, we could score with anyone at our level. Hirsch surprised everyone but Max and me by holding onto a starting spot, and along with Marcom and Brown made sure the left side of our line was very good.

The defense needed a lot of work. "Big Dummy" Eichorn was the best athlete on that side of the ball, but he needed more time to learn the system. The defense had nine new starters, and most were freshmen or sophomores so that was to be expected until they could figure things out.

So we kept throwing. Sure, we could have made the scores of a couple of losses closer and might have even won another game if we had played conservatively, but we were having fun and so were the fans who started coming in bigger numbers. Even our losses were fun games to play in and exciting to watch. Coach wanted us to keep firing, and our offensive numbers were sick. Idaho Tech gave us a shootout, but we outlasted them 54-47. The weather was perfect, and we always had perfect footing to run on so defenses had no chance because we were so fast and in such great condition.

The Homecoming game against Nevada-Carson City drew the biggest crowd in UC-Camarillo history, about 15,000, and we rolled 45-14. Everyone wanted to come to the games, which had become a party atmosphere. Halfway through the season the band started staying for the second half of games following their halftime show. Before that, they always left early.

"This is going to help us recruit better players," Coach Schebig told me. "If kids see we're having fun here playing this system they'll consider coming to play."

And it was fun. We finished 8-3, the second-best record in school history and good enough for second place in the conference. We didn't qualify for the national tournament, but that became our goal for the next season when we would have a ton of returning players with experience. Max and I made the all-conference team and received honorable mention all-American notice as he finished with 80 catches for 1,200 yards and 18 touchdowns, and I threw for 3,300 yards and 27 touchdowns.

Coach said some top-notch athletes were considering us. Several strong junior college standouts committed to the Thunderbolts, especially on defense which seemed to be getting bigger and faster every week. Because we didn't lose that many seniors, we were getting deeper, too, which meant there would be plenty of competition during spring ball.

CHAPTER 11

We expected our second year on the West Coast to go even better. This time everybody stayed in Camarillo for the off-season workouts, at least partly because they have started to understand the new recruits coming in might be good enough to take their jobs. Because of the workouts and better recruiting, the roster average was about an inch taller and 20 pounds heavier per man than the year before we arrived. It was also about 10 wins better.

Maybe because the defense had more good players, or because they are used to going against us every day, they expected to have a big advantage over opposing offenses. They never seemed to get tired. As soon as fall practice started, it was obvious "Big Dummy" wasn't so dumb and had a better understanding of what the coaches want him to do out there. He had become the leader of the defense, and Coach added him to the captain roster with Max and me. That was OK with us because we didn't have to be the ones always pushing for an extra wind sprint.

"C'mon you guys! If you can't keep up with me, there's no way you'll stand up to Oregon Coast!" Eichorn yelled. He had a point. Oregon Coast had finished second last year in the Pacific Northwest and won the Buttercup Bowl over Florida Bayside. The Meadowlarks had most of their starters returning, including Heisman Trophy candidate Joey Mawhorter who could run and throw. He ran his offense like a basketball point guard, changing directions all the time and dishing the ball off to his backs at the last second. Preparing for him was always a fun week in practice for me because I got to do whatever I wanted with the ball to help the defense adjust.

Despite all of "Big Dummy's" yelling, everyone was in much better shape this season. We also all knew what Coach Schebig and his staff expected and what the schemes were. We all felt comfortable and were anxious to show what we could do.

We also had some new talent, especially on defense. Some of our key recruits were linebackers Nik Hoot and Jake Ryan, linemen Cory Hoersten and Reid Sproat and defensive backs Cole Trammell, Dyer Ball and Tucker McClure. Everyone was a tad undersized, but they'd all come in early to work out and take summer classes to get ready for the fall.

Even better, Mikala came out to spend some time with us over the summer. She trained on the beach with some of our women's volleyball players while we were doing our morning workouts. The great thing about long-distance relationships today was they were not as tough as they used to be thanks to Skype, cell phones and e-mail, but they were still not the same as being there with each other all the time.

``Good thing she's coming, because I'm tired of hearing you whine,'' Max said at the end of the spring semester. ``I was about ready to wrap a clock in a blanket for you like a new puppy.''

``Shut up! You'd feel the same way if Natalie wasn't from here and if you didn't get to see her every day. She might as well be my sister, I see her so much.''

Max finding Natalie was like a lightning strike. Shortly after he turned 21 around spring break, we went to a karaoke bar over by the beach, and she was running the show. After about an hour, she came right up to him and gave him a song to sing and then pulled him up to the stage. I about died laughing listening to them try to sing ``Look on the Bright Side of Life'' from Monty Python. And he actually sang!

While Max was always quiet and somewhat shy, Natalie was all about attitude and communication. Ten minutes after meeting her, you know her whole sassy story. She could even make Max talk, which is something I haven't even been able to do. She's got a very sharp, quick wit so she can keep up with us pretty well. After handling some of the drunks with the karaoke performances, she said talking to Max was easy. Sometimes she's a little jealous of how Max and I can communicate without talking, but she's catching on. I think she's starting to realize I'm no threat.

I'm just worried she's going to rub off on Mikala. Natalie is older than we are and has a 2-year-old daughter named Emma, who is also a pistol and always sitting on one of our laps. Emma's got so much energy, even Max and I had trouble keeping up with her. She's also just like her mother in that she babbled constantly. Life with Natalie and Emma was never boring, and Max was smitten with both of them. I kind of wish they'd move a little slower but so far I hadn't seen anything wrong.

I never thought I'd see Max fall in love this hard, and Max's family back in Indiana freaked out a little bit. One day I answered the phone at home when Max was over at Natalie's, and it was his mother who for once wanted to talk to me. Rather she wanted to yell at me. I tried to tell her it was OK, and that I would never let him do anything too stupid.

``Right," she said. ``Hearing that is not helping me relax too much. There are too many examples I can think of where you were the instigator."

``Hey! Well, that may be true but there were never any cops involved, and this is different," I pleaded. She wasn't buying it. Why is it all women see right through me?

``Yeah, sure." Momma Curry said. She also had a point, because I always was the one who instigated things, and usually the cops weren't involved because they always knew where to find us if they had to.

And we didn't leave any permanent damage. Sometimes I wished they'd have just come and got us because they always called Coach Snuff instead, and that was 10 times worse for us.

``First you take him out there, and now he falls in love and may never come back," she said. ``This is all your fault. You should have stayed closer to home where I could keep an eye on you."

I was never going to win this discussion or even get an idea across.

``OK, tell you what. Call Mikala and talk to her. Tell her what you want to know and what kind of things you're looking for. Don't tell me any of it, just talk to her, and she can report back once she comes home next month. You know I'm horrible at getting information out of women, and you trust Mikala, don't you?"

That finally bought us a few weeks peace. I did not tell Max

As usual, this plan backfired on me in a way I never expected. Emma LOVED Mikala who suddenly wanted to talk about how many kids we were going to have someday. Yikes! Mikala volunteered to babysit just about every day which saved Natalie some money but seriously cut into our time alone. As soon as Emma wobbled in the door, she always ran right to Mikala, begging to be picked up and cuddled. I get along OK with Emma (Mikala says we're on the same intellectual level. Thanks, Babe), but I didn't do too well with diapers. I was the king at rocking her to sleep with a bottle, though. Usually we both fell asleep at the same time. It was a gift.

I'm not sure what the deal was with Emma's father, but he wasn't around anymore. His loss.

Mikala liked Natalie, but as she said, what can you really tell in a few brief visits?

``That was a stupid idea you had," she said before smacking me in the shoulder a few days before she was to fly home.

"Ow! What did I do?"

"What am I going to tell Max's mother? She's going to drill me, and I don't know half the answers she wants. I feel like I'm responsible for Max's future love life here, and all you did was pass it off to me."

"Would I do that?"

"Hah! Of course you would."

"Well, at least it worked."

"Of course it would. Why would Momma Curry believe anything you said anyway?"

"Aw, c'mon now, that hurt. She knows I'll always look out for Max and never let him do anything too stupid."

"No, she knows if he does anything stupid, you'll be right there with him in the middle of it."

"Wow, you guys must have had a long talk."

"Honestly, it didn't take us that long to get into the exploits of you two. They weren't news to me."

There really weren't that many. I mean, what kind of trouble could you get into in a town like Talbott when you were the star quarterback and receiver? It wasn't like we were anonymous kids because you couldn't be anonymous in a small town, and I never would have messed around with anybody else and have taken a chance on ticking off Mikala. I may have been quick with the lip, but I wasn't that stupid. Some girls tried, and there were a few rumors over the years, but thankfully she never believed them because they weren't true. She always knew where I was at, with her or with Max.

We did go to a few fraternity parties at IWU, which sounded a lot more dangerous than they actually were. One time someone called the house to say there was fight going on with one of the brothers at their rival house, and everyone took off running down this hill to go back him up. Being stupid and slightly inebriated, Max and I ran right along with everyone else, and this stocky guy running next to Max was carrying a beer in a little plastic cup. He tripped over something in the dark and did a full 360-degree turn in midair to somehow land on his feet about 10 feet further down the hill. Even more amazing than the fact he wasn't injured, he didn't spill a drop of his beer. It might be the most amazing and athletic thing I've ever seen by one of the least-athletic people I've ever met.

It turned out the frat brother didn't need any help anyway because he had already talked his way out of the situation. Bubba always could talk his way out of anything – until he met his future wife and then he was a goner.

We hadn't had too many parties like that in California so far because everybody was so laid back from partying all the time. It was kind of boring really. I would have to try to get "Big Dummy" fired up some night to see what happens.

"So here's what you tell Momma Curry. You tell her how precious Emma is and that Max seems happy with Natalie. Tell her he's not stupid drunk in love, that he's simply Max and seems to have a handle on everything. If you hadn't seen Natalie or Emma, could you tell a big difference in Max?"

"Not when he's on his own," she said.

"See, that's what I'm talking about. She wouldn't believe me when I told her that, but she'll believe you. Besides, they've only been going out for two months. It's not like they are getting married this year. I'm going to be the best man whenever Max gets married, and I think I'd know. And besides, usually Max is not the one we have to worry about doing anything stupid, right?"

As soon as the words were out of my mouth I wanted to swallow them back. I walked into that one with my chin pointed out for the knockout shot. Sometimes I just hand her ammunition..

"Hello, stupid!" Mikala said, laughing.

Yeah, real funny.

It didn't matter anyway because when I talked to Max about all this, he had it all figured out.

"She's not going to believe any of us until she sees it with her own eyes," he said. "And even then, she won't trust it."

Told ya, Max was pretty smart. He was already planning on taking both Natalie and Emma home for Christmas.

That was a long way away because our season was going so well. With the improved defense, we rolled through the regular season. The only team that gave us a challenge was Oregon Coast, and that was our best game of the year. We were 4-0 going in and they were 3-0, but we crossed them up and messed with their heads all day. We had a new running back named Anthony Tomlinson who was a junior college transfer. He wasn't very fast or elusive, but he was tough. No one defender could bring him down with an arm tackle, and it usually took two players to wrestle him to the ground. He loved following Hirsch into the hole or around the end and sticking his helmet into some linebacker's chest.

The Meadowlarks expected us to throw on every down, so they used a nickel package with five defensive backs from the start. We expected them to do that, so we ran Tomlinson for the first 10 plays from scrimmage. Our idea was to keep them off-balance and also to keep Mawhorter off the field. We'd run him left behind Marcom and Brown for two plays and then had Hirsch pull to the right on third down. They never knew where Tomlinson came from.

To mix things up, we also threw to the tight end Eastin over the middle. Thanks to a blocked punt, we were up 17-0 before the end of the first quarter and 24-10 at halftime. We got a break at the start of the third quarter when Mawhorter tried for a bomb after the opening kickoff and our safety Tucker McClure picked it off. Then we put together a 15-play drive that rode out the rest of the quarter and put us up 31-10 when I hit Max on a slant at the goal line. We finished them off 34-24.

Though they didn't have great stats, I gave Max, Alexander and Andrews all the credit for making that gameplan work because they blocked their backsides off. Coach always preached that blocking was just as important at catching passes for his receivers, and they hustled the entire game and just threw themselves in front of OC players, allowing Tomlinson to gain a few extra yards each time.

My numbers weren't that good, but I was happier with the win, which was pretty obviously the biggest in school history. We shot up to No. 2 in our division polls after that one and rode the momentum to winning the conference title.

We also qualified for the playoffs for the first time, reaching the semifinals before we lost to No. 1-ranked Lehigh Valley which eventually won the title. Because of the way the pairings worked out, we had to play the game in Pennsylvania in mid-December. It was cold and wet, and we couldn't get much footing. The Great Danes were the better team and beat us 31-27. We were coming from behind the whole game and never caught up with them.

We finished 13-1, and it was a great year. UC-Camarillo was on the map as far as football was concerned, and we lost only two seniors from the starting lineup. Our goal for next year was to be ranked No. 1 so we could have the home field advantage throughout the playoffs.

We were satisfied, but also sore and tired. By the time Christmas break came around we were all ready for a rest on our trip home.

Of course, Momma Curry loved Natalie and especially Emma who started calling her Gramma. At first she accused Max of putting her up to that, but that was actually my idea. The way she spoiled Emma, I wondered where this nice old woman was when we were growing up because that kid got away with murder! Stuff I remember getting yelled at or backhanded for was now suddenly the cutest thing ever!

Anyway, we all had a great Christmas, and Momma Curry and Emma both cried when we all left to return to school.

Served her right for stressing me out all semester.

CHAPTER 12
JUNE, THE PRESENT

Before we can begin thinking about preparing to earn the home field advantage in the playoffs for our third and last season at Camarillo, we need to decide what to do about Indiana Western first.

Max doesn't want to do it, and I'm still deciding, but Brown, Haley, Marcom and Eastin all want to play them, and Hirsch is with them on this one. You'd think they would be smarter, but they are mostly offensive linemen so they have all suffered numerous head injuries.

Coach has been nice enough to tell me to take a few days and think about it, but he also told me we had to meet with the school president after the weekend. She wants to put her two cents in, which I'm guessing will be about how this is money the school can't afford to turn down. I really could not care less about that.

This time, I haven't bothered asking Mikala what she thinks I should do because I know she won't give me an answer. She sure can be stubborn sometimes. I suppose I should be thankful because that's probably partly why she's still with me. Plus, I figure I've got the next 50 years or so when I get to look forward to never having the opportunity to make a decision.

She's still the first person, other than Max, I talked to about it after we left Coach Schebig's office. We Skype at least twice a week. It's easier now to be in a long-distance relationship than it probably ever has been in history with emails, cell phones and all other forms of computer communication, but it's still not the same as being there every day.

"This has to be a trap," I say. "There's no way Coach Jackson would go for this unless he's totally confident he can just kill us. There's no way he'd take a chance on us making him look bad."

"But he's right that it will be an easy sell," Mikala says. "The buzz on campus will be amazing. This will sell out in about two days."

"Which means he thinks he's getting to put us in our place once and for all," I say. "I still can't figure out why he'd want to do this, though, because we're out here in complete limbo from IWU. We're totally irrelevant, but he's giving us a chance to be relevant again."

"Maybe he didn't have a choice."

"What do you mean? Of course he has a choice, he controls everything in the program."

"But who controls him? Maybe the athletic director said he could move the Ohio Valley game only if he accepted this game in that spot. There's no way an athletic director is going to move a Homecoming game at the last second unless there's a perfect fit waiting to replace it. The alumni would scream bloody murder. They wouldn't care if it was because of national TV or not."

"Plus, like you said, you guys are irrelevant out there. He sees you as no threat or he'd never consider it. He figures his team has gotten a lot better and you guys must have gotten a lot worse because of the lack of competition. He probably hasn't even thought about you guys in two years. Why should he have? You're history here because his team has moved far past that."

She's probably right about that.

"So in other words, as much as we think this is about us, it really isn't. He isn't considering us at all and just sees us as practice fodder, an easy week for his boys in the middle of the season. He doesn't see us as any threat. He's probably right because I can't remember the last time a Division I-AA team beat a good Division I team. He probably gave the AD the go-ahead and never thought about it again. We know he's that arrogant, but are they really that good?"

"You better figure that out pretty quickly," she says. "You know, that might be to your advantage if they completely overlook you."

"I don't see how they can with Max and me and all the guys who are still there that we played with. They know what we are capable of, or at least what we used to be capable of. If we decide to play this game, maybe we can use that."

As usual, it's Max who figures out Coach Jackson's plan. He thinks Coach Jackson has us trapped.

"He's got us cornered in a way he never could while we were there," he says. "He thinks he can force us to come in and take a beating from his best team, but if we don't go in there to play them, he'll leak it to the media that we were afraid. He never thought for a second we'd accept."

That would end all discussion about us from the alumni, meaning Coach Jackson could win without ever taking the field. That's pretty smooth.

"He's figuring your ego will put you right where he wants you," Max says. "If it doesn't, he'll smear us or let the media do it for him. He can't lose."

That should make the decision easier because we really have no choice not, but... I'd love to say no, but the animosity is too much and my competitive fire too strong to let it go that easy.

As I walk to classes and workouts, I think about the possibilities all week. If I say no, will Coach Jackson think we are afraid of him? Will I regret it 15, 20 years from now? What about the other guys on the team? Will I be taking away their only chance to play on national TV?

I also wonder if it's worth the hassle because I know it will be a huge one. We might get to spend a few extra days at home, but the press conferences will be a mess, and how focused can we really be for the game? Do I really want to rehash that part of my life again?

Mom and Dad and Max's parents will want to make a big deal out of it for the whole team, which also makes me worry about wearing them out. Our folks won't stop until we leave, and it's a lot of work to host 100 people for anything, let alone 100 people who can eat through a buffet line three times a day like massive swarms of locusts.

When I still don't know what to do by Friday, I decide to ask Coach Schebig for Coach Burgess's phone number. He tells me the best way to reach Coach Burgess is to call the Trolley Bar around lunchtime. There are rumors that Coach Burgess is a part-owner and actually has a sandwich named after him on the menu.

"Yeah, it's made with tongue and it's really rough on one side," Coach Schebig jokes. "And it wouldn't surprise me if he owns part of it because he's never paid when we've eaten there."

"I was guessing maybe bologna and hot mustard," I say with a chuckle.

"That would be Coach Jackson."

It takes three days to finally reach Coach Burgess. He is splitting his retirement between Arlington and fishing in Texas, once in a while throwing in a TV or radio interview. One of his sons is a high school coach in the area, too, so he's still regularly going to practices.

"Tell Schebig I'm putting this lunch on his tab," he says, laughing, "and he needs to get in here and pay it off sometime because it's getting pretty high."

He sounds so relaxed, it's obvious Coach is enjoying retirement.

"My wife kicks me out of the house every day whether I've got somewhere to go or not," he says. "There aren't that many places to go in Arlington so I've seen a lot of movies and played a lot of golf so far."

"You should come out here and help us put some new twists in our offense," I say.

"You know what, that's not a bad idea. I might just do that. I really miss a good, hard-hitting practice every once in a while. Plus, I could use some work on my tan."

Maybe the oddest thing about Coach Burgess is that he's always talking about his tan. The calendar could say February, and he'll be talking about taking off for the weekend somewhere warm so he can work on his tan. Even when he's dead and all the blood is gone, he'll look like he's just gotten a brown paint job.

"I wanted to ask what you thought about us possibly playing IWU. I don't know what to think, and I'm tired of everyone telling me to figure it out for myself. My first thought is why should we do them any favors? What's in it for us besides being punching bags?"

"You don't owe them anything, but is that what you're really worried about, or are you worried about maybe being embarrassed? I figure that's what IWU wants. For two years they've been haunted by you two and the Lily game. They were a .500 team two years ago and went 8-3 last year, but everybody asks how much better they might have been if you two were still here. Part of that is because their offense is so dull. I figure Wally's plan is to bring you guys in here, try to put you through a major whipping and shut everybody up. That way, he can finally prove to everyone that it's his program."

"That's what I'm thinking, and I'm afraid my teammates have no idea what they are facing. Yeah, we're good for I-AA football, but we're not good enough for Midwest Conference football."

"Well, that all depends. Who says you have to play them in Midwest Conference football? You didn't let Oregon Coast play their style of ball. I'm guessing you've got a few surprises this year for Northern California as well. Plus, you have a couple of big advantages going for you. No one knows Wally's schemes like Schebig does. The other thing is you know his defense is going to be set up to smash you and Max so you already know exactly what he's going to run and how. They'll have 99 percent of their focus on you two, leaving a lot of holes to be exploited.

"His offense is so basic it makes Woody Hayes look original. They just try to run people over, control the clock and win the turnover battle. They give up the fewest points in the conference, but they also don't score very many. If you can crack their defense, your chances go way up."

That is obviously all true and should have been helping me make my decision but it isn't working that way in my head.

"Have you figured out what your main question is yet?" Coach Burgess asks. "Because I have."

"What do you mean?"

"I'm not saying this to be rude, but you're scared," he says. "You've got it pretty good out there in Camarillo. Your team is very good, and you and Max are playing great. You don't have to prove anything to those folks, but there are still the questions back here, aren't there?"

"We showed everyone what we could do in the Lilly game," I say.

"Yes, you did – in that game. Was that a lucky fluke? You and I know it wasn't, but nobody else does. Did that game legitimize you as a big-time quarterback? It must not have because no other school called while you were available. That must make you wonder a little. Then you're worried about what happens if you guys get smacked around. What will happen then? What will everyone back here think then? Will it burst the bubble of how good your team is in Camarillo?

"Look, Lars, it's OK to have those doubts. They are real, but that's not the kid who talked me into letting him walk-on, or the one who stood up to Wally every day in practice with the scout team, or the kid who beat Lily. You have to figure out how much you want to challenge yourself and your team. Are you satisfied with where things stand, and if you are, that's OK, but are you going to have questions later about all this? Just how good can the Thunderbolts be? Just how good can you be?

"If you decide you want to do this, you have to quit thinking about the bad things that might happen and start focusing on the good things that can happen. You can't play not to lose; you've got to play like you have everything to win. You can't worry about protecting everybody else and everything you have built with this game; you've got to get the drive back you had as freshman when you were so desperate to play so you could prove what you could do.

"If you're done growing as a player and decide you don't want to accept this challenge, that's fine, but understand why you are making that decision. You don't have to do this and you don't owe anybody anything, but you might owe it to yourself later on to be sure about your reasons. Am I making sense?"

I don't say anything for a few seconds to let what he's saying sink in.

"It's your turn to talk, Lars," Coach says. "I'm needing a second or two to sip this here beverage. Why is it that talking to you always makes me thirsty?"

"Yes, sir, as usual, you're making more sense than I would like to admit. Must be nice being old so you can have wisdom."

``See, there's that kid again. You've got to be cocky about this; you can't be hoping something good is going to happen. You have to know you are prepared and ready for it. This is not going to be something you can just start preparing for that Monday on the first day of practice that week. You have to start working on that team now if you're going to do this. You've got to take all summer and the entire season to get them in the right mind frame for this game, yourself included. You need to start molding them now."

``OK, I get it. But I have one condition. If we decide to play them, if it's OK with Coach Schebig, I want you to come out here for a week in early August so we can sit down with you and design some plays. I'm not asking you for plays against whatever defense they are going to run. I wouldn't ask you that, but I have some ideas that need tweaked a little. No one else has to know you're even here."

``I think we could maybe make that happen, Lars, and I don't really care if anybody knows I'm there or not. It's nobody else's business what I do now. I've been off their pay clock for a while now."

``Why create trouble for yourself?" I say. ``If we do this, I plan on creating enough trouble for everyone."

``That's my boy."

CHAPTER 13

UC-Camarillo president Dr. Betty Stein stands 5-foot tall and walks with a cane, but I've never met a more commanding presence in my life. She never misses anything, and always sees the other angles you are ignoring. She's sort of like your grandmother, but the one you don't want to have to admit to when you've messed up because you respect her so much. She's also not an academic who pretends to like athletics, either. She shows up to games and likes to say that the athletic, theater and music departments are the university's marketing arm. Unlike many college presidents, she's smart enough to let her coaches do their jobs and doesn't try to give them tips.

Each year she addresses the team and asks for only a few things.

``I want you to win, but I don't need you to win,'' she says. ``There's a big difference. If you don't understand, ask a coach, or better yet, your parents.

``The two things I need you to do is first, don't break any NCAA rules. It's simply not worth it for yourselves or this institution. We can't know everything you are doing so we have to trust you in this, and we are. The only thing breaking the rules will accomplish is embarrassing yourselves, your parents, myself, Coach Schebig and this school, and none of us need that. You may get away with it now, but eventually it will get out, it always does, and then we'll all pay for it long after you're gone. So will your reputation and the respect others have for you which someday you'll realize is much more important and more costly than scholarships or trips to bowl games or going on probation. You can never get it back no matter how hard you work.

``The other thing is, please take care of your grades. Do that for yourself, though, not for me. You may not fully understand this right now, but doing that will do you more good in the future than any tackle you make or touchdown you score. No matter how many people praise you for those things, they are temporary. This is a wonderful opportunity, but I won't tell you to not blow it. I will say to you, take advantage of it.

``Always remember that 99 percent of the people in the world are being exposed to UC-Camarillo through you so please continue to make us proud.''

She shocked the bejebbers out of Max and me one spring during our sophomore year. Walking to class, we passed her going the other way as she was talking to a student. About five steps later we heard, ``Mr. Curry, Mr. Preston, aren't you going to say hi.'' She remembered us, obviously, and Max and I were suddenly wishing we had shaved that morning.

She's a sparkplug, and I'm always glad she's on our side. I went to hear Dr. Stein speak one night and she was fascinating, funny, sarcastic at times and always thought-provoking. She must have been great in the classroom where she taught English.

I also really wonder what she's going to say during our meeting because everyone seems to enjoy throwing me curves on this situation. As we walk into her office with Coach Schebig and Athletic Director Jim Stovall, she's laughing loudly on the phone. Stovall is a pretty good guy. He and Coach Schebig were fraternity brothers here so they still get along well. In fact, it was Stovall who decided to bring Coach Schebig back to Camarillo. He tries to give us what he can, but we all realize we are Division I-AA.

``Before we get started,'' Dr. Stein says, ``Mr. Preston, have you come to a decision. The way I look at this, if you say we're going, then we'll play IWU; and if you say you'd rather not, then we won't be. Where do things stand with you?''

"Gee, thanks for all the pressure," I say, hoping for a laugh. But it never comes.

"I'd say you're probably used to it," she responds, with a twinkle of mischief in her eye. "It's been my impression you prefer to be in the middle of everything all the time anyway. Start talking."

"Yes, ma'am."

So much for easing into this.

"I've decided I want to play them, but first, I want us all to understand and talk about all the ramifications of that. We need to have a game plan for all the off-the-field things so we can concentrate on our regular game plan. If we're going to do this, I want to have the best chance to compete."

"Agreed. We all want what's best for the team and for you. What are your suggestions?"

I had actually written them all down as Max and I talked about the situation all weekend so I pull the list out of my pocket.

"Indiana Western has promised to take care of our expenses, and I've got a list for them, which means somebody else had probably better present it to them. I know my folks and Max's folks will want to throw some kind of a party for us, but I don't want them to have to worry about any other meals or anything like that. I want them to be able to enjoy this as well. Is there any way we can ask some athletic department workers or alumni from that area or someone to help them out for that party? I'm not asking for them to pay for it, just to help Mom and Dad by pitching in for some of the work. Maybe as payment, they can travel with the team and get comp tickets to the game."

"I think we can arrange that easily," Mr. Stovall agrees. "We'll treat this like we're going to a bowl game and set up travel packages and such. I have a feeling a lot of people will want to say they were at this game."

"Then we also are going to need to quadruple our ticket allotment of 500 that IWU is offering for the game," I said. "The last thing Max and I want to worry about are all our friends from Talbott asking us for tickets, and they will. And I would imagine most of the players' parents would like to go to this game if they can make it out there. This will be the first time most of our parents will have to make a big trip with the team. And if IWU balks, remind them they need us a lot more than we need them for this game.

"The next thing is we're going to need a bigger training staff for the football team. Maybe this will be a one-time or one-year experiment, but we need to be able to be at our best for this game. I know I can ask Dave and Joni Kuhn and their staff at Indiana Physical Therapy to pitch in on gameday and during practice that week if that's OK with you. We're going to need some more support staff at practices leading up to this trip, too, because we'll have to push everyone even harder than they have played before.

"We're also going to need more help for the Sports Information Department. Randy James is a great guy and he's top-notch for this level, but there's no way he can handle this week all by himself. Even he can't talk to everyone who's going to want a piece of this. There's going to have to be a press conference every day, too, and Max and I have already decided we are not giving one-on-one interviews outside of the press conferences that week. They'll overwhelm us if we let them. If they want a one-on-one with us, they better get them done before we leave here."

So far everyone is just nodding on every suggestion.

"These are all good ideas, Mr. Preston, and I'm sure Director of

Football Operations Mr. Ed Rose and Mr. Stovall can handle all of them, especially with this much lead time," Dr. Stein said. "In fact, I think we need to set up a meeting within the athletic department and my administration to discuss these matters. We probably even need to appoint a head of delegation for the trip to help things run smoothly. What would you think of Mr. Anthony Davis for that, Mr. Stovall?"

"Sounds good. As special events coordinator, he'd be the perfect man to coordinate between everyone. Plus, you know he'd love to go. We might be able to give Sports Information some help by organizing a team to go along and document what we do with video and photographs as well. Anything else, Lars?"

"Most of the rest of it is internal team stuff that we'll talk with Coach about after this meeting, but the one thing I think can make a big difference is we'd like the school to fly Coach Burgess out here for a week in early August. He can assess where we're at, help us with some plays and give the rest of our players some good advice. I'm worried they're all going to think they are better than they are and then they'll get knocked flat on their backs on the first play. He can help us with that."

"Is there any restriction against that with NCAA rules?" Dr. Stein asks.

"I'll look it up, but I don't think so," Mr. Stovall says.

"If it comes to that, he can just come out and stay at my place," Coach Schebig says. "There's no restrictions on that."

"OK, anything else, Mr. Preston?" Dr. Stein asks. "Are you absolutely sure this is what you want to do? I worry about the repercussions for you if things don't go well. Again, this is an opportunity, not an obligation."

"I understand, and lately I've begun to understand just how big of an opportunity this is in many different directions. I'm focusing on the good things that can happen with this."

"Then I think we're done," Dr. Stein says and stands. "Just remember, I'd like you to win this game, I don't need you to win it. And one piece of advice: Don't let this one game take over your entire season. It's big, but it's not that big."

That is something we are all going to have a tough time keeping in mind.

CHAPTER 14

After that meeting, we have another with Coach Schebig and then he calls a team meeting on Friday for all the players who can get to it. Since most of the players have been away from school for a month since the spring semester ended, that gives most of the guys some travel time to get back if they need it, but it also gives them all time to call Max and I and wonder what's going on. For the next two days I want to throw my cell phone into the ocean. All we can tell them is that the news isn't bad and that they'll all enjoy it when they got here. We can't even tell Big Dummy Eichorn because we know he'll blab to everyone he knows. He never has an unexpressed thought, and I know that's saying something coming from me.

Part of our discussions with Coach Schebig this week are about new team rules before we go over them with the leadership council and then the team. We also hash out a few surprises for everyone.

Despite the anticipation of the meeting, the rest of the week flies by – except for the blasted cell phone calls.

All the players seem a little uptight when they walk into the auditorium for the team meeting on Friday afternoon. For one thing, all the coaches and most of the athletic department staff are already here which is extremely odd to the players, so everyone must be thinking Coach has been fired for some reason or he's retiring because he's facing an illness.

It doesn't help the tension when Mr. Stovall starts talking by thanking everyone for coming. He points out Max, Eichorn and me standing up front with Coach Schebig and then introduces Coach Schebig to the lectern. Everybody is fidgeting and whispering. You'd think they were waiting to take a one-test-decides if you graduate exam just like in the nightmares.

"Before we recruited you here," Coach Schebig starts, "each one of you thought you were good enough to play big-time college football. Maybe you were a little small or a little slow or maybe your high school conference wasn't that big and no one from the big schools noticed you. But you all thought in your hearts that you were good enough, and for whatever the reason, you all ended up here. Deep in your guts you all still wonder if you could play at that level, don't you? You all wonder if you're still going to think about those 25 years from now when you're lying in bed at night.

"Well, guys, we have a chance to find out the answer. On Oct. 24, we're going to play at Indiana Western."

He may have tried to say more, but it's futile because the players are all roaring. They jump to their feet in excitement and everyone is hugging, giving high fives and back slaps all over the auditorium. Everyone is also talking at once, so much so that it takes four minutes for everyone to quiet down and even then everyone is still beaming and trying to catch their breath.

"OK, yes, that is exciting and I'm tickled to death you guys are so happy about this. That means I was right and you do still want to prove you can play with the big boys, but there are some conditions to that. There are some things we'll need to do that we would not normally do as part of our regular routine here. Just playing against them isn't the reward I'm looking for. I want a bigger reward out of this one. I want to beat their asses!"

At first everyone is in shock that coach swore, and about three heartbeats later they all roar again and start chanting "Coach! Coach! Coach!" Max and I are laughing our... um, butts off.

"Yes, I'll run the laps for that one, but I want to stress to you guys, this is not going to be fun for us. I would not have accepted this game if I thought we couldn't win it. I say that in all seriousness, even though I know we'll be the underdogs, substantial underdogs. I STILL think we have a chance to win, and what we have to do from right NOW is work on maximizing those chances.

``This is going to be work. The only way we have a chance to win this game is if we are so prepared that we know what we're going to do on every play going into that game. That's going to require more sacrifice, more commitment and more of your best effort EVERY day than any of you have ever given before. We are not going out there to be humiliated. I want to win! No excuses! Which means we start working on this game now.

``We can't start practices yet officially, but Lars, Max and Big Dummy... oops, sorry Jordan... I mean Jordan, are going to start two-a-day practices next week.''

That draws a few groans from the audience and finally settles everyone back into their seats.

``Hey, that's what it's going to take,'' Coach continues. ``We are being as totally upfront with you as we can be, and I'm serious when I say this is going to take quite a bit of sacrifice from all of us. I'm not allowed to and don't want to know what they are going to do with these workouts, and I can't make them mandatory, but you should all consider attending if you can. That's about all I can say about that.

``This is also going to be a difficult process, but I think you'll be surprised how good we can be and what we can do at the end of it. I ask you to all support your teammates. Help them in practices, in games and in the classroom. Don't cheat or anything like that, but look out for each other. If we are to have a chance in this game, we have to be as close as brothers. We have to all pull together and know we can count on each and every one of us to do their job. And we need everybody on this. We can't go into this game thinking that Max or Jordan is going to out-play his man so that can make up for somebody else getting beat by his guy. That won't work. We have to have everyone playing at their best and holding their own or better. No one else in that stadium is going to give us a chance, but by the end of our preparation we'll know we can do it.

"That also means we need everyone. We can't afford for one player to be ineligible because they didn't want to get out of bed for class or because they were out drinking too many nights. GO. TO. CLASS. Help each other there, too. Encourage each other so we don't have to worry about that side of things. If you need help, don't be too proud to ask. We need to be able to prepare as if everyone on the team is going to be available that day to help us.

"We will have some fun at this, but it will be because we will be achieving our best. I owe it to you guys to push you in this, and you owe it to yourselves and your teammates to give it your best effort. You also owe it to your parents who will be sitting in that stadium watching us. We may be the underdogs in this game, but we will not be overmatched, I promise you that. You'll be as prepared as I can possibly make you, and that's going to mean some different things around here. Those will only work if you trust us starting right now. Can I get an Amen?"

"AMEN!"

I think the entire building shakes with that one. It's a good thing it's late June and no one else is around this part of campus.

"Good. Whenever you're tired this summer or you're sick of my voice this fall, remember how you feel right now, ready to take on the world, like you could go out right now and take on the Pittsburgh Steelers. We're desperately going to need that passion and energy at different times this season. No excuses! No excuses!"

"No excuses!" everyone roars.

"That's more like it. I don't say that lightly because very soon you are all going to have to make that commitment to yourselves as individuals and as a team. If five of you don't live up to that commitment, the true goal of what that means, then we will be in trouble. I'm dead serious about that because I need you to be committed as well.

"Now Lars has some things to say."

How the heck can I ever follow that up? He's the master.

"To be honest with you guys, at first I didn't want to play this game."

That gets a few murmurs going around the room.

"I didn't think it would be worth it to break up our schedule and go out there and get hammered."

Now everyone is focusing right in on me.

"Didn't think I'd say that, did you? Well, that's what could happen if we aren't totally focused on this. Indiana Western is a very good team. They'll probably win the Midwest Conference this year, and there's about a 75 percent chance they'll just crush us if we're not totally ready. They are that good. Max and I and Alex, Erik and Bob and Randy all know exactly how good they are and how hard they work and the tools they have to work with. There's about 10 guys on their team who will be playing on Sundays in the near future. How many of us do you think will be?"

No one raises a hand or offers an opinion.

"Good, now everyone is paying attention. I'm not saying that stuff to intimidate you, just to scare you a little, to try to force you to follow the program we are going to attempt. Now, I think we can be that good, but I don't know it yet. We have to build to that level. We can't go toe-to-toe with them because right now they are bigger and stronger than we are, and you should always keep that in mind. If we try to play their game, and I mean any part of this entire next six months, we'll get creamed. Our advantages are we are faster and we MUST be smarter than they are. We must be more determined, more organized and more motivated. That will give us a CHANCE, and we aren't any of those things right now! If I had to bet today, I'd put $100 on them, but instead I'm betting on you and what we can become over the next four months.

"That means we have to do some things differently and begin preparing right now. These are not going to be things you'll enjoy, but they are very, very necessary and we've already cleared them with Coach and Mr. Stovall and the training staff. Summer practices are going to start at 6 a.m., and..."

As I knew they would, everyone groans loud enough that I can't get any more out so I step back let things settle down.

"Guys, this is what we are talking about. How badly do you want to do this because this is all part of it? What time do you think IWU is going to want to play this game? Do you think they'll think of us, be considerate and decide to play it at 7 p.m.? No, they'll force the network to show it early and want to play it at Noon, which is 9 a.m. our time. Half of you guys don't roll out of bed until 10 a.m., so how well do you think you're going to play at Noon out there? They know that! If anyone disagrees with me, I'll bet them right here, right now the game will be at Noon or even earlier. Anyone want to take that bet? You can name the wager.

"No? Then this is the way we have to do things if we want to make the most of our chance. That's what Coach is talking about when he says commitment to this team and to each other! Everyone thinks it's going to be great to play them, but really will it be?

"You really want to know why they want to play us? They want Max and I and Coach Schebig, and Bob, Erik, Alex and Randy to come out there so they can bury us! You have no idea how much they hate us. Oh, they'll say all the nice, polite things to the newspapers, and we didn't do anything to them, but I guarantee you they are talking about us every day at workouts this summer and they will be at every practice this fall. They want to humiliate us! They're so overconfident; they aren't even going to think about any of the rest of you until the opening kickoff! They don't care about you, they don't respect you, they don't even know about you. You are insignificant to them.

"Don't like to hear that? Well, it's true right this second, but this is also where and how we start to earn that respect. We have to suffer now so we're used to it when we play that game and nothing they do can affect us. We have to be so ready that no matter what they do, they can't wear us out. And then we give it back to them! We have to earn their respect, and we will if we pull together and follow this program to a man. No excuses!"

There are a few nods at that, but there are still plenty of scowls.

"Because of the early practice times, the university has agreed to furnish us with another training table every day at 10 a.m."

That brings everyone's heads back up.

"Yeah, I thought you'd like that one.

"There's one more big rule change that you aren't going to like, but it is necessary. From here on out, not one of us can Tweet, post on Facebook or even send an e-mail that talks trash about this game or about how excited you are to play there or about how you like our game plans. Don't even mention the game. I'm completely serious about this. We cannot get into a battle of words with those guys. Let them do all the talking they want, we'll show what we can do on the field. That will be a major part of our focus. If you have any questions on whether you can do something or not, ask one of the captains. We can't give them any ammunition to get fired up.

"We have to be like a Marine unit preparing for a deadly mission, totally focused and committed to each other and the goal. Think about it, no one is going to believe anything we say about ourselves right now anyway, are they? We can say how good we think we are, but really no one is going to believe us anyway, so what's the point? So what good would responding to them or talking do? They've never seen us play and that's great! Let them get overconfident and prepare for this just like it's any other game; because of that lets us sneak up on them and surprise them. We're going to do everything we can to make sure it's not just another game for them! We will be ready to play our best game ever. We ARE going to prepare to kick their Asses!"

Once again the room is rocking.

"Coach, I'll run those laps with you," I say and everyone laughs.

"We need to use this emotion to prepare, but we can't show it to anyone else but the people in this room. I am dead serious about this. This is about us! Not them so don't give them anything to use. Heck, they'll make up enough stuff anyway, and we better be ready for that, too. We know the truth about everyone in this room so who cares what anyone else says, no matter how bad it is?

"Guys, we must be stealth and precision. We CAN do this but we have to start preparing for this right now. This game is going to help us the rest of the season, too, because we are not forgetting those goals, either. I still want a ring. I just want to take IWU out along the way. Imagine the benefits to all of us, to this program the rest of the season and in the future if we can pull this off. People will never forget us if we can sacrifice together for the next four months. Four months to be remembered for a lifetime, and even better than that,

106

we'll have all those memories no one can take away from us.

``We'll see you Monday morning at 6 a.m. No excuses!''

CHAPTER 15

When Indiana Western sends out the press release announcing the game the next morning, Sports Information Director Randy James calls to warn us what is coming. Max and me and Coach Schebig are scheduled to be in Randy's office at Noon for a teleconference with all the media from Indiana. We know this is just the start of it.

We get one phone call before that from Win Rood of the Talbott Chronicle. Besides having the coolest name ever for a sportswriter, Win is a good man and has been friendly with both Max and I since we were growing up. It just always seemed he was there to cover whatever we were doing, and we learned to trust him over the years. We know he'll be listening in on the teleconference, but we agree to call him back later that afternoon so he can have some exclusive material.

As we expected, it's going to be an 11:30 a.m. kickoff, which is actually 8:30 a.m. our time, so I would have won the bet. We'll adjust. Max and I have already talked about how we'll be doing a lot of adjusting for this game.

The first question also goes as expected.

"This is Wendy Bartle from Sports Illustrated. Lars and Max, do you feel like this is a revenge game for you? What kind of emotions do you feel for Indiana Western?"

"We don't have any hard feelings for IWU," I start. "We've still got some friends on the team, but this is a great opportunity for us to play in front of our hometown fans. Because we went so far in the playoffs last year, we didn't get to come home for Thanksgiving, and this year we're hoping to go far enough we won't be home for Christmas, either."

``Max?''

``I'm just happy my folks will get to see me play again somewhere besides on the computer screen. As for the rivalry, how can there be bad feelings when most of the players and coaches there have never heard of us? They weren't even there when we were there.''

The rest of the questions all kind of hint around the same subject, trying to get us to say something it should be obvious by now we aren't going to say.

``Coach, this is Rick Rimelspach from the Cleveland Plain Dealer. Do you see this as a chance to match wits with Coach Jackson?''

Safe in the SID's office, all three of us look at each other and try not to laugh out load.

``Well, Rick, I'd say we're pretty even in that area since we went head-to-head in practice every day for 10 years. Sure, we'd like to win, but that's because it's a game, not because it's anything personal. I'm using some of Wally's stuff in our defensive schemes, and I'm sure he's using some of my stuff in his offense.''

Yeah, like maybe a snap count, but that's about all I can think of that Coach Jackson might be using.

``This is Pete DiPrimio from the Fort Wayne News-Sentinel. Besides the money on the payout, why do you guys want to play this game? No one would have known if you'd turned it down. You wouldn't have lost a thing.''

``I'll take this one,'' Coach says. ``We know Indiana Western is going to be very good this year, and we think we're going to be pretty good, too. We'd kind of like the chance to find out how good, and this is one way to do that. We'll also see our weaknesses exposed so we know what to work on before our playoffs start. Plus, we all get to come back and see family and friends. Basketball teams schedule these kinds of Homecoming games for players all the time, so why can't a football team do it as well? Plus, I hear I have to pay off my tab at the Trolley Bar."

Everyone, at least all the local writers from Arlington who know the situation, get a good chuckle out of that one.

"I can't believe you feel the same way, Lars," DiPrimio says.

"Max and I played pretty well on that field, but I didn't get to play enough to get it out of my system. I'd still like to see what we can accomplish."

That's about as close to the line as I can get without charging over it.

"Max, this is Rich Griffis from the Indianapolis Post. How will your teammates match up individually with the Sagamores? What's the main difference between Division I and I-AA?"

Max looks at both of us before answering, and Coach Schebig just nods his head at him.

"Well, Division I players are usually bigger and faster and because of that think they are a lot better. We're going to find out if they are. I've found heart wins a lot more games than any stats or measurements."

"That'll do it for this one," Mr. James says. "We'll see all of you out there in October. If you need anything before that, call me. If any of you want to come out here and see a game, you're more than welcome. I'll supply the suntan lotion."

That didn't go too badly. We were honest, but we also didn't tip our hand too far.

When we get back to the apartment, we wait an hour before calling Win because Coach Jackson is supposed to hold a press conference right after ours was finished.

``So what did he have to say, Win?"

``Pretty much the usual bluster. He tried to stick to talking about his team, but finally Pete DiPrimio stood up and said what everyone really wanted to know was his thoughts about you two and Dennis. He tried to talk around that, but Pete got him when he basically said the game wouldn't be of any interest to anyone except for you guys, so what did he really think?

``He finally said he didn't want to play this game because it was going to be so tough on you guys. He figures it's a no-win situation for his team because if they win it won't be by enough. He even said they'll use it as a practice week to prepare for Grand Rapids the next week which he thinks could be for the conference title. He said it's great that everybody else is getting so excited about this, but he and his team can't afford to be. He's not exactly helping sell a lot of tickets."

``Good old Coach Jackson, He never changes," I say. ``Wait until I tell the guys about that."

``Yeah, sometimes Wally isn't as smart or as smooth as he thinks he is. Who knows? Maybe he's just telling the truth from his perspective. Let's admit it, guys, they are going to be heavy favorites. Now start giving me some stuff I can use."

We both talk about how nice it is to have the chance to come home and play again, something we never thought would happen. Neither of us ever thought we'd talk about IWU again. I have to admit, while I'm talking to Win, in the back of my mind I'm already starting to make plans.

CHAPTER 16

By the time we get to the locker room Monday morning, most of the guys are sitting in their stalls reading copies of Coach Jackson's comments I put there last night. That wakes everyone up in a hurry.

``I can't believe this guy," Eichorn grumbles. ``He just thinks we're going to be a pushover. A practice week?"

That draws a few murmurs.

``He might be right," Max sys.

``What?" a shocked Eichorn asks. ``How can you say that, Max?"

``You guys have got to start understanding this situation right now. Lars, Randy, Bob, Erik, Alex and I are among the best players on this team, right? A couple of us are even all-conference selections, maybe all-Americans this year."

Everyone nods at that.

``What's your point?" Cory Hoersten asks.

``We were nothing on that team. We couldn't even get many reps in practice because we weren't big enough, fast enough or frankly good enough. Now all of you think we're going to just ease in there and somehow beat them?"

The locker room is real quiet now.

``So, if that's true, what are we doing here?" defensive secondary leader Miguel Perez asks. ``Why are we wasting our time?"

``You're not," Max says as he walks to the center of the room. ``Not if you are willing to listen and work harder than you ever have before.

You have to understand the circumstances and how we can make the most of them. You have to buy into the plan."

"Coach Jackson hates us," I say. "You may think we're exaggerating or making it up to impress you, but he really hates us, and he'll do whatever he can to embarrass us in this game if we aren't all perfectly prepared. If 15 of us aren't ready for that game, we're dead. If 10 of us don't play our best game of the year, we have no chance and it will be awful. This will be a defeat you or nobody else will ever be able to forget because they will run it up on us and keep trying to score no matter how far ahead they are. If they get the ball back with 30 seconds left and have the lead, they will not be taking a knee to run the clock out. They'll throw to try to score more points.

"This isn't war, but the biggest chance we have is to stick to a plan and prepare to execute it perfectly. We can out-smart them, but we have to be physically and especially mentally ready to do that. We can't afford to make mistakes if we are tired because they have the physical capability to score on every play. Because of their physical ability, they can afford to make more mistakes than we can. That's why we're here today and every day, so we can start preparing so that doesn't happen. We have chances, but they are fewer, so we must take advantage of them. We can't afford to miss on more than one or two.

"Max, Jordan and I are not smart enough to start talking strategy with you guys. We can't design the game plan, but what we can do, what we all can do, is get as physically prepared as possible so when the real practice starts, we can buy the coaches some time. If they don't have to spend two weeks getting us into top shape, that's two weeks we can start working for the Indiana Western game. That can be an advantage we have."

Most of the players are nodding at this. Though none of them are looking forward to what it's going to mean over the next two months, it makes some sense to them.

``And don't we want to be in the best shape possible anyway? We talk about how this could be a national championship year, one we'll never forget. Let's make sure we're ready for it. That is still our No. 1 goal, not this game. No excuses!''

We go out and start with stretching and calisthenics before running two miles. Then we hit the weights and finish up with a light scrimmage and some sprints. We have great numbers, better than we've ever had. In the afternoons we do it all again, each day a little bit harder.

Every football player hates this stuff, even though they all realize how necessary it is. You have to toughen up your body to take the bruises and the punishment that is coming. If you're not ready, it will be worse. You have to do the same thing to your mind. We push everyone. One time we'll say we're going to do this for 10 reps and we'll ask for 12. In another situation, we'll ask everyone to beat a certain time. The coaches can't be present, but we can still go talk to them or the strength and conditioning coach about what are legitimate goals to meet. When everyone surpasses the standard, we'll push it out a little further for a new goal.

We also do a lot of research. Though Max and I haven't been there for the last two years, my dad still records all the IWU games so he sends me a box of DVDs which Max and I sort through to make up scouting videos for each position. It's not the same as having a coach to go over stuff with us, but it definitely gives us something to look at and to study for tendencies. It also keeps us out of trouble by giving us all something to do away from practice.

I personally sit down one night after practice with Perez to go over Sagamores receiver Jim Wallace.

"I think one thing we can have an advantage on is if you can take him on one-on-one and keep him away from the ball," I say. "He's big at 6-4, 228 pounds, so he's got five inches and 38 pounds on you."

"You're asking a lot," Miguel says.

"I think you can give a lot. He's not real tricky, but he's great at running his routes perfectly. If you can determine what his routes are, you'll have a great chance of sticking with him. They don't like to throw the ball that much, but when they do, they mostly look toward him. The way I look at it, they under-utilize him. He's very good, but he might be under-used. Because they don't throw much, we can dictate a little when and where he can get to the ball.

"If you can slow him down, then their entire offense is limited to running the ball. That leaves 10 guys to bring down one."

To help him get ready, he's been covering Max in every workout, trying to match him on patterns and speed and tenaciousness. Though Max is shorter than Wallace, he's a tad bit faster and everything else is equal so it's a good test. After following Max around for months at a time, Miguel will be extremely ready to face Wallace head up.

Besides getting in shape and working on a little strategy, we're also trying to make sure at least part of these workouts are fun, and every couple of days we'll do something different on the beach in the afternoon to shake things up. One day we play 16-inch softball because none of us have gloves, offense vs. the defense. The next week we play soccer, and the week after that it's dodge ball. It's stupid, it's mindless, but it's also a pretty decent workout, and everyone is laughing and having fun while they can still breathe from running in the sand. It's like our own form of intramurals within the team.

"Just think," I tell them all after we finish playing a football game where everyone had to play their exact opposite positions, meaning

Big Bob was the safety and I was the nose tackle on defense and he was the quarterback and I was the center on offense, "if we work this hard during our real practices and the games, nobody will be able to touch us. How much fun will that be?"

That message is starting to sink in.

Near the end of July we come up with the idea for a Thunderbolt Olympics where the defense is taking on the offense in a week-long event. The losers will have to buy all the goods for a team party on the beach. We've all been working hard, and just about everyone but the biggest guys can run the two miles in under 14 minutes. We are in the best shape we've been in since Max and I got to Camarillo, even better than when Max and I first went to IWU. We think we're ready to go for the real practices next week so we decide to celebrate a little and even let the guys pick events they want.

One day we play a beach volleyball tournament, and it doesn't hurt our performances so we ask the girls' team to serve as officials. No one wants to look bad in front of the ladies so the intensity picks up even though we're all dog tired. You have no idea how good your legs are until you play all day in the sand. I have a lot more respect for Mikala and the girls and I already thought they were amazing.

Tuesday we play softball because it allows our legs to recover a little, but the next day we play a soccer tournament on the sand again. The big guys try to influence things by forming a wall in front of a player kicking the ball upfield, but the soccer coach/referee says that's illegal – when he stops laughing long enough to blow his whistle.

On Thursday we're holding our own track meet – on the track, not the beach, which is a lot more fun than I expected. It's fun to see how fast Max actually is and who is the second-fastest player on the team. Trever Andrews gives him a good race, with Keaton Alexander finishing third as the offense sweeps the top three places. The defense owns the field events, so the meet comes down to the 1,600 relay. Three cornerbacks and Eichorn go head-to-head with Max, Andrews, Alexander and me.

We thought we'd surprise them by having Max go first, but they keep cutting into his lead as each new man takes off. I figure halfway through I should have put Andrews on the anchor leg because he'd have killed Eichorn. It's all I can do to lean at the tape, but that's when a huge argument starts over who actually won.

Finally, "Big Dummy" yells, "It's a tie. Guys, it's a tie! C'mon, there's no reason to destroy what we've built over one stupid race! Let's all relax here. Lars, I had no idea you could run that fast, brother."

"I think I have to quit calling you 'Big Dummy,' " I tell Jordan a little later. "That was a pretty smart move."

"I'm learning," he says. "I'm learning."

The team score is very close and the final outcome comes down to dodge ball. You've never seen dodge ball until 80 in-shape, determined college athletes try to kill each other with rubber balls on the beach. You've also never heard this much trash-talk before, and it's a good thing Coach Schebig isn't around or we'd be running laps for weeks. The scary thing? We'd have no problem finishing them.

Referee? We don't need no stinking referees for dodge ball! Hirsch nails one defensive lineman so hard in the forehead, it knocks him flat on his back. The defense has a couple of guys who had been high school pitchers, and nobody is stupid enough to try to catch their balls. They'd leave a mark on a stomach or back for a long time. We're all going to be limping and complaining the entire weekend.

It is so much fun!

It takes an hour to get down to the final two players. Am I one of them? Heck, no! I get knocked out early when three linebackers gang up on me. It's finally down to Bob Brown and Eichorn's defensive co-captain, Nate Higgins, who is bigger, quicker and pretty sharp than Big Bob. He and Bob already knocked heads a few times last year in practice. It's obvious our training is working because Big Bob is down under 300 pounds for the first time since his sophomore year in high school, and he's still standing after an hour of dodge ball.

``Tell you what,'' he says to Higgins. ``We can keep throwing and fight this out, or we can drop these balls right here and start the party that we'll never forget. I don't know about you, but I could use a beverage, and I'll buy you the first one.''

``Make it two, and you've got a deal, big man,'' Higgins replies and throws his ball down as we all start cheering. Then it's a group hug in the middle of the beach. We're all dog-tired, smelly and in the best shape of our lives. We're also all friends.

``Way to go bro,'' Jordan tells me. ``We did it and we didn't kill each other.''

``We sure did,'' I say.

With that, the party starts, and it won't end until sunrise tomorrow. We're all tired, but happy and having fun. With two days off before the real practice starts, we are as prepared and together as we can be.

We've finally become a brotherhood.

CHAPTER 17

Coach Schebig also has another big surprise for us in early-July. Well, two of them, actually.

Once again, Max and I get called to his office, this time along with Jordan Eichorn. As we are shooting the breeze with Mrs. Nation around her desk, Coach's office door opens and the biggest man I have ever seen walks out. At least he's the biggest I have ever seen until the next guy walks out behind him.

These two are only about 6-foot tall, but they were also about 6-foot wide. They aren't exactly built like fireplugs, but more like dump trucks whose grills have been smashed in. They look almost exactly like footballs that have been a little over-inflated by about 50 pounds.

"Guys,' coach says, "This is Malosi Savaiinaea and Mataio Fialua. They're our new defensive linemen."

None of us know what to say, me mostly because I am already afraid of them. They both weigh at least 350 pounds but somehow it seems to be mostly muscle. Their forearms are corded with muscle, the kind you get from working every day as a kid, not something you can just earn in a weight room.

They look like God decided one day to build the perfect nose tackle and couldn't decide which one He liked better. They have huge heads, bigger shoulders and their thighs are bigger than my waist. They also have that tremendous low center of gravity. There's no way anyone on our offensive line can move them even with pads on and maybe not even two-on-one.

There are not going to be any problems getting Savaiinaea on the back of the jersey for one of these guys because it will fit with plenty of room to spare.

"Wait a minute, this is a joke, right," I say. "You guys look like you could be twins, or at the very least cousins or something, right?"

"We've never met before today," the one on the left says.

"Now I know you're pulling my leg."

"Actually, Lars, they are Samoans, but they have never met before. Malosi grew up in American Samoa, but Mataio is from San Diego. Both are junior college transfers who'll be joining in us in the fall after they go home for the summer.

"I'm thinking it will be interesting to see how many teams try to run up the middle against us, don't you?"

"Yeah. Well, welcome to UC-Camarillo guys! I think you'll enjoy it here because we plan on having a lot of fun this season. The only problem will be that I don't think anyone is going to have an easy time pronouncing your names."

"I'm stumped," Eichorn says.

"All my friends just call me Joe," says the one on the left.

"How about I call you Little Joe, and you," I say pointing to the one on the right, "what would you think about Big Joe?"

"My daddy is called Joe so that could work. If I don't like it, I'll let you know."

"Please do it gently. How in the world did you guys end up here? How come none of us have heard of you before?"

It turns out Little Joe, the one who grew up in American Samoa, had given up football after high school but found out he missed the game too much while attending community college. His uncle teaches philosophy at UC-Camarillo and is friends with Coach Schebig. Big

Joe, who grew up in San Diego, had been an all-city player who was recruited by Northern California and ULA but lacked the grades to get into either school.

"My mom kicked my butt for two years," he says. "I'll have bruises for the next decade, but it worked and I got my grades up. Then she heard Coach speaking at some conference and decided this is where I was going to play next. I never had a chance to say what I wanted."

"Aw, c'mon, Big Joe, you'll love it here. I know we're going to love having you here. You two just made all of our lives a lot easier."

They are really something. You've never seen anything that big that can move that fast outside of a "Jurassic Park" movie. Both are tremendous athletes. I think Big Joe could jump over Max's head, and Little Joe is the strongest player in the weight room.

They are also jokesters. They told everybody else on the team they were fraternal twins even though they had different mothers.

"Our dad impregnated two different women on the same day," Big Joe tells everyone. "Our moms picked our names."

Uh, huh. Most people buy it because they obviously are smart enough not to disagree with them. The "brothers" never let on.

When someone asks why they have different names on the back of their jerseys, Little Joe says, "In our culture, it's the women's surname which passes on. If you don't believe it, you can take it up with Mom, but I wouldn't advise that. She's meaner than even Big Joe."

Nobody can argue with that, even if it's total balderdash, because Little Joe shows us this picture of a woman who is so astonishingly mean looking she makes him look like a puppy. No one knows if it's his actual mother, but no one is quite sure how to comment so they say nothing from pure fear.

Other than that, the two Joes don't say a whole lot which means they love hanging with Max, and they've found kindred spirits in Big Bob and Gabe who love going out to eat with them. They start at one restaurant and then drive to another and finish off at a third. It got so crazy that a couple of restaurant owners made a deal with them for advance notice when they were coming.

The local wings place has become a hangout on Mondays for all of us. At first the owner, Rick Hazeltine, panicked, but then we started to draw more business for him so now he loves us. Once in a while we'll all pitch in and help him move equipment or packages or do favors to thank him. His wife Sandy adopted most of us anyway and is always asking how we are doing with our grades. Because of NCAA rules, they can't pay us and we can't do promotions for them, but everyone knows we always show up on Mondays, and we also let it be known we'll be hanging out there on Sundays to watch the NFL games. It works out for everyone.

They aren't Camarillo graduates, but they have quickly become our biggest fans. It doesn't hurt that we've adopted their son Spencer and made him a ball boy for the home games. He just loves hanging around with us and we all keep an eye out for him. We make sure his grades are pretty good, too. One time when he was having trouble with bullies at school, Little Joe and Big Joe showed up for a class presentation to talk about their heritage. They also made sure to point out that Spencer was their little brother and would be untouchable from that point on.

Then they told him if he tried to bully someone else because of their presence protecting him, he'd have to answer to them.

It's obvious they are going to fit in just fine, and Coach has some pretty big plans for them.

CHAPTER 18

When Coach Schebig and his staff start the real two-a-days on the last Monday morning in July, they can't kill us, and they are trying to. Stuff that normally wears us out, we are tearing up. Grass drills, up-downs, nutcracker drills, we are ready to go, and everyone is encouraging one another, even the freshmen. It's not that everyone is having a good time, but we are ready to work and Coach can move through things quickly. He finally calls a stop to the first practice 30 minutes early.

"Guess I'll have to come up with some new stuff for you guys tomorrow," he says and earns some cheers. "I'm proud of you guys. This is awesome. It makes me want to work that much harder, too. Since we obviously don't need two-a-days to get everyone in shape, we'll continue our regular workouts in the morning, and we'll start putting in work on offense and defense in the afternoon. I still expect the same effort, though, and if I don't see it, we'll bring all this back in a hurry. I don't think we'll need to.

"Everybody but Jordan, Max and Lars head in and enjoy the rest of your afternoon and evening. Good job! No excuses!"

Then the team surprises him again by sprinting to the locker room, something the three of us came up with as a way to stay sharp.

"Nice work, men," Coach says. "Looks to me like we're about three weeks ahead of schedule. I'm calling Coach Burgess tonight and telling him to get here by next Monday. Maybe he can even stay a few days extra. I'm guessing you guys have some ideas on stuff to work on, so let me know what you think tomorrow. Heck, you know the drill."

"Just as long as we stay away from beach volleyball tournaments," Eichorn says with a laugh. "They are fun to watch but lousy to play in."

"I still think we should still do something a few times on the beach," Max says. "We've got that resource that few teams have, so we should be using it. It's great for your legs."

Despite Jordan's groans, Coach agrees, and once a week we'll go down to the beach and play our games at the end of practice instead of running sprints. Everybody hates it at first, but it really seems to help team camaraderie. We all work hard, but we laugh, too, and our legs feel amazing.

When Coach Burgess arrives, Max is the happiest man on the West Coast because I've been peppering him with play ideas for weeks. I filled up two notebooks with potential strategies for trick plays and different options we can try. My first idea is that we should script out our first 25 plays and practice them until we can do them backwards. My second idea is if we are this far ahead, we should take advantage by concentrating one day a week on Indiana Western. We have 20 starters coming back and we all already know the schemes so well we could teach them.

Coach Schebig likes both ideas but as always cautions us to remember the real goals of the team. It's our responsibility to make sure there are no problems with the rest of the schedule first so we can concentrate on IWU. Any losses or problems, and we go back to our regular preparation schedule.

Max also comes up with the idea that we should have one senior speak at the end of each Indiana Western practice about what the game will mean to them. Jordan says he wants to go first.

I give Coach Burgess a few days to check us out and get acclimated before we have our first meeting with Coach Schebig. Notebooks in hand, I'm ready to start the real planning for the Sagamores in the coach's office.

"I'm impressed," Coach Burgess says. "Dennis told me a little bit of what you guys did this summer to prepare, but I thought he was kidding me. There's only a few stragglers out there."

"We've been working hard, trying to save some prep time on the physical side so we could spend more on the mental side," I say.

Then I start flipping pages, showing them what I've been working on. They nod at first, but eventually, they both look at each other before Coach Schebig tells me to stop.

"Lars, it's great that you're so excited about this, and some of those plays could work, but you can't use more than 10 of them," he starts. "For one thing, if we spend as much time as will be needed to teach all of those plays, it will take away from our preparation for the other games, and we can't do that. The other thing is, how much new stuff do you think everyone can learn? We can't overload them, and we also can't overload you."

"What do you mean? I'm ready to go right now."

"Yes, and the game isn't for three months yet, and there are eight games before that which are probably more important to us as a program in the long run.

"You know the real reason I agreed to bring Coach Burgess out here? It wasn't really to work on the team, but to work on you because I knew you'd be so excited you might be on the edge of losing control."

"Now wait a minute, I've done everything you asked of me this summer, and you know I'll be ready no matter what."

"And that's a little bit of the situation because we have to make sure you're not too ready, too fired up that you explode. The one thing you guys can't do is go in there so fired up that you let the emotion take over. You have to use the emotion. You need to be smooth and efficient and act like you've been there before. For one thing, emotion doesn't last and it has peaks and valleys which you can't afford on the road against a team like this."

"That starts with you, Lars," Coach Burgess says, "because the one thing Coach Jackson is really counting on is that you'll lose your cool in this game. He never had any doubt you'd want to play this game, none of us did. He knew eventually you'd go for this because you are so competitive, and he's expecting that to lead to mistakes in the game. He expects you to implode and try to go for things you're not capable of just so you can show him how wrong he was. He's counting on that.

"You have to go at it from a different angle. This is where you have to show how much you have grown up and matured as a quarterback and as a team leader because everybody on both sides of that field is going to be looking to you. You can't crack."

"I haven't shown a hint of cracking on this. Remember, I'm the guy who debated whether we should do it all."

"Yes, and now, three months before the game you are pushing yourself harder than you ever have before. This is even more than when you and Max were getting ready to walk-on because now you know more about football and about yourselves so you think you can handle more," Coach Schebig said. "Right now you're in the ultimate mind frame and physical conditioning to play that game, but that's not what we need right now. Do you understand what I'm saying?"

"Yes, I think I do. It's fine that I'm that way now, but I really need to be that way in the middle of October."

"Exactly!" Coach Burgess smacks his hand on the table. "Your teammates may think they are ready right now, too, but they still have a lot of room to grow, and you have to lead them there. You have to make sure this team is peaking at that time, not next week. It has to be a process, not just the end goal.

"Lars, let's be blunt, the only chance Camarillo has in that game is if you play the best game of your career, and that has very little to do with statistics. Who cares if you throw for 300 yards if you guys get stomped 37-10? That's exactly what Coach Jackson wants. That will prove his point for him. Again, you have to be smarter than that because as much as you think you know what he'll do, he knows exactly what you'll do because he's been a football coach for 25 years. That's his job. He'll also be watching video of every game you play this year.

"You think you guys have motivation for this game? Nobody has more motivation than he does. He may say it's a practice week in public, but behind the scenes he'll be whipping those guys hard. He'll spend two months promising them how bad things will be if they lose."

"I'm counting on that," I say. "I want them to feel all the pressure so when we are successful at something, they are the ones who start to crack. I want the crowd to have doubt, and I want them to have doubt. I think we can use Coach Jackson against them."

That statement shakes them up and both lean back in their chairs a bit.

"What do you mean?" Coach Schebig asks.

"I'm hoping we can get him rattled before he gets us rattled. I know he's going to be focusing totally on Max and me, and I think we can use that, which is what I've tried to do with some of these plays. We'll be the decoys and we'll take the punishment because it will open up other areas for us to attack. I even know how to make sure that happens."

``What are you talking about?" Coach Schebig asked.

``You know how the most important person in pro wrestling is the bad guy? Well, I'm going to draw so much attention that they'll all want to kill me and forget about the game. I'm going to be the bad guy."

CHAPTER 19

``Oh, that's good," Coach Burgess says and nods.

``Wait a minute, Mike," Coach Schebig says. ``We have to be very careful about this. As good as he thinks he is, Lars is still just a kid here and we have to protect him, even if it's from himself. We can't let him do that."

``Sure, you can," I start again. ``Here's why: You're going to be in on it from the start. You're going to know it's all a fake, all part of a plan.

``The whole plan is to present the picture that I'm out of control when actually it's all going to be totally under control. That will take pressure off everyone else here and allow them to prepare normally. I'll appear like some cocky punk who doesn't know his place. I figure we'll draw at least three personal fouls from them in the first half on late hits and cheap shots."

I can see that Coach Schebig is finally starting to get it as he says, ``We'll have to make sure the rest of the team doesn't follow along in that aspect, but you're right, this could work. Instead of letting Wally bait us, we turn it around on him."

``Exactly, and you'll know it's not `real' since I'll still be my normal self in practice and during our games and stuff. I'll only let loose when I'm asked about Indiana Western so it looks like I'm so focused on them that I'm losing perspective on that game.

``At first, I thought our best hope was that they would overlook this game and come in flat, but I realize that's never going to happen because Coach Jackson won't let it. He may talk down the game, but you know he's going to want to beat us by 30 or 40 points. He'll have those guys foaming at the mouth, so we just have to push them a little further, and I think I know exactly how to do that."

I lay out some of my plans for them, and then some of the plays and the reasons behind them. They both agree some of them might work but will need some work on the field. We all agree maybe the biggest difficulty with new plays is we can't try any of them live on the field during games before that one because Coach Jackson will pick them up on the film. In fact, I suggest we have to get them all worked out before we head to Indiana because we won't even be able to try them out in practice there. We have two options right now when we go out there, practicing at Moord Stadium or at Talbott, and in either place, there's no way to make sure we're not being filmed. I expect to be.

So, we really do have to start working on these plays now during our Indiana Western practice days for them to have a chance to working then.

"In fact, I think we should tone down our offense maybe all the way until that game," I say. "We aren't going to need too many special plays to beat the teams we're going up against, except maybe Northern California. IWU is going to expect us to use that game as a test run, so they'll have four scouts there watching everything we do. What would happen if we played conservatively? We might cross up NCU enough to mess up their schemes as well."

Coach Schebig says he'll think about it, and the next day agrees to sit down and start plotting out our first 25 plays. At first he thinks maybe we are rushing it a bit by doing that, but I convince him there's no reason to wait. The three of us already know what schemes "The Green Monsters" will use, and it's not like we have to wait for a scouting report or even to watch video. We can actually save time later by doing it now, especially with Coach Burgess here.

That doesn't mean we won't watch the video later, since we'll want to make sure there are no last-second changes or surprises.

"Besides, half of those guys aren't smart enough to teach new things to," I say with a grin.

"Hey, hey! I recruited those kids," Coach Burgess jumps in.

"So did I," Coach Schebig chimes in.

"Well, then it's a good thing you got smarter," I say to Coach Schebig and we all laugh.

"Sometimes you are just too cocky for your own good," Coach Schebig says.

"Let's hope everyone thinks that, especially Coach Jackson."

The preseason practices go smoothly, as do the first few weeks of our schedule. We're rolling so good, the starters barely have to play into the third quarter for the first two games and get to sit out the fourth quarter in the third game. You might think the locker room would be giddy after the games, but we have a new team rule that we can celebrate the win that night, but by Monday we have to practice like we just lost the game.

We also establish a kangaroo court with Max as the judge and Jordan as his sergeant at arms. Their mission is to make sure nobody is getting too happy with all this and help us all keep things in perspective. It turns out to be another team-building thing because we all laugh so hard during the "hearings." For one thing, somehow Max found the head of an old-fashioned mop which he uses as his judicial wig. Then Jordan came up with a list of team rules that no one can remember all of them. Some of them are things like not stepping on the Thunderbolt logo in the locker room, or spitting on the floor, not picking up towels, etc. Then there are the strange ones he makes up. He fined Nate Higgins because he had a date with a girl who didn't live up to the standards of the team. "Hey, don't talk about my sister that way!" Big Bob yelled. Then he came up with one for the worst suit worn on a gameday. Everyone can get fined, even coaches. I nailed Max by recording him talking baby talk with Emma. We hold the meetings on Sundays, and it gives us a chance to blow off some steam.

We also start our weekly IWU practices, putting aside a couple of hours on Wednesdays to go over offensive and defensive plays. One week, the defense uses IWU schemes so the offense can try things out, and the next week the opposite happens. It's not a tremendous benefit, but it does remind us all of what we're facing and keeps us all thinking and dedicated to staying extra sharp.

We also start the senior speeches to help maintain focus.

"When Max and Lars first showed up on campus," Jordan starts in our first one, "I didn't like them. I was pretty sure they thought they were better than us and we were lucky to have them even consider playing with us. I didn't like their attitudes at all. If Coach wasn't standing there and I didn't want to run any more laps, I'd tell you what I really thought of them."

That draws a few chuckles.

"Now, I realize they weren't being cocky, they just had the confidence of knowing they could compete at a high level. It was a good kind of confidence, a physical and mental maturity maybe. I think we all need that same kind of maturity for this game because we'll need it to help them. I realized the other day that the only reason we're getting to play in this game is because of these two, and maybe not in a good way. This is a great opportunity for us, but maybe not for them. If we get crushed and humiliated, we can still come back here, and really, nobody will know the difference. Our families won't care that much, our fans will forget about it after the next win, and we'll go on with our season and our lives pretty easily.

"Max and Lars won't be able to do that. This is their Homecoming Game, and if the worst happens, they won't be able to go home that much again. Think about what a bad performance by us could mean to their families who have to stay there and listen to all the snide comments when they go to the grocery or the mall or even church. A lousy performance here would wipe out everything good they did in the Lily game.

"And then I asked myself why we are doing this? Why is UC-Camarillo really going to play Indiana Western. It's all because of those two making these sacrifices for us. They could have said, 'No,' and we never would have known better because none of us even knew the offer had been made in June. We had no idea. As much as he talks, Lars is actually doing this for us more than himself. I would have said as much as Max talks, but we all know he doesn't.

"So what I'm saying is, we need to be ready to help them do this. We can't let them down after they have done so much to lift us up. You know, we talk a lot about 'No excuses!' but we never really talk about what that means. We need to think about that because truthfully, the rest of us are still Division I-AA players and we do have that excuse if we fail, but Max and Lars don't. They can't have any excuses going into this game. They believe so much in us that we have to make sure we truly live up to those beliefs. We have to perform to the expectations they have for us and work extra hard to make sure we don't have any excuses when this game is over. No excuses!"

Coach Schebig, Max and I are standing off to the side stunned when everyone starts chanting, "No excuses! No excuses! No excuses!"

"Shoot, if I'd have known he was going to be that good, I'd have saved him for the pre-game speech," Coach Schebig says with a grin. "Who knew 'Big Dummy' had it in him?"

"I think we're just starting to find out what all Jordan can do," I say.

The next day we all have "No excuses!" T-shirts in our lockers.

It's great that everyone is excited about IWU, but we all know the Northern California game is coming up. It's our first road game, and even though it's not in our conference, we know it's a big game against a Division I squad. They are giving us some good money to come in and lay down, but we're not going to.

But as ready as we think we are, they are just as ready for us.

CHAPTER 20

Northern California is always a tough game for us because it's on another level of skill, and it's hard to get to Fremont. The Pathfinders are never a great team, but they are a solid, good team and they are known for their hard-hitting defense. It always takes a couple of days to recover after playing them because the games are so physical.

This is our third trip to Fremont after we lost there during our sophomore year and beat them last year. It's a beautiful city, and you can easily get distracted, but we're all quietly ready to go for this one.

We kick off, and they run the ball right down our throat. They stomp off an 80-yard, 15-play drive that almost runs out the quarter, and there's nothing the Joes or Jordan and company can do to stop them. When we get the ball back on the ensuing kickoff, Anthony Tomlinson fumbles on his second carry. When NCU scores a minute into the second quarter, it looks like a very long day for us, especially since we don't want to use any trick plays to keep them off-balance.

It's a slugfest up front, but my offensive line is doing a pretty good job. I get hit a few times after I've released the ball, but nothing major. Tomlinson is having a hard time running the ball, but he's great on screens and finally breaks one for a score so we trail 14-7 at halftime.

"That's OK, we didn't expect this one to be easy," Coach Schebig yells at halftime. "We wanted a good test, and we've got one. This is where all that summer work pays off."

We keep trying to run Tomlinson early in the third quarter, just to keep them honest more than anything. That opens the middle for Alex Eastin to catch a few passes at tight end, and then Keaton Alexander breaks free for a deep ball. The drive stalls at their 25, but Manuel Jimenez boots a field goal to cut the margin to 14-10.

But they get another long kickoff return to start their next drive deep on our end of the field and they score to go up 21-10. We're trying to stay patient, but the running game isn't working so I use a play-action fake to Tomlinson to set up Max on a bomb. He catches the ball at their 10-yard line, and Jimenez kicks another field goal to end the quarter.

We need a break and we get one when Eichorn steps in front of the tight end to pick off a pass on our own 23-yard line. We finally pull off a little bit of a big play when I fake a handoff to Tomlinson and toss it back to Max on a reverse. Their inside linebacker on the left side buys the fake, and Randy Marcom takes care of the left end to free up Max to take off.

Sometimes it's just fun to watch him run. Everybody thinks because he's short and doesn't weigh a lot he'll go down on the first touch, but Max is always moving those hips so they aren't that easy to grab. When the cornerback on that side tries to get him with an arm tackle, Max breaks it and he's good for another 40 yards. He finally gets shoved out of bounds at the 7 by the safety.

With all the running and the way our offensive line has been pounding on them, the Pathfinders' defense is starting to wear down. Tomlinson runs a sweep left and shoves behind Gabe Hirsch and Marcom to get close, and then Coach pulls a surprise by sending Big Joe in to play fullback at the goal line. He plows ahead and Tomlinson trots in behind him untouched for the touchdown.

Because there's still five minutes left, Coach Schebig decides to have Jimenez kick the extra point so we're still down 21-20. Jimenez is one of the greatest kickers I've ever seen. Of course he started playing soccer, but he can make the ball dance when he needs to, and it's fun to watch him try trick kicks in practice. He'll bet us he can hit the goalpost within three kicks from the 30-yard line, and he almost always collects. He's also gotten pretty good at making his kickoffs land where he wants them to. This time his onsides kick travels exactly 11 yards on one bounce, and Eastin and Higgins pounce on it to give us another chance.

By now, the stadium so quiet you can hear the linemen grunting as their pads smack up front. Tomlinson goes behind Brown up the middle for two plays to get us past midfield. Then I hit Trever Andrews on a slant over the middle. We've got three minutes left and we're on their 40-yard line.

I call my own number on the next one, and their middle linebacker falls for the fake slant to Max to leave a hole for me. I tuck the ball, reach up and grab Big Bob's beltline and let he and Gabe shove forward into the middle of their defense. We get to the 33 before enough of them drag us to a stop.

We're within field goal range, so I hand it off to Tomlinson for 3 yards and another first down with two minutes left. Their linemen are all bent over, hands on hips trying to suck oxygen in. Coach sends out a double tight end formation and we let Tomlinson pound away on them two more times to get inside the 25. With 30 seconds left and facing a third down, I call time out.

"All right, good job, Lars," Coach says. "Get some rest while Manuel wins this game for us."

Big Bob's snap is perfect, and Manuel does exactly that with his kick which would have been good from 50 yards.

On the final kickoff, NCU tries a bunch of laterals, but our guys all stay in their lanes until they have nowhere to go and eventually one of them throws a forward lateral. We win 23-21 in what is probably the hardest-played game I've been in at UC-Camarillo. My uniform is caked in dirt that became mud because I was perspiring so much.

Max and Tomlinson need IVs in the locker room, and all of our offensive linemen are beat up. But they are also happy.

"There were a lot of heroes today," Coach Schebig says. "That's what 'No excuses' is all about because that was a heck of a football game! Let's enjoy this one for a little while."

After making sure to thank all my linemen and credit NCU for playing so hard, I get my first question about IWU during the post-game press conference. Somebody asks if that game scares me because the beating I took today could be easy compared to what that game will bring.

"I'm not scared of them at all," I say. "We're not scared of anyone. They could never stop me in practice, and I'm a better player now than I was then. If anything, they should be scared of me."

That's the truth, but maybe a little over the top. It's also the first thrust that Coach and I have planned.

CHAPTER 21

When we resume practice on Monday, I've already initiated phase two, texting with my former teammates Andrew Crow and Duncan Welker. One of Mikala's teammates had Crow's number, so I poked some fun at him on Sunday after our kangaroo court. I told the guys during the meeting what we were doing and why we were doing it. "Still keeping your head down on reverses?" I send Crow. Then I sent a few choice words to Welker, ending with, "Caught any good alley oops lately?"

After sitting out red-shirt seasons, both those guys are seniors this year and the leaders of "The Green Monsters." Because of their responses, I can tell right away I'm getting under their skin. "We'll see who still has a head on his shoulders when the game is over!" Crow sends back. Welker just texts back, "I can't wait to see you lying on the field again."

I'll be keeping a dialogue going with these two for the next few weeks heading into the game. I even plan on keeping copies of the texts and sharing them with Win Rood for a story the week of the game. That should get the entire team boiling at me, though I'm guessing that part will be taken care of a long time before then.

Speaking of the media, I have my first visitor from the Midwest after practice on Monday when Max and I meet with Pete DiPrimio from The News-Sentinel in Fort Wayne. For some reason, he thinks we're going to be big news in Fort Wayne, and I prove him correct right away when he asks about my relationship with Coach Jackson.

"It's a love-hate relationship," I explain. "He hates me and I loved playing for him. I say that sincerely because he made me a much better player. I needed to be a little quicker releasing the ball, a little more elusive and a lot smarter or I'd have gotten killed by his players. There were no-holds-barred when facing the defense as I was running the scout team, but it made me a better quarterback because I learned to be ready for just about anything."

"That's a pretty strong statement," DiPrimio says.

"Maybe I'm not being totally fair," I say, sitting back a bit. "He may not only hate me, but he loathes me, despises me. For some reason we offended him by even being on the same practice field with his players, and he always let us know it. He encouraged his players to try every dirty hit, cheap shot or illegal tactic to injure me. Except for the guys on my side of the ball, I never had any protection. We had to learn to handle things on our own."

"Is that why you left IWU?"

"Sure. It was obvious that we weren't going to get a fair chance to play there under him, and even if we did, it was going to be open season on us. He never protected us from potential injuries when he was the assistant coach, so I doubt it would have gotten better with him as the head coach. We also weren't given the option to stay. If he could have, he'd have kicked us off the team two minutes after the Lily game ended."

"How can you believe that?"

"Less than a month later, he told us he was going to remove us from scholarship at the end of the school year. Then he wanted us to red-shirt the following season and said there was no reason to plan on dressing for spring ball, taking part in summer workouts or even planning to practice with the team in the fall. How many red-shirt guys who aren't hurt do you know who don't even practice? When we said we wanted to transfer, he wasn't going to release us until after he knew where we were going, which we couldn't even think about until we had been released. We had to force a meeting with the athletic director to get any consideration."

"So this is going to be a grudge match?"

"It may sound like it, but at least this time I'll have officials there to protect me from the worst of it, and my guys will take care of me. I still don't trust some of their guys like Crow and Welker, though. All they need is one clean shot, and anything can happen. They'd love that."

"Then why did you agree to play this game?"

"I could not take this opportunity away from my teammates. This is probably their only chance to play on national TV, and I'm also not going to let one man decide what I do or don't do with my life. He's not nearly as powerful as he'd like to think. Besides, I think we can give IWU quite a battle because it's going to be fun to match wits with him on the field. For once, I get to call my own plays and he won't know what's coming ahead of time so he can't stack his defense against it. I'll finally have a fair chance. It should be a lot of fun."

"You can't think you're going to win, do you?"

"What have we got to lose? Nothing. The most dangerous human being or animal is the one who doesn't have anything left to lose. Think how much pressure is going to be on those guys to crush us. Coach Jackson will be hounding them for weeks, their fans expect nothing less than a rout and they all think they are that much better than we are per man. If they don't step on us early, they're going to have to deal with doubt, and I like our chances if I've got the final snap with the game on the line. They all know what I can do then.

"I will say this definitively, win or lose, I'll be standing at midfield at the end of the game waiting to shake hands with Coach Jackson and anyone else on their team. Will they be there?"

I'm laying it on thick, but it's also 100 percent true though I have never said any of that publicly before. Coach Schebig and I had talked about what I would say as part of our preparation. SID Randy James had come up with a list of questions he thought media members would ask, so I had time to study those and think about my responses. We decided I should just be honest and say what I felt.

Will there be consequences? So what? Can Coach Jackson hate me anymore? Can his players be even more motivated to knock me out of the game? Maybe that will work in our favor.

Like Coach Burgess predicted, everyone will be focused on me anyway, and I'm used to it. This was just a way to make sure IWU's players would be as well. If that means they leave my teammates alone and able to prepare properly, bring it on.

CHAPTER 22

The one person I should have let in on the plan but didn't was my father. That also explains why he has some tough questions for me tonight.

We talk at least twice a week, mostly just to touch base with each other. He asks about my practices, I ask about his latest doctors' appointments or how work is going at the shop. I think this time he just wanted to reassure me that everything was planned for and there would be plenty of help available when we arrived in Arlington and Talbott. Besides having the other parents visiting, he's asked about 10 of his retired buddies to pitch in and act as hosts and guides. They've made up Talbott Thunderbolt T-shirts, and we're going to instruct the guys they can always ask for help from those people if they see them in town. Some have even volunteered to drive us around on a limited basis.

The other thing he wanted to know is why I'm showing so much bitterness in all these interviews. He's seen Pete DiPrimio's story which is causing all kinds of ripples in Indiana.

``You've got anger in every sentence, and that's not you," he says. ``It's certainly not how I raised you, so what's going on? I don't believe you are still that upset over what happened three years ago. If you are, that doesn't say a lot of good things about Camarillo, either. Are you?"

``Not especially, but it's part of our game plan," I say.

Then I tell him about trying to get everyone on the IWU side of the ball to concentrate on me so they leave my teammates alone. The texting with Crow and Welker has gotten pretty nasty, and I've decided to pull back a little on my end of it. I need to let them simmer a bit. It's done being funny.

"You know you can't win using anger," Dad says. "It's not strong enough to carry you through."

I agree, and try to explain some more of what I'm trying to accomplish. I also tell him how I'm mostly concerned about the rest of my team.

"Dad, a lot of these guys have no idea what we're facing. They have never played against these kinds of athletes or this kind of atmosphere before. The goal is to use me as the decoy so they can just play, but I'm not sure they understand how hard this is going to be."

Dad has always been my biggest fan, but that also means he knows me better than anyone so I have never been able to hide anything from him. No one has ever seen me play more games, good or bad. He's the one who taught me every sport at the beginning, but he's never pushed me to excel in any of them. He always allowed me the time to develop my skills and didn't force me to. He's always been my balance and my barometer. Sometimes he lets me go and work things out myself, and other times he makes me talk about what's bothering me.

He just always wanted me to play with class. I still remember getting yanked out of a Little League game at age 9 because he saw me talk back to an umpire. It didn't matter if the coach said it was OK because it wasn't OK to my dad. It never happened again, either.

"Well, I think you're pushing it a bit far and need to tone it down some. There are a lot of people who think this is some kind of blood feud between you and Coach Jackson, and you need to pull back before it gets beyond your control. Maybe you should just say some of that stuff in the locker room and leave it out of the media conferences."

A lot of people who don't know me already think I'm cocky and a jerk, but I'm really not. I'm a quarterback. That means it's my job to be a leader and instill belief in others that we can get the job done on the field.

I also have to believe in myself. Because of my size and coming from a small town, if I didn't have confidence in myself during this process no one else would have. I had to first believe I could do these things or I never would have gotten the chance because I always had to convince someone to let me try. There's a difference between confidence and cocky, and I've had to live on that edge to prove to people I was worth taking a chance on.

Sometimes I push it too far, but if I let up for a second, I know I could lose any chance I have. There's too much there for the doubters to pounce on so I've had to learn to fill the role. It's sort of like a police officer or an umpire, in that no matter the circumstances, you have to project confidence so people will believe in you and that you'll do the right thing even when you have no idea sometimes. Why do kids often cause more problems for substitute teachers? They sense a lack of confidence and push to see how far they can go. They'd rarely dare to try anything with the regular teacher because they know the limitations.

For this game, I have to get my teammates to believe they don't have any limitations.

My dad taught me a lot of that whenever we were driving home from games. We'd always discuss not only what happened but why it happened, too. Then we'd focus on what I could have done differently to help prepare my teammates or to pick up somebody who had dropped a pass or missed a block.

I have also learned that sometimes the best leaders are the ones who can make others believe something can happen even when they themselves aren't quite sure. As long as everyone else believes, there's a chance. That's the hardest part of playing quarterback for me at times because as cocky as I appear, I also sometimes have doubts.

"I'm worried about this game, Dad. Max and I know what's coming at us, but I'm afraid the other guys are going to panic once something goes wrong. They could get overwhelmed in a hurry, and I'm afraid they are going to see my doubts and then everything will fall apart."

I swear, he's the only person I would dare admit anything like that to.

"I understand," he says. "I really do, but that shouldn't bother you too much. When are you always at your best? When everything else is falling apart and you have to rely on yourself and Max to make something good happen. That's why the scout team worked together so well, and that's why you guys beat Lily. You quit thinking and just trusted your instincts. That's when everyone else followed you. Those players believe in you not because you talk a good game, Lars, but because they know you can play one.

"You're prepared for this in so many ways. It's what you've been dreaming of, and you have all worked so hard for it, but you have to trust that extra work and yourself. I'm not afraid you guys are going to get blown out or even beat. I'm looking forward to seeing what you can do with all the preparation you've had. Trust your teammates and your coaches the way they always trust you. Most of all, believe in yourself. You're ready for this even if you don't fully realize that yet."

"I guess so."

"Well, I know so. What have I always told you about which opponent is the one you have to worry about?"

"It's not the one doing all the talking, it's the one who's quiet because he's confident enough he doesn't need to do any talking."

"Exactly. And you know what? Even if it all falls part, it doesn't really matter because that's what everyone else is expecting to happen anyway. Either way, you can't lose. I still can't believe Coach Jackson was stupid enough to schedule this game because out of everyone, he should know best of all how good you are when you are so motivated. You're nervous? He better be scared to death."

I hadn't thought of it that way. And better yet, Coach Jackson had no idea what style of game we were going to try against them.

"It will be fun to see how these trick plays will work against them," I say.

"This is an amazing opportunity. Just like the Lily game, you should just seize the moment. Quit worrying about what might happen and plan for what will happen. Relax and trust yourself like you always have."

"Yes, sir."

"The other thing is, no matter what happens, your mother and I will never be disappointed in you. Every time I think about this game, I can't believe the courage you are displaying and the sacrifices you are making for your team. I know deep inside you didn't want to play this game, but you put what everybody else wants ahead of your own desires. You're doing what a man does. Just by coming back here you have made us very proud, and nothing that happens during that game will change that."

"And that's always the most important thing," I say.

"Yes it is, and you better never forget it. If you play and live up to the stands we taught you, everything will take care of itself. Whatever anybody else thinks or says doesn't matter."

"Guess now it's time to shut up and play."

"That's my boy. I love you, Lars."

``I love you, too, Dad.''

I am so blessed to be able to tell my dad that.

CHAPTER 23

With three weeks left until the IWU game, we continue to pound away at our schedule. Idaho Tech falls 40-20, and University of Los Angeles gives us a big test before Tomlinson scores late to give us a 37-30 win. Our running game is finally gaining momentum, meaning it's difficult for any defense to scheme us. We are scoring 38 points per game and we're still holding back a big part of what we can do for the Indiana Western game.

Even better, we've been able to overcome some small injuries so far with our depth. Alexander and Andrews are really showing what they can do as receivers, and the offensive line is knocking people off the ball the entire game. We are wearing teams out.

While our offense has been scoring and playing very well, I'm worried about our defense, but Coach says everything is OK. He's about to focus more on that side of the ball and has a few tricks he wants to try in practice. The defense is giving up about 24 points per game against our schedule, which makes me worry that Indiana Western might score 40 against us. As good as our offense is playing, I'm not sure we can out-score the Sagamores on their home field if we have to.

``You take care of the offense, and I'll work on the defense,'' Coach tells me. ``Jordan, Nate, Miguel and I have been talking and we think we know something that will work. Those three are taking over the leadership responsibility.''

As I expected, my comments about Coach Jackson are sparking a lot of talk in Indiana. Several reporters have tried to talk to Coach Burgess about it, but he just says, ``There's nothing Lars said that I know to be false, but he never complained to me about the situation. When I asked him about it, he always said he'd handle it himself.''

That only increases the speculation. Instead of answering questions about Southern Michigan, this week's opponent, Coach Jackson is getting asked a lot about things that happened three years ago, and he was not handling it well.

"Lars Preston and Max Curry were not treated any differently than any other walk-ons who have come here," Coach Jackson said.

So of course the next question is, "How are walk-ons treated differently than other players?"

Coach Jackson just grumbles and says, "Anybody got any questions about this week's game?"

Several reporters ask to speak to Welker and Crow, but IWU says they are unavailable. Smart move.

Mikala keeps e-mailing me the newspaper stories from Arlington which are asking some pretty pointed questions. Suddenly, the game that was supposed to be a walkover for the Sagamores is turning up some significant interest. Thanks to all the reporters, the Sagamores are spending more time worrying about Max and me than they are about preparing for their next game.

Gotta love it when a plan works early!

Our last game before heading East is against Nevada-Carson City at home for our Homecoming game. No matter how much we keep stressing to everyone not to get caught looking ahead or get distracted by everything else going on around campus this week, we come out flat and trail at halftime 20-14. The Dolphins are a good team, one game behind us in the conference race after a last-second loss to ULA on the road. But they aren't that good. We have some dropped passes, and the defense is getting shredded by their running game.

"C'mon, defense," Coach Schebig yells at halftime. "You've got to start pulling your share of the load around here. I want to see some turnovers in the second half. Get them going Jordan. No excuses!"

When I gather the offense together, I never get to say anything before Max starts jumping on everyone, starting with me!

"When are you going start focusing on this game?" he asks. "So far you've missed the open guy five times. You haven't missed that many all season. We've dropped a few, but you've had plenty of time to throw, and you've just missed them!"

I think I know what Max was doing, so I just nod and say, "You know what? You're right. I'm ready to go. No excuses."

He's using me as an example to get through to everyone else. I had been playing fine, but Max knows everyone would be more shocked if I was the target instead of themselves.

We got a break on the second play after the second-half kickoff when Perez picks off a pass. We decide to go deep on the first play, and I hit Max on a bomb at their 5 for an easy score. The extra point by Jimenez gives us a one-point lead. Big Mo has switched sides, and we never trail after that. Knowing their offense would be shook up, Coach lets everybody blitz and take off on defense, and Eichorn buries their quarterback on the next series.

"I figured we've been doing it all wrong," Coach Schebig says after the game. "We've been playing too passively and reacting to what everybody else is trying to do on defense. We can't beat IWU that way so we need to mix things up. We need to dictate a few things."

All year long he's been using Big Joe and Little Joe one at a time, switching them whenever they get tired. For the first time he tries using them together, and suddenly NCC can't run the ball any more.

I hit my first 10 passes in a row in the second half and we get two more scores out of them to go up 35-20. NCC gets only one first down in the second half and we win big 49-20. With the Joes clearing things out in front, Eichorn gets 17 tackles, and Perez nabs two interceptions.

``Finally, everything we've been working for is here,'' Coach Schebig tells us in the locker room. ``I think we're finally ready, how about you?''

``No excuses!'' everyone roars back.

``That's what I want to hear. Everybody enjoy tonight and take tomorrow off. We leave at noon on Monday. Have fun but don't do anything stupid over the next day and miss the trip. We've worked too hard for this chance to blow it. No excuses!''

``No excuses!''

It's finally time to go home.

CHAPTER 24

Sometimes, like everyone else I suppose, I get these songs stuck in my head and I have no idea why. I don't know when they start, and I'm not really sure when they end, but somehow they run their course. Right now I've got Elvis Presley singing "I'm caught in a trap, I can't walk out," ringing through my brain on an unending loop. I've never been a huge fan of the king, but I have an appreciation for his gifts most of the time. And yes, I know he meant the song to profess love, but I'm not feeling a lot of love right now even though we're traveling to the home of my loved ones.

As I suspected/intended, my quotes about Coach Jackson have not gone over well in Indiana. I think that's partly because they shocked so many people since Max and I have never spoken publicly about why we left IWU. Well, we didn't leave so much as we were essentially escorted off campus. They're the ones who started this up again by asking us to come back and play against them. That means I get to set my own terms this time.

About the same time we left three years ago, IWU came under an NCAA investigation for alleged improper payments and recruiting violations. Max and I had nothing to do with that, but the timing was very suspicious to some. The NCAA investigators talked with us three times. C'mon, who's going to waste money on walk-ons, even if they are the most famous ones since Rudy? By the time we were even noticed by 99 percent of the fans, we were already headed out the door.

Our detractors probably thought we left because we decided we weren't getting paid enough.

We've continually let it be known that we didn't know anything or suspect any recruiting violations in the first place. Nothing has been discovered publicly so far, which is as rare today as one of the Khardasians actually doing something truly noteworthy. Still, anytime the NCAA is poking around everyone assumes the worst.

That's easy to do since usually it's true, and everyone knows it. About 50 percent of the players out there know someone who's cheating, and not just in football, either. For one thing, it's almost impossible not to technically be cheating. For example, the rule book stands on its side higher than Blake Griffin's vertical. If you are a coach who tries to do the decent and morally right thing for a player, you're more than likely breaking one of the rules, and no one knows all of them.

Head coaches always say they didn't know of any violations their assistants might have been instigating, like their job is too busy to know everything that's going on. Then why are you the head coach? Aren't you getting paid enough to know? They don't care about doing what's right; they care about not getting caught.

It's not really the NCAA's fault, either. They work for the school presidents, who continually pass rules to amend rules because there was an application of a rule that no one considered before. Everything is twisted in knots worse than the U.S. tax code. There's book smart and then there's common sense, and college presidents are usually brilliant in only one way. That's part of what leads to the cheating, too. Nobody figures they'll get caught, and if they do, they can just say they didn't understand the rule.

There's also the problem that there's one investigator for about every 200,000 NCAA athletes. There's no way the NCAA can be effective without help from the media or other whistleblowers. It's not that the NCAA wants to jump into investigations after someone else exposes the problems, but the NCAA often has no choice.

Some of the problem is a ton of these players have no right to be in school except for the fact they are exceptional athletes. The academic system sold its soul for money and publicity and fame, and that genie is never going back in the bottle. Now it's tradition. Most people have no idea how many athletes never graduate or really care to, most going to class only enough to stay eligible. As soon as they are eligible for the first semester of their senior seasons, many quit going to class at all. They don't want to be there, they want to play professionally, but going to college is their only route to the pros. If there was another option, most of the athletes, at least the non-academic ones, would take it.

Nobody in the pros or the colleges wants to take that risk so the NCAA and the schools try to make the athletes adjust by holding them to the rules and making scholarships renewable every year. Doesn't that somehow seem to be the antithesis of what our universities are supposed to be all about, academic freedom and exploring our world and ourselves? The hypocrisy is astonishing.

The odd thing is everyone would lose money with a true minor league system for football, just like everyone who ever gets involved with the basketball minor leagues always does.

Every athlete knows the system, and following the rules is an option. That's all it is.

In an effort to try to keep athletes happy, schools overspend on them like crazy. Year-round training tables, new sweat suits about once a month and staying the night before a home game in hotels are examples of wasted finances. When teams are lucky enough to go to bowl games, most lose money because the athletic department has to ship the band out, along with a lot of alumni, and most schools can't sell their allotment of tickets. Last year Indiana Western purchased eight pairs of shoes for every football player so they could be prepared to play in any conditions. They do that every year. The players also got new sweat suits for their conference championship and bowl games. Imagine how much it cost to buy 150 sweat suits twice in a month.

Wonder how many of the players still have them, and how many have sold them? "Uh, sorry, Coach, I took mine home and left it there." Or, "I gave it to my dad to wear."

The craziest things are the stupid college boosters who never get any smarter about the whole process. They are so transparent, and I'm not just talking about the jock sniffers. They all want to buy immortality by getting their names placed on the side of buildings, which will eventually be torn down and replaced by something bigger with a new, more expensive name on it.

Some have this impossible ideal about what they think college football is like or what it was when they were playing. They are so far out of touch the only thing that makes them the least bit relevant is their money, and the schools have administrators set up like Madams to try to entice that money from their hands. They can call it marketing or development or whatever, but they are really the greatest con men alive because they really don't have anything to sell – provided they follow the rules. They can't and shouldn't be selling access, which is really what the boosters want, so what are the schools really peddling? Success? No, it's ego.

The really crazy thing about all of this is how many schools lose money by sponsoring Division I athletics. Despite the billions of dollars going around on television contracts and merchandising and such, only about 10 percent of the athletic departments break even each year. And those few are so scared, they are always looking for new avenues to make more money because they know one bad year could put them in the red.

The college sports world has truly become just as big a bureaucracy as any in Washington. Anyone who protests or tries to institute reforms gets ignored until they fade away. Most of the time, any president who makes it a point of emphasis to run a clean program is worked around by the other administrators or alumni until he or she leaves. No one believes a totally clean program can win, at least not consistently. Everyone tip-toes up to the line and then tries to balance on it without falling past it.

No one wants to rock the boat, because there's too much money involved. There has to be a better system possible, but no one wants to try it because they'd all have to give up a little bit of the little control they think they have.

So it'll never happen.

Maybe I'm too cynical, but too often I see people who have no insight into what college sports are really like talking in theoretical terms. There's what they think it's all about, and then there's the reality.

Ironically, the athletes I see who abuse the system the most are not those who come from poor backgrounds, but those who come from middle class or privileged homes. They are used to having everything and never doing without, so they figure they shouldn't have to now. Mom and Dad gave them everything whenever they put their hands out before, so why shouldn't someone put something in those same hands now?

Maybe they should hold a freshman seminar before practices start just like they do with rookies in the NFL. Here are the facts about how few of you will make it to the NFL, so you better wise up and take advantage of this free scholarship you are getting. Why do you think you're going to be the one who makes it when every year less than one player from each senior class ever plays at least one year in the pros? Why will you make it when you're not even going to start this year, but last year's all-conference starter didn't make it? What's your back-up plan?

Except so few of them want to be in school in the first place.

You want to know how you can tell this is truly such a farce? Whenever a student-athlete really succeeds as a student, they are the ones the schools make a really big deal out of. Shouldn't that be the rule rather than the exception? This whole system has it backward.

Somehow that song needs to change, but it never will.

CHAPTER 25

Max must have taken 45 minutes to say goodbye to Natalie. You'd have thought he was leaving for boot camp and then off to war and not just going home for a week. It takes less time to get out of a parking lot after a NASCAR race than it did for those two to let go.

"Oh, sweetie I will miss you so much, and I'll call you four times a day. I'll think about you just before I go to sleep and first thing when I wake up in the morning. I'll miss you so much my heart will hurt."

At that point, I finally had to jump in and tell Max to shut up about all that because it was getting pretty embarrassing. TMI! Finally, Natalie drops the leash and I hand Emma back to her so we can leave. If I'd have been smart, I'd have gotten it all on video, but then I'd have had to juggle the baby, and she was sleeping. Man, I wish just once I could relax enough to sleep that hard.

"Take care of him, Lars!" Natalie yells.

Uh, sure.

"Do you need a shoulder to cry on, my little sweetums?"

"Oh, you should talk," Max says. "You've been packed for this trip for two weeks just so you could cut down on the time to see Mikala. You're 10 times more whipped than I am. You're so hung up you could be an exhibit in an art gallery."

"What can I say? She's addicted to me."

"Ha! You are so full of crap. Everybody back away! There's about to be a toxic spill over here. Keep your feet up so you don't step in it!"

"At least I didn't look like a Kindergarten kid trying to let go of

Mommy's skirt on the first day of school."

"No, you'd be the one wearing a skirt if Mikala asked."

"Depends how she asked."

OK, this part of the conversation has suddenly gone too far.

"Aren't we a pair," Max says.

"Aren't we both very lucky," I say.

"Amen to that, brother. Thank goodness Emma was asleep or it would have been a lot worse for both of us. We all probably would have been crying."

"Speak for yourself, Sweetums. I've got $25 that says your mom calls Natalie and talks most of the time we're in the air."

"No bet. That's too easy. I'm just glad we're on the team plane or Mom would load us up with stuff to take back for Emma."

Even though we are the last two players to arrive, we are still ready to go five minutes before the bus leaves for the airport. We're used to traveling to games so the only thing we had to do was pack an extra couple pairs of jeans and some shirts. Because the managers have to get everything through security and packed onto the plane, we dropped off our travel bags the day before. Luckily, we're traveling on a charter or the security details would be much worse. The managers still have a very difficult job.

Maybe the toughest part of this for us was telling everyone they should pack jeans instead of shorts. Big, tough Little and Big Joe balk at that right away. Everyone tries to tell them how cold it can get in Indiana in late October. Gabe even suggests they consider dressing in extra layers for when they get off the plane, but they aren't having any of it.

"Have either of you ever lived anywhere where the temperature was less than 40 degrees?" Max asks.

"I'm hoping it snows," Little Joe says. "I've never seen real snow."

I hate to disappoint him on that one. As huge as he is, he still acts about 5 years old as he talks about snow.

"Wait until we go to Lehigh Valley for the playoffs," I say. "You'll see more snow than you'll ever want to see again."

We get to pick our seats based on seniority, and each player has been given an itinerary for the week. We practice first thing in the morning each day, there are study tables in the afternoon after lunch and then there are some team events in the evenings. Even though school is out for our fall break, we still have projects and papers due when we return. Just like kids, we're used to and need routine and structure. Some of the players' parents are arriving in Arlington early to visit so those players are allowed to miss some things to be with their families.

Other than that, I have no idea what kind of reception we're going to get. It's not like we're the returning conquering heroes. We're the enemy now, which has me a little on edge.

We've convinced Coach Schebig that the team should headquarter for the week in Talbott before riding the bus to Arlington on Saturday morning for the game. A few of us will have to go into Arlington tomorrow for a press conference, and there will be post-practice media conferences every day. We're trying to contain that stuff as much as possible. We've got 10 athletic department officials traveling with us on this trip, when usually only a handful fly up the day of a game and leave afterward. This is more like the way big schools do things.

I think I've got myself mentally prepared for whatever may come up. Max and I have talked a lot about things we need to be aware of, but I'm sure there will be something we haven't thought of. We've stressed again and again to everyone that we have to stick together, nobody goes anywhere without at least two teammates and they need to be very careful with the girls they may meet. The last thing we need is some kind of police charge, warranted or trumped up, to disrupt practice and everything else in case something goes wrong. Stranger things have happened on road trips before, and this time we'll be there for seven days instead of the normal two.

``Remember who you are and who you represent!" Coach Schebig yells at everyone the day before we leave.

``Yeah, and always remember no one wants to be the one who has to explain to Dr. Stein what they did wrong!" I quip.

Except that really wouldn't be that funny.

In some ways, Max and I both feel like we're assistant coaches rather than players. We're practically hosts for this trip, showing everyone our hometown. A lot of these players have seen tons of beaches and mountains, but they've never seen a farm or a field of corn. It would be hilarious if we were going to be there a couple months later to see how some of these guys would react to snow.

Talbott also won't have seen as many minority people as we have on the team. There were three in our graduating high school class, and we've five races represented on our roster.

I guess I should just trust everyone, but that's a little hard to do as the quarterback who is used to setting the pace and the tone on everything. I feel responsible about this entire situation, and I know anything positive or negative will reflect on Max and me who hope to and will have to return here someday. This week will have a lot to do with determining if we can ever live here again if we choose.

I don't want to let my teammates down or my family and friends in my hometown. Someday I'd like to be able to get married here at the least.

There's a lot to think about.

I'm very relieved and glad we're bringing along some extra help from the athletic department. Mr. Stovall is flying with us on this trip, and Anthony Davis has been designated as the head of delegation, working for months to arrange meals and hotel rooms and a few other side trips. Because this is our annual fall break, we've got the week off classes off so that isn't too much of a problem. We've arranged for a room at the Talbott Public Library to help with studies, and there's also a trip to the cinema on Friday afternoon so everyone can relax a bit. We're also holding team meetings and press conferences in the high school auditorium after practices.

We know we're going to be an odd group. It's not every small town that can accommodate an extra 150 people moving in for a week, even if we are fairly self-sufficient and used to being organized. Still, we eat more like 250 people. We're used to eating a specific way with lots of chicken, vegetables and carbs, but it still takes some effort to organize that much food to all be served at the same time. There also aren't too many places in town that can sit that many people at once so we're going to eat our meals in our church's cafeteria. I had suggested the school cafeteria, but there was no way to work it out where we could not be a problem for the lunch times of the regular students and staff.

Instead, my mom has organized plenty of help from family, friends, church members and local restaurants. I'm going to be thanking a lot of people over the next few days. If Indiana Western wasn't paying the bill for all of this, there's no way it could work.

Dave and Joni Kuhn are assisting our training staff if we need it, along with Talbott High School's trainer, Joe Baer.

Within reason, I think we've got everything covered. At least I hope so.

CHAPTER 26

When we get off the plane and walk into the terminal, I am dead meat. Mikala comes running up to jump into my arms just like a TV Movie of the Week scene, except there really are some television news cameras filming the whole thing. I look at Max over her shoulder and he just winks and smiles before showing ultimate mercy by turning to walk away. Whew! The rest of my teammates aren't so nice about the whole thing and are hooting and hollering, even though they all know who she is.

``That looks just like what happened with the girl at the airport when we left,'' Jordan Eichorn says.

Thanks, Jordan.

``Hi, honey, how's my girl?'' I say into Mikala's ear.

``Better now,'' she says.

``I love you and missed you.'' I tell her. ``Let's get through this mess so we can go somewhere a little more private.''

Of course, before we can do that, I have to give a couple of interviews to the TV crews, but I make sure Mikala stays by my side. I can't remember what they ask, but it isn't too tough. I also quickly yield the face time to Coach Schebig.

Because the managers are taking care of all our luggage and equipment, it only takes us a half hour to get everyone onto the buses for the 25-minute ride to Talbott.

I get to ride in Mikala's car. Because her volleyball season is also in the fall, we haven't gotten to see each other in person since mid-July. Her team is doing well this year and will likely make the NCAA

Tournament. One advantage of coming into town this early is I get go see her play tomorrow night. I'm sure some of my teammates will want to tag along.

We've been together for seven years now and have so much to talk about, but you know what? It's nice just to ride along with her in silence, my hand on her knee, soaking up her presence. Finally, she pulls up to a stop light, leans over and kisses me.

"Hi," she says.

"Hi, Babe. I'm very happy to see you."

"Shut up and kiss me."

"Yes, Ma'am!"

Just then a horn honks behind us and I throw up my arms like I am a struggling, drowning man. We both laugh and a blushing Mikala resumes driving. I look back and see one of the team buses right behind us.

"I would appreciate it if you could hurry up and get to another stop light," I say.

"I'm trying."

This time no one honks.

Needless to say, somehow we get behind the buses which beat us to the church. I get a little razzing from my teammates, but I expect that.

"Dude, I can't believe that girl can drive like that with her tongue stuck down your throat!" Gabe Hirsch says before stepping up to give Mikala a hug. "Hi, sweetie! Are you sure you don't have a younger sister?"

I so badly want to say, "You should see what else she can do!" but I know that will get me smacked so hard I wouldn't be able to play in the game. Figuring that wouldn't look very good on the injury report ("Concussion, insulted girlfriend") I just blush and keep walking. She smiles at Gabe and gives him a peck on the cheek which is probably what he really wanted.

As soon as everyone gets off the bus, it's time to eat. With a football team, it's always time to eat. Just like soldiers who learn to sleep whenever possible because they never know when they'll get another chance, that's the way football players look at eating opportunities.

We scarf down spaghetti, garlic toast and salad. My mom wanted to make sure we had a welcome home dinner so she started making spaghetti sauce three weeks ago and asked all the neighbors to pitch in with the salad, garlic bread and boiling water for the pasta. When she finished, there were 50 gallons of sauce and 75 pots full of spaghetti. Everyone pulled their pots off the stove and drove them to the church, which in a small town is at the most five minutes away. The Army should be so organized and would be lucky to eat half as well.

Within the quietest 30 minutes you've ever heard from a football team, everyone is done eating and Max and I are carrying the trash bags to the dumpsters while Gabe, Keaton and Trever help wash up in the kitchen. (Their parents would have been A) shocked to see them actually holding a dish towel in their hands; B) very proud; C) ticked off wondering how they could get them to do that at home.)

The scary thing? There are no leftovers and maybe the most impressive thing about the entire operation is that everyone got enough to eat. I'd say no one could ever pull that off again, but I know Mom and Grandma probably could. I'm also pretty sure they had a back-up plan in case more people than expected showed up.

After dinner, the team rides 10 minutes back toward Arlington to the hotel to start work on its own back-up plans during a team meeting. I've been itching all season to try out some of our special plays. In fact, it's been killing me to run a straight offense with no gadgets, trick plays or having all that much fun. We've even taken to having Max run behind the line of scrimmage like it's going to be a reverse just to keep teams guessing, but we've only run one so far. After spending all summer diagramming plays, I am literally giddy at the opportunity to finally show what we've been working on in practice.

To me, that's the fun part of playing quarterback, letting your offense reflect your personality by showing some flair. I love confusing the defense and watching them run around trying to figure out who has the ball. It's worth it to see them so out of breath from running that they can't talk for once. They're like little dogs yapping all over the place until they hit the wall and collapse.

Except we haven't been running any of that stuff this year. We've been trying them in practice once a week, and everything has been working fine, but it's not the same as a game. Practice speed is at most 75 percent of game speed, and on these trick plays timing has to be perfect. I have to give the guys props that they've kept their focus and have tried to go as hard as they can most of the season, but this is still going to be the toughest team we have or ever will face.

I'm tired of talking about what we've got planned, and I can't wait to see it go on the field!

So does Alex Eastin who is going to be the focus of a lot of those plays. It was his turn tonight to give the talk about this game.

`I can't believe we're finally here. Once I left, I never expected to come back to IWU, even to drive through on the way to somewhere else. That's how upset I was after everything went down here. I felt like I was betrayed, but worse, so were my friends. You can mess with me all you want, but you don't mess with my friends, even if they are just Max and Lars. Nobody messes with them but me!"

That draws a few cheers and laughs from the guys, but Max and I don't laugh because we know we get messed with by everybody.

`I'm very proud of what we have accomplished so far and the things we have done to prepare for this game. Even if things don't turn out like we hope, I will always look back on this as a positive experience. We've all come a long way, and I'm looking forward to this challenge. I think we've all grown up quite a bit as football players and as people.

`As much as we look out for each other on the field, that's also how much we have to look out for each other this week when we're away from the field. Be aware of what is going on around you so you can stay out of trouble. There are some people on that team who would take advantage of any situation to make us look bad. This may feel like a hometown, but we are definitely the visitors here.

`I really never expected to have this chance, especially with you guys. I don't say that because I don't think you are good enough, but let's face it, if other people thought we were good enough we wouldn't be here, would we? Well, you know what? Right now I think we're good enough. I'm proud of the way we have prepared for this game and the way we have fought to come together as a team. I consider you guys to be my brothers, and I know 25 years from now I'll still be talking to you on the phone or at our kids' weddings or whatever. I think we have built something very special here, and I am so excited because this is where we get to prove it. No one knows how strong faith is until and unless it gets tested. This is finally our test.

`Nobody believes we can do this, but I do. And I can't wait to see everyone react when we do it."

CHAPTER 27

We still have our usual morning practice, though by this point in the season it's mostly stretching. We just go through the motions, aware there is the possibility of a few spies checking us out to see if we will work on any special plays.

Now would Coach Jackson stoop to that level? Oh, heck, yeah he would. I'll be disappointed if he doesn't try. There's one story going around that during Coach Jackson's high school coaching career, he got caught in a tree near an opponent's practice field. Now that's a bad day.

Despite the threat of a spy, that's not to say we didn't run through a few things in the gym after Coach Snuff kicks everyone else out for about 30 minutes. After we finish running plays, he calls everybody together which I think shows a lot of guts since it's not his team, but, hey, it is his gym.

"I just want to welcome everyone to Talbott," he says. "If you don't already know it, this game has a little bit of controversy to it. There are a few folks around town who are die-hard IWU alumni and fans, so they have some hard feelings about you guys staying here. I just want to remind you to be aware that there are some people out there who are looking for any little slip-up you make so please act like the gentlemen I know you are."

Everyone nods to that.

"I also want to tell you that Talbott is inviting all of you to come to Friday's football game where we are going to retire jerseys for Max, Lars and Mikala at halftime. I know you'll all want to be there to honor Mikala, especially."

I am totally floored. I have never even considered that, since usually that's an honor that is given to players who are, you know, old, retired and sometimes forgotten. There have been only two retired jerseys in the history of the school, and one is the No. 56 for the 1956 sectional basketball champions. They are still revered in town and eat breakfast together on the second Monday of every month. The other is the No. 1 for the mascot. The school decided to make it a triple play this time.

"We've never had any athletes who have done what you three have gone on to do," Coach Snuff says once everyone finishes clapping. "And we're all just as proud of the people you turned out to be."

I didn't know what to say to that, so I just shake his hand. He then scares the crap out of Max by telling him he has been chosen to represent the three of us and needs to give a speech as part of the ceremony. I think Max is about to mess his drawers!

"Let Lars do it," Max pleads. "He's the talker."

"Actually," Coach Snuff says, "We've got to start the second half on time so we know we can't let Lars speak, and if we let Mikala speak all the players will be too distracted to play."

Who could argue with that? And who knew Coach Snuff has such a sense of humor?

This ought to be good! Max already has to give the speech to the team on Thursday, so that's two speeches in two days. Somebody get a tape recorder! We may need to put this up on YouTube for posterity so in 20 years we can show his kids, "See, your dad could, too, talk!" The idea of Max talking in front of a packed house is too much!

"I could write it for you," I tell him.

"Like I could trust that."

``Aw, c'mon, really I'll play nice. Besides, if I don't, you'll never talk to me again. Doh!"

``Funny."

We are still laughing about it when Max, Coach Schebig and I drive to Arlington for the daily press conference. After today (Tuesday), we'll hold a daily media session after practice at Talbott.

This could be interesting. Press conferences are never anything like what they show on TV with people leaping up to shout questions. They are much more sedate, usually with people walking in and out of the room. Only three or four people usually ask questions and everyone else writes down the answers from those. Coaches are so used to every question, it's like they don't even think much any more about their answers.

Turns out we'll have to think of some answers quickly today.

``How ya doing, Win?" I say as we walk into the room behind him. ``Got any good questions ready for us?"

``I don't, but I'm pretty sure some of these folks do. The NCAA just announced they are starting another investigation into the football program."

``Aw, that's just great. How convenient that we're having a press conference today. Max, Coach, we're about to get ambushed. We better start thinking fast."

I quickly get on the cell phone, call Mikala and ask her to bring me something.

It doesn't take long because the first question we get is about the NCAA. I defer to Coach.

``What are we supposed to say to that? It has nothing to do with us, but I'm sure few people around here will believe that. We've all met with NCAA representatives, that's no secret, but the meetings were at their instigation, and we just tried to answer their questions. The only answer is that none of us know anything that could lead to an investigation."

But the next question sets coach off.

"Are you staying that because of your loyalty to Coach Burgess, or because you were warned by the NCAA not to say anything?"

"I'm a little offended by this because to me you're really trying to think of a smart way to ask us if we had anything to do with starting this investigation, or if we know of any violations under Coach Burgess's program. The answers are emphatically, no and no. I really feel for Coach Jackson and his team during this time because this is a no-win situation for them, and they'll all be changed people by the time this is over. This kind of process wears people down no matter if you are innocent, and it's likely the folks who may be accused are long gone."

"Anything you want to add, Lars?"

"You bet. Even if there were things going on that were suspect, we have never heard of or seen them then or since so the only thing we could tell the NCAA people was that we didn't know of anything. I do not personally know of any players receiving money or extra benefits from boosters. C'mon, again, how many times are boosters or anyone else with money looking to give things to walk-ons? And if we did, how come it didn't work to make us feel more appreciated or make us want to stay? I can't emphasize enough that neither Max or I know anything."

"But what might your girlfriend know?"

``Who asked that?" I ask, looking around. No one steps up.

``The things I talk about with my girlfriend are none of your business," I start, ``but I will say this – why would we want to waste any more time than we already have in our lives talking about IWU football? Believe me, we talk about everything but that. Talking about that would be the quickest way possible I could get kicked to the curb by her. Again, for the record, I do not know of any past or present NCAA violations or any questionable conduct, and that is exactly what I told the NCAA. I am not hedging on this, and I have nothing to hide. I. DO. NOT. KNOW. ANYTHING. I hope you believe me, but if you don't, there's nothing I can do about it."

Everybody is scribbling frantically, but I really don't expect that to end the questioning.

``How many times did you speak with the NCAA?" Pete DiPrimio asks.

``Three times. Once on the phone and twice they came to Camarillo. We spoke for about two hours combined. There's not a lot to say when my response is always, `I don't know.' ''

``What did they ask you about?" DiPrimio follows up.

``Really nothing very specific. If you are asking in hopes of getting a clue into what areas they are looking into, Max and I have talked about that many times, and neither of us can come up with a target for you. They really seemed to be scatter-shooting, hoping to hit something."

``Do you think IWU cheated or has violated any other rules?" Rich Griffis asks.

``Again, I don't know of any violations. If you are asking me what my gut says? There is no way any athletic program can go through a four-year period without breaking some kind of rule because the rules are so confusing, the book is so thick and nobody knows everything in there. Even those with the best of intentions have probably broken some rules. To prove that I am not picking on IWU, I will admit that I have probably broken some rules inadvertently, though I don't know which ones, and for that I apologize. No man is perfect, and that's what those rules require."

That gets a few rumbles from the crowd. Max leans over and whispers in my ear, "As usual, you say too much rather than too little."

"Let's end this with this," I say. "I am asking the NCAA to release the transcripts of my discussions with the investigators. If I need to write that out and sign it, I will. I have nothing to hide with this. I don't know how else I can prove that or if that's even allowed since the NCAA is not a public institution, but I'm willing to do that if they are. If I get any transcripts, I'll be happy to release them."

Finally, one of the IWU administrators stands up. I recognized him as soon as we walked into the room.

"You have to admit Mr. Preston that it's awfully convenient that the NCAA has spent so much time questioning you and then all of a sudden when you are in town they announce this investigation. It certainly looks suspicious. It would also serve your purpose to shake things up around here and provide a distraction heading into this weekend."

For one of the rare times this entire fall, I take a few seconds to think out my response. While I'm pondering, I notice Mikala slip in and give Win something which he brings up front.

"OK, let's do it this way," I say, taking the Bible from Win and putting my left hand on it. "If you know anything about me or my family, which most of you do, I want you to record this. Let this be my answer to all of this. I swear on this Bible that I don't know anything about the NCAA investigation other than what I have relayed to you today. I have said nothing to the investigators that reflects poorly on IWU. I am as clueless as anyone in this matter, and again I call on the NCAA to release the transcripts of our conversations. I have nothing to hide."

The room is incredibly silent as I pull my hand away from the Bible and scoot back into my chair.

"Now, has anybody got any questions about football?"

That sermon seems to have gotten through to the folks in the room because for a few seconds no one says anything. This is turning out to be a really strange day.

"Are you going to predict a UC-Camarillo victory?" Wendy Bartle from Sports Illustrated asks, cracking a grin.

I'm sorry, but that's the funniest question I have ever been asked. I start laughing, then Max and Coach, and pretty soon everyone in the room is laughing. It's the perfect way to break the tension.

"Oh, you'd like that, wouldn't you, Wendy?" I say when I regained my breath. "No, I'm not going there. I will say I think my team is as prepared as anyone could be. I think we're going to represent our school and ourselves well."

"Aw, c'mon, Lars, you know you want to. Besides, that's the only way to top what you've already said."

"That's why I let Max answer all of my tough questions. Ready to take over, Max?"

Everything settles down after that and they ask questions about the strategy of the game. I don't give anything away, but instead talk about how I am playing a more-disciplined game this season.

For somebody who loves to talk, I can't wait for this press conference to end.

CHAPTER 28

Because we've essentially taken over a hotel halfway between Arlington and Talbott, it's no secret where we're staying. Though Talbott has one hotel that's barely big enough to host all of us, it's a good thing we aren't staying there because this is also the week of the Talbott Street Festival.

That's going to be our team activity for Wednesday night, and I'm truly hoping it gets real cold over the next 24 hours because I want to see how some of these beach boys react to real weather. Because they refused to listen to advice, a good stiff breeze should test all of their willingness to continue wearing shorts. They're not as tough as they think they are.

I don't have to worry about that tonight as I'm going to watch Mikala play volleyball in a key conference match against Lily. The winner will have the inside track to the MWC title. Right now, I'm much more excited about this contest than I am for my own later in the week.

Though our seasons are both played during the fall, and I don't get to watch her perform very often in person, I love watching her play. For one thing, it's fun for me to simply watch a game and be a cheering fan instead of trying to figure out what is going on strategically. Watching football games isn't too much fun for me anymore because it's become part of my job. I'm always watching for the little things that can make such a big difference during a game.

When we were in high school and our first year in college, I attended all of Mikala's matches and now I watch as many as I can on the internet. The Sagamores also made a West Coast tour early in our junior season so Max and I drove a few road trips to see her play.

It's no secret where Max and I are going tonight, and though it's not an official team function, about 10 teammates decide they'd like to come along. Basically, it's Alex, Randy, Big Bob and a bunch of guys from California who actually like volleyball. They also have nothing else to do right now because many of the guys wanted to go see some vampires vs. zombies movie and a few of the others are using tonight as a chance to get together with their parents.

"Won't we freak everyone out by cheering for IWU tonight?" Big Bob asks.

"Yeah, but who really cares?" I say. "The only way I'm shutting up is if Mikala makes me."

"So what else is new?" Max puts in. "We can only hope."

"Ha, ha."

We meet my parents, Max's folks and Mikala's mom and dad out front. They have all been season-ticket holders for four years and sit with a group of friends down low. My group figures it will be better if we sit back a ways from the court so we're less of a distraction for the other fans.

When we finally get situated, the girls are going through their warm-ups. Mikala glances up and I give her a little wave which she tersely nods once at.

She's just like me in that she has incredible focus and she loves to compete. All she cares is that I'm safely there, not what I'm doing or what I'm wearing or anything else. This is about her, as it should be. Because she's 6-foot tall and so athletic, she's a monster talent. She's so graceful and quick she can play any position, but she's the Sagamores' opposite, mostly because that lets her do a little bit of everything.

She's also a little bit mean. Totally unlike she is off the court, she's hyper aggressive during matches. She'll even talk a little trash to opponents – and here I thought it was just me who brought that out in her. She's just as competitive as I am which has led to a few arguments over the years when we've played cards. Or tried to pick a movie. Or bought Christmas presents.

Because Mikala's been playing so well, she's the consensus player of the year in the conference and a likely first-team all-American pick. After she graduates, her options include playing professionally in Europe, trying out for the national team or getting a real job. She hasn't said much about what she wants to do, but I'd love to see her take that chance and go for the Olympic team. After everything she's put up with by being with me these past seven years, I'd love to be able to support her in something like that.

Tonight, Lily just wishes she was already on the national team. The Appleknockers have no chance of stopping her because she's tall enough to dominate the net and can jump high enough to hit over any block they can put up. Their only chance is to dig her a few times, but she's also the smartest player on the court and keeps mixing up her targets so they have no hope. At the top of her leap, she can sense with her peripheral vision where the defenders are and make adjustments. They end up with more floor burns than digs. A couple of times she just taps the ball out of bounds off the blockers' hands which must be incredibly frustrating.

The Sagamores sweep through three games or she might have had a chance at the school record for kills during a match. She finishes with 25 kills and only one hitting error all night as I yell and scream like an idiot the entire time. We basically all make fools of ourselves cheering her on, and tonight she's the best player on the floor no matter where she's at in the rotation. She even gets off some great sets to her teammates.

I may play a sport that most people recognize as a major sport, but

Mikala is twice the athlete I am by comparison. She has real pro and Olympic potential, something I'll never have. She can do things in competition with a grace and style that dwarf my ability. We are both very similar in the way we approach our competitions, but she has so many more ways to win than I do. If she's not hitting well, she can win a game defensively or with her mind anticipating where to be to make a big play. She has a great ability to instantly forget a bad swing and then come back strong on the next one. She's everything you'd like your senior leader to be: tough, inspiring, smart, disciplined and focused. She's playing the best volleyball of her career at the end of her final season when some players are starting to break down physically and mentally.

In some ways, there's an injustice to our sports system where she plays before 1,800 fans every night. and I'll play in front of 80,000 on Saturday. She's a far superior athlete and human specimen. On my best day, I can't compare to what her physical abilities are. She's an once-in-a-lifetime talent at IWU, and I was the fourth-string quarterback.

`Dude, she rocks," Randy says to me after she belts the ball over a three-person block for a point.

Maybe because there was a small crowd and we were obviously rooting for IWU, no one gives us any trouble during the match. Afterward, as we're waiting for Mikala to come out of her locker room, we run into Duncan Welker and a couple of his friends from the football team. Turns out he's dating one of Mikala's teammates, Katie Mettler.

As soon as I see him, I think we should all veer off and spend the time with our parents, but of course just then he looks up and spots me and starts walking toward us. I can't really say anything because I've been texting him all fall and really started all this if there's going to be a confrontation. I just thought it would come five days from now.

"Duncan," I say. "Congratulations on making all-conference last year. How are you?"

"Shut up," he says. "You don't really care how I am, and I don't care how you are. I just want you to know I can't wait to get a shot at you Saturday. If I get a chance and something goes wrong for you, I won't have any regrets. I'll say all the right things, but I want you to know the truth."

I stand there, trying to think quickly because I know if I respond with what I want to say, this is going to turn into a fight. Even though I've got 10 teammates with me and he's got three, I know we can't win this. Oh, we can win the fight for sure, but we'll lose in every other way possible. We'll get creamed by the community, someone will probably get arrested, Dr. Stein will kill me, two or three players will get hurt and somebody will get suspended from the game. Worst of all, I'm embarrass my folks and Mikala.

Nothing good can come of this, so I turn and walk away.

"Have you turned into such a chicken that you can't even respond?'" Duncan yells. "Or can I expect a text later? Are you going to anonymously slam me on some message board? Is that how it's done now?"

There's nothing I can say about that because he's right so I just keep walking, grabbing Randy and Big Bob to make sure they come with me. If anything is going to escalate, I know it's going to happen with these two. After all, they are used to protecting me. Once they get started, they won't stop, either.

"Let it go until Saturday," I say low enough that only they can hear. "All he's doing is talking, and it doesn't matter. We'll get our chance."

"But Lars..." Big Bob starts and tries to turn around.

"Bob, does 'No excuses!' mean anything to you? This is exactly the type of situation that's about. There will be no excuse big enough if we let this get out of hand. Just think about the consequences for a second. It's not worth it."

Bob just nods and turns around and everyone follows. We find the parents about 30 feet away and stick to them, though my dad knows me enough to easily tell something happened. I just nod at him and make sure everyone is being cool.

"Letting your Mommy and Daddy protect you now, Lars?" Duncan taunts. "What a loser. Just like you'll be on Saturday."

"Good night, Duncan," I say, refusing to turn around and shaking my head at the rest of my teammates.

He stands there for a bit, glaring at me as if he's intimidating us and then his girlfriend walks out of the locker room to distract him. She's talking with Mikala and laughing about the match when Duncan interrupts to grab her arm and start to stomping away.

"What's up with him?" Mikala asks as she gives me a hug. "He better relax pretty quickly or Katie won't put up with that. She's already said she's got some doubts about him."

"Everything is fine, babe" I say, leaning in to smell her wet hair. "He just wanted to cause a distraction from your night, and I won't let that happen. That might be the best match I've ever seen you play. You were spectacular."

Everyone agrees and we talk for a few minutes. Then a couple of my teammates see some of her teammates walk out of the locker room and ask Mikala to introduce them. I am so glad Duncan has left because the addition of pretty girls to the mix a few minutes earlier would not have helped. Then there would have been way too much testosterone trying to show off.

Mikala tells everyone which girls are already attached, and says she's been talking up a few of the fellas. I can tell she's already been playing matchmaker and might have some plans for later in the week at the hayride.

When defensive specialist Ruth Wiegmann tells Alex, "I heard you yelling all match! You were so cute," I think Alex may become the first person ever to suffer from permanent blushing. Instead he just says, "Not as cute as you."

Yep, taught that boy everything he knows! He may use what I gave him quite a bit better than I do, but at least I taught him in the first place.

Everyone decides to go to the local diner where we can sit down and talk. After a short drive and before we all go in, I ask Mikala to check the place out and make sure there aren't any IWU football players around. Things are almost too tense around campus, and we don't need to take any chances.

It's been a very odd day, even by my usual expectations. I can't believe the school is going to retire our numbers, then there was the press conference and Mikala's volleyball match. I still think the highlight is sitting next to her in this restaurant, sharing a strawberry shake and holding her hand.

As much as I want to go find a couch and snuggle up with her, my group goes a different way from hers after we finish eating. A goodnight kiss will suffice for now.

Somehow I wonder if tomorrow is going to be even stranger.

CHAPTER 29

As soon as we get back to the hotel, of course we report what happened to Coach Schebig what happened. Since there were so many witnesses, including Indiana Western fans, he tells us to blow it off but to be more careful the next time.

"Don't even get caught in a position to be in a potential situation," he tells me. "We just can't be there, you especially."

Then, before practice in the morning, he tells us to continue to be careful and make sure we stick together in groups. It kind of sucks that I have to be so on guard in own hometown. I probably have more right to be here than anyone, but I'm the one who has to act like the outsider, always looking over my shoulder.

"Remember, guys," I say, "if something happens, do not turn it into a brawl. Just pull together and let them make fools of themselves. That's the plan. We'll wait to win the fight on the field. This is all part of our plan. We keep our cool while they lose theirs."

After practice, it's Randy's turn to give his senior speech about the game. He's so emotional he's been thinking about this for weeks, trying to make all the words just perfect. I'm sure he's written at least 10 rough drafts, but instead, when it was finally his turn, he just let it rip. He's the type of guy who always wears his heart on his sleeve anyway, which means he's just whom you want watching your back on the football field. His grandfather played and his dad played, both for IWU, and I'm betting he's the best of the three even though he never got the chance to show it here.

"I've got $20 that says he ends up crying," Max says to me as we gather up.

``No bet,'' I say. ``Our M&M is just a teddy bear.''

We call him M&M because he's hard on the outside and soft on the inside. He tells the girls the name's because he's got a great rap. Uh, huh. Not something you want to picture in your head considering Randy weighs 310 pounds and he's only 6-1. Somehow he makes it work, though, and the ladies all love him. Or maybe that should be love all of him.

``I don't have a lot to say because I think you guys all know how much this game means to me,'' he tells the team. ``Truthfully, it's the one thing I want out of this year more than anything else. I'm being totally honest here when I say that, and the reason why is because this game will last forever with me. My family still thinks I made a mistake by going out West, but they have never understood that I never had any other choice because I was friends with Max and Lars. We all looked out for each other when we were freshmen, just like with Big Bob and Erik and Alex, because it was obvious to us at least that nobody else was.

``This is my chance to show my parents and the rest of my family. That's why even if we go on to win the national title, which I hope we do, I want to win this game more. Maybe that will mean more to me in the long run, but this means more to my family right now.

``Can anyone else tell me who won the national title three years ago? Who did they play? Do you think there's anyone outside of the teams in our division playoffs who can answer either question? That's what I mean. We'll remember if we win the title, and we'll have a ring to show off which is great, but everyone will remember if we win this game. No one will ever forget us. Think about that. How many times in our lives do we get a chance to do something that so many people will never forget? Coaches will be talking about us in their pregame speeches for decades when we pull this off.

"Yeah, this is a team game and we're representing our school, but just this once is it wrong to want to be selfish and do this for ourselves? We've earned this! We have trained for this! We have sacrificed for this! No excuses!"

"No excuses," everyone else roars back.

As he's talking, Randy can't stand still. He's bobbing and weaving all over the place. Like a gymnast on a floor exercise, I'm guessing he's walked over every blade of grass in the circle in the middle of our gathering.

"That's what I'm saying! We don't owe anything to anyone else for this game, except to each other... except to each other. I think we've all come a long way this year. We've bonded, we've gotten better individually and I think we are quite a bit better as a team. I also think we are good enough. I don't think IWU has a clue what they are up against... and I like that.

"They treated me like garbage when I was here. I was the lowest of the low and they made sure to step on me every day to make sure I stayed there. Well, I'm not garbage any more. We aren't garbage any more that nobody else gave a chance. We have our chance right now, and I want that chance! We have earned that chance! We will take that chance!

"That's all I've got to say. No excuses!"

It's more than enough. As Randy finishes, tear free, everyone rushes in to bury him with their bodies and yells. Like I said, his emotion is wonderful to see because, dang, is he an inspiration. You always get total honesty from Randy because that's just how he is and he always says what he's thinking from the heart. I am so proud to call him my friend and have him protecting my back.

``Maybe we should have saved him for closer to game time, Coach," I say to Coach Schebig. ``There's no way Max will live up to that."

``You watch," Max says.

``I'd rather hear," I say.

``You will," he says.

All Coach Schebig says is, ``Randy's going to make a great coach someday. Max, you're up tomorrow."

The rest of the day is pretty calm, spent studying and making sure we've got every one of our trick plays memorized on offense. The defense doesn't have to worry about any of those because we already know everything IWU runs, and it's basic, boring traditional football. They will make it a point of pride not to make any changes for us because they think they're good enough to beat us without making any adjustments. That's part of what we're counting on.

Take us for granted. Please.

There's fried chicken for lunch, but we're all skipping the normal supper later to attend the street fair. There's plenty of food there everyone can enjoy. Anything that can be dipped, battered and fried will be available, and I mean anything.

Fried butter? Tried it.

Chicken-fried bacon? Haven't tasted that one yet.

Fried Twinkies? Oh, yeah, baby!

Fried avocado bites? Do I go to school in California? But I don't think I'll try it again. I'll also pass on the fried guacamole. That's about as appealing to me at fried green tomatoes.

Spaghetti and meatball on a stick? Give me some garlic bread and I'm good for two.

Krispy Kreme burger? No thanks, not when the real beef is right there, dripping with cheese and grease and requiring two hands to hold onto. It tastes better anyway.

Deep fried peanut butter and jelly sandwich? That and a glass of milk and I'm ready for a sugar coma nap.

I'm more of a traditionalist when it comes to street fair food, sticking to tenderloins, Mettler's Fish Stand, pulled pork and elephant ears, but my favorite of the heart-stopping junk food is fried cookie dough. It probably takes six months off my life every time I eat one, but it's so worth it. Every year someone comes up with a new taste of heaven that has never been considered before as a fried food.

The best part of food alley this year is watching Little Joe eat fried frog legs on a dare from Gabe. The deal is, if Little Joe can eat them without any problem, then Gabe has to eat something that Little Joe will come up with when we get home. We're all figuring that will be sautéed testicles of something we've never heard of before so Gabe dips the frog legs in the meanest hot sauce he can find, but Little Joe just keeps chewing.

"You're eating Kermit!" Randy says, cracking up everyone but Little Joe. "Miss Piggy's going to kick your tail."

Even though we're all wearing our civilian clothes, 100 college football players walking through food alley clears out the rest of the crowd at least for a few minutes. Everyone in town knows who we are and is very friendly. There's a little trash talking from the IWU fans, but nothing too serious, as everyone is here to relax and have a good time. Everyone on our side seems to have the right attitude about tonight, we josh them back a little.

Maybe it's a good thing we can all walk this food off a little while seeing the sights. Our street fair has been around forever, and because it's Wednesday night, there's a parade that includes high school bands, choirs and sports teams, 4H winners, local service organizations, youth organizations such as dancers, pee wee football and Future Farmers of America and of course the clowns and the local motorcycle club (definitely not one and the same). It's the same stuff every year, but to the California guys, they've never seen anything like it.

"When do the animals come through," Nate Higgins asks.

"When they do, you better watch your step," I say.

Yes, there's also a horse troop and the local animal shelter is walking a group of dogs who are looking for new homes. I have to hold Nate and make him give a puppy back, but it's killing him. The Shriners finish everything up by coming through on their mini cars, driving through patterns while throwing candy to the kids.

"I want one of those," Big Joe screams. "Can you imagine me driving that around campus?"

"No, because you couldn't even fit in one," I say. "You already weigh more than two of those things."

"You've at least got to get me a hat with the flashing lights," he says.

Alex Eastin and Ruth Wiegmann have met again tonight and are walking around holding hands. They're so cute even though he's about 6-foot-5 and she's about 5-foot-2. So far he's carrying around three dolls that he won at the ring toss, the ping pong ball bounce and by throwing darts at balloons.

"I hope you're planning on giving Ruth at least one of those, Alex," I say. "I'm not sure you'll be able to carry them onto the plane."

He just blushes some more. It might be all over for Alex.

Besides walking around with Mikala and watching the local We've Got Talent competition, my favorite part of the street fair is seeing all my high school friends. It's the first time I've been back for the fair since graduation and it seems word got out that we would be here tonight. Everyone was already coming out for the parade, but I'm running into all kinds of folks I haven't seen in three or four years.

We end up gathering on a side street in front of the Elks Lodge with about 50 former classmates, pretty good considering there were only 75 in our graduating class at Talbott. We're all talking and hugging and having a great time catching up. One thing about growing up in a small town, you know everyone in your high school class and you usually know everything about them. There are no secrets in small towns. It's fun to see who married whom and even see some of their babies.

With Mikala standing by in case I have any problems, I'm holding the baby of one of her best friends. The little boy, about three months old, is asleep in my arms despite all the noise and attention he's receiving. He's relaxed, I'm relaxed and Mikala is smiling at me like she's already got big plans how often I'll be doing this in the future. I hope so.

But seconds after I hand the baby back to its mother, something big and hard smacks me in the right cheekbone and I drop to my knees. Luckily I saw the shock in the mother's eyes so I was turning my head to see what was coming or I might have smacked the pavement as hard as I got hit in the back of the head. It's like a giant gong is going off inside my head. I can hear the screaming, but my head is numb and my eyes are showing me this big red splotch like fireworks are going on behind my eyelids. I can also hear the baby crying since it has been awakened up by all the raised voices.

"No so tough now when the rest of your team's not around, are you,"

I hear Andrew Crow snarl. "Couldn't wait for you to give that baby back."

Because my teammates are everywhere else at the fair, I've made a huge mistake by meeting on a side street with my high school friends. Though I was hanging with friends, I realize I'm cut off from my teammates when I can finally open my eyes and look up to see what I think are six IWU players standing over me. Mikala is screaming at Duncan Welker, but he shoves her aside.

I'll remember that.

"Just like always, Andrew," I finally speak, "always hitting me from behind when I can't see it coming."

That just ticks him off even more, and he pulls his arm back to add some more lumps. He never gets to throw the punch, though, because a few of my high school friends grab me and pull me back across the ground while a few more jump between Crow and me.

My head is still buzzing, but I hear some feet running as the argument continues. I played football with some of my high school friends, but none of them are half as big as Crow and some of his teammates. Luckily, help arrives as some of my teammates heard the commotion and came running.

"Figured if there was trouble, you'd find it," Jordan Eichorn says. "Why do people always want to punch you?"

"Cause I'm so cute," I mutter, shaking my head. That only hurts worse.

By the time he and Miguel Perez help lift me to my feet, my head is still spinning, but the IWU players have walked away into the crowd. As I lean on Mikala, a few seconds later county deputy Rich MacIntyre shows up and starts asking questions. Everyone else knows who hit me and what happened, but the last thing I want is for this to turn into a big thing that embarrasses everyone.

"I'm fine, Rich, no harm no foul," I say, holding up my hands.

"Doesn't matter, we can't have this kind of thing happening at the street fair," he says. "I want names or I'm taking you in instead. I want somebody's butt for this and I'll start with yours."

Mikala starts to argue with him about me being the victim here, but I understand where he's coming from. He's got to stand up for the standards of the community, and with a big incident like this – big for Talbott at least – he can't appear soft or to play favorites in any way.

"Rich, I can't tell you who hit me, but if we pursue this, it's just going to make Talbott look bad, Please let us handle this on the field. If you want, you can call Coach Jackson and Coach Schebig, but really, I'm fine and I'm not willing to press charges."

He thinks about it a few minutes, and realizes the incident is over with no serious injuries. He also knows my head is too thick for anything to dent it.

"OK, but I want you and your teammates out of here in 15 minutes. If you're not going to tell me who did this, then I want any chance of another altercation eliminated. You all go home and that way there won't be any revenge beatings tonight. Too many of you young guys think you're invincible and unbreakable."

"That's fine," I say. "This way everyone else can enjoy the fair. Guys," I say to Jordan and Miguel, "gather everyone up and meet at the buses."

"I'm not leaving you alone again," Jordan says. "That was a mistake."

"You can because I'm sure Rich here will escort me to the bus and not even those guys are stupid enough to attack me when there's a deputy here."

It takes us 25 minutes to get everyone together, which is OK because Coach Schebig gets to spend a few minutes listening to Rich, and then another 10 reaming me for going off without my teammates. I think Rich enjoys that a little, and finally says the incident is closed before we pull out.

By then my right eye is puffing up pretty good and I can barely see out of it. It's going to be a whopper in the morning.

By the time we get settled in at the hotel, my cell phone is buzzing constantly with calls from what I'm guessing are reporters and sportscasters from Arlington, but I ignore all of them. I do call my folks and tell them to call Mikala's and Max's parents to let them know that I'm fine.

Because it happened at the street fair, there's no way to contain the news and it leads the 11 p.m. broadcasts. Head of delegation Anthony Davis goes on camera to say that I'm fine and it was just boys being boys and trying to impress some girls. He tells the broadcaster that I'm fine and unwilling to press charges, saying we'd all prefer to handle this on the field rather than in the courts.

Any tickets that were left to sell probably were sold right there.

CHAPTER 30

Now we'll see how tough these California boys are because when I wake up, finally, there's frost on the ground! That also describes Coach Schebig's mood today when we get to practice as he's growling at everyone, particularly me.

The story of the punch is on the front page of the paper. The details are correct, thanks to the baby's mother and her husband telling Win the details. I'm sure it'll be another fun press conference today.

My eye is swollen shut, but Joe Baer says I'll be able to see fine in two days on Saturday.

"You'll be pretty ugly, but that's nothing you're not used to dealing with," he says.

Thanks, Joe. Love you, too.

Turns out Coach Schebig and Coach Jackson have already talked. It was cordial, Coach Schebig says, especially since neither side wants Duncan and Andrew suspended for the game. Coach Jackson needs them to play, and we need them to lose their cool during the game, though Coach Schebig didn't say that to Coach Jackson. It's obvious I'm getting to them.

Other than that, practice is pretty calm and methodical. We go through our stretching and run a few dozen plays. It's our usual Thursday routine until Max calls everybody in and starts his speech. His topic, as usual, is perfect.

"I know we all want to kill those guys after what they did to Lars, but my biggest concern about this game is that we're going to be too fired up, that we're going to play only on emotion. Then we might let it get away from us because we'll take stupid penalties or we'll run out of energy early. Just like last night, no matter what happens, we can't retaliate. We can't get into a fistfight with these guys because we'll lose. We're already the enemy, playing on their turf. Everybody already hates us. That doesn't mean we can't win the football game, though, if we're smart.

"I just want to remind everyone that we have to be a team under control emotionally and physically to do this. That's not saying we can't use that fire to push us, but let it burn inside, let is smolder, let it focus us on what we have to do each play. Play with passion, play with fire, but we'll win because we're the smarter, more under-control team. Let them lose their cool, let them implode because we won't make mistakes. Let them play dirty and throw punches because we won't respond and we won't let them get under our skin. It's Lars' job to get under their skin, and it's our job to protect him enough that he gets to do that.

"We have to stick to our game plan. We have to trust everything we have worked on, and we have to trust each other. It's only going to be us out there, and I trust each of you. Do you trust everything we've done this year to give it a chance to work?

"Remember, we are stealth, we are calm, we are precision, we are prepared. I want every one of you to think about that because when the emotion hits us we have to remember to use it the right way, not let it use us.

"Does that make sense to you?"

Everyone nods, and someone says, "No excuses."

"I also have an idea. During the pregame introductions, they always announce the offense or the defense, but I don't want to walk out there as an individual. I want to walk out there with my team. I don't want us to run onto the field with everybody jumping up and down and yelling. Everybody does that and what does it prove? I want us to walk out there together as one unit. I want us to be calm, show we have class and know what we're going to do on this job.

"And then I'd like us all to turn and point to the section where our parents are going to be and bow our heads to them in respect and thanks. They are every bit as much a part of this as if they were a member of this team. They have sacrificed every bit as much as we have, and this may be the only time they are all together in one spot so we can thank them and let them know that we are playing because of what they taught us, and that we are representing them in everything we do.

"What do you guys think of that?"

"I love it!" I yell and start clapping. Soon the clapping grows to include everyone.

"Thanks," Max says, "Is that OK with you, Coach? That's all I've got to say."

It was more than enough as everyone else continues clapping for Max. It wasn't the longest speech we've heard through this process, but as usual, it was the one that put it all in perspective.

"Great job, buddy," I say as I wrap him in a hug. "That was perfect."

"It's what I feel," he says.

"I know. We all do."

Randy James approaches Coach to set up the players for the media conference and says I'm the only one everyone wants to talk to. I'm not surprised but tell him I'm bringing Max and Jordan with me, even though neither was there last night.

The first question is, "What happened last night?"

"Obviously," I say, pointing to my eye, "I didn't see anything."

"But you know who hit you, right?"

"Yes, I think I know who hit me, but I'm keeping that to myself. Just like we always have, we'll handle this on the field."

"So it definitely was one of the IWU players? Reports have said it was Andrew Crow, can you confirm that"

"I'm not going to identify the person in any way. I'm not positive anyway because I never saw the punch coming."

"Are you going to be able to see well enough to play Saturday?"

"Well, I might have to squint a little more than usual to find Max downfield, but I'll be fine. This won't be an excuse in any way. I'll just have to switch my blindside this week."

"Did your mouth get you in trouble again?"

I wasn't expecting that question, but it's not too hard to send it back. "No, I never said a thing during this incident. I was talking to some friends from high school when I was hit from behind. I just happened to turn that way a split-second before I got hit or it would have landed on the back of my head.

"Anybody got any football questions, I really wouldn't mind answering a few of those sometime this week?"

Maybe they think those kind of questions are irrelevant this week because everyone believes we have no chance. If that's the case, then my overall plan is working because no one has been pestering my teammates for strategy points. Maybe IWU will be way overconfident, too.

"I've got a football question," Wendy Bartle says. "What do you think of your counterpart Mason Parker?"

Though he's a year older than I am, Mason is still playing at IWU because of a red-shirt year and then the NCAA granted him an extra year of eligibility because of a shoulder injury. He's started the last two years for the Sagamores.

"Mason is a great guy and a great leader, and I'm happy his career has worked out so well for him," I say.

Then I can't resist sticking the needle in.

"I'm sure he's happy I left here because there's no way he can throw with me, and he probably wouldn't have gotten much playing time if I was still here. I mean, c'mon, have you looked at their passing stats? Maybe none of that is in his control, though."

There are no more questions after that, but I add a quick reminder, "Again, win or lose, I'll be at the 50-yard line at the end of the game waiting to shake hands with whomever is willing."

With that, I turn and run into the locker room. I'm sure that will stir things up some more for IWU, and maybe Mason will try to come out and prove he can throw the ball on Saturday. That would be great for us because we are a lot more worried about trying to stop their running game. B.J. Cowen has developed into an all-American tailback, and I'm not sure we have the speed to keep up with him.

With all the commotion last night, we have an official team function tonight which should keep everyone out of trouble, even me. When we were planning this trip, I wanted to make sure to do something that I was guessing most of my teammates had never done before, and I think 90 percent of them have never been near a farm.

I knew all of our parents would want to throw some kind of a party while we were in town, so I jumped the gun a little and called Ken and Joyce Knipstein, long-time family friends, to ask if it would be OK if we held a hayride at their place. They agreed, said they'd rev up the tractor and start the bonfires. They also offered their pole barn as a place to eat and even dance later. Max has asked a buddy of ours named Larry Schmitt if he would mind being a DJ for a night. Mikala is bringing some of her friends along to provide the dance partners.

Max and I also have special plans for the Samoans.

Before that, Randy, Coach Schebig and I go on Win Rood's weekly afternoon sports call-in show. Most of the questions are pretty tame until the final call. The owner of the Trolley Bar calls and demands to know when Coach is going to pay up his bar tab.

"My tab or Coach Burgess' bar tab?" Coach asks. "If it's just mine, we're OK, but I didn't bring enough money to cover his. If it's just mine, I'll be there in a few. Set a cold one out for me."

That draws a big laugh from the owner who hands the phone to someone.

"Boys, how are you doing?" Coach Burgess asks. "Just wanted to call in and tell you good luck and stay healthy. I'm very proud of the way you have all progressed and the way you are handling this circus."

Of course, that starts Randy's eyes to watering, and he can't talk.

"Thank you, Coach," I say. "That means a great deal to all of us. Just like the rest of our family and friends back here, we always try to play to make you proud. We're hoping we can do that again on Saturday."

After that, Coach takes off for the Trolley Bar, and Alex and I head back to the hotel to get ready for the party. I've also got some preparations I have to make for the festivities.

It's already starting to cool off significantly, and the breeze is picking up out of the North. It's already dropped into the high-40s, but the sun hasn't gone down yet. The farm is also on flat land with little to slow down the wind so it's going to get quite a bit chillier tonight.

Bwa-ha-ha! Good!

By the time the team buses arrive at the farm, it's 6:30 p.m. and the Knipsteins and everyone's parents already have things started with help from the athletic department staffers.

Because the temperature has dropped to 40 degrees, as soon as they step off the bus most of the players run toward the three bonfires to warm up. They are complaining so much, you'd think they were naked.

"Shorts?" my dad asks. "Didn't you tell any of these boys to bring jeans?"

"Of course I did. Do you think they listen to me?"

"Probably about as well as you used to listen to me," he says.

Hey, I resemble that remark.

I'm bundled up with long johns, jeans, two pairs of socks, a sweatshirt and my winter coat, hat and gloves. This isn't my first hayride. Despite all my warnings, most of the California boys have showed up in shorts and T-shirts because that's pretty much all they have packed. Most of my teammates are begging the equipment managers for their game day parkas that are used on the sidelines. At my "suggestion," the equipment managers all plead ignorance, saying the equipment is already unpacked at the stadium.

"W-w-w-w-h-h-h-h-h-y-y-y-y-y?" Big Joe whines, with the wind freezing tears on his cheeks. "We need it now!"

I swear his hands and legs are turning blue, his belly is jiggling from all the shivering and his teeth are chattering so much it sounds like a machine gun is going off. The poor guy really seems to be showing the symptoms of possibly dying from hypothermia which is understandable considering I'm guessing he's never experienced temperatures below 55 degrees before.

"What's it worth to you?" I ask.

"W-w-w-w-h-h-h-h-a-a-a-a-t-t-t are you t-t-t-t-talking about?"

"What will you owe me if I can provide warm clothing for all of you? Even you big, tough `I always wear shorts' Samoans?"

"The heck with everybody else, I just want to take care of me!" Big Joe stammers. "I swear to God my hands and toes are already numb and it's crawling up my legs and arms."

When I stop laughing, I pull out my cell phone and make a call. "OK, you can bring the truck up."

Within five minutes, the equipment truck pulls up, followed by another bus, both of which will do wonders for morale and everyone's body temperatures. The equipment truck includes all the parkas, everyone's game day sweats and some hand warmers. The bus gets things even hotter as it is carrying Mikala and all of her friends. There's Sherry Springer, Hannah Olsen, Emily Miller, Dawn Findling, triplets Maria, Brittany and Jordan Tomlin and Ashley Combs from the volleyball team, along with about half of Mikala's dorm wing, including Jami Hahn, Deb Talbott, Kim Boroff, Kathy Zoucha, Tara McClure, Sue Tilbury, Mitzi Toepfer, Heidi Skorjdahl, Carol O'Brien and Eryn James. I don't know how she did it, but that bus is packed. I'm going to owe her pretty big for this one... So I better start building up some favors due me from my guys.

``Big Joe, may I suggest that next time you listen to me? Like right now I'm suggesting the best way to get warm is for you to go snuggle up to one of those ladies.''

His reply is unprintable. At least I don't know how to spell that word, though I've heard it often enough used as an adjective to describe me.

I thought the idiots who wore sandals and no socks were on their own because there's nothing I can do about that, but Max comes through with about four dozen pairs of white athletic socks.

Still, nobody is too eager to move away from the bonfires – at least until the girls start dragging guys off for hayrides. ``C'mon, I need somebody to keep me warm,'' they coo.

A couple of guys whimper and looking longingly back at the fires but allow themselves to be pulled along. The fools! They don't realize yet that a hayride is guaranteed to be 20 degrees colder than the announced temperature because you're sitting up and catching the wind full on. There's nowhere to hide, either, as the girls are smart enough to use you as a windbreak. That's really the main reason they want you along.

Thanks to help from the neighbors, there are two wagons going at all times as two more are being loaded up. This might be the biggest hayride in state history.

``T-t-t-t-h-h-h-h-a-a-a-a-t-t-t-t w-w-w-w-a-a-a-a-s-s-s-s-s f-f-f-f-f-u-u-u-u-n-n-n-n!'' Little Joe sputters when he finally can straighten his stiff legs and crawl off the wagon to hobble toward the bonfires. Yeah, it looks like a whole lot of fun.

The entire time there's two long lines going through for food. Again, Mom, Mrs. Knipstein, Carol Booker, Patty Abbott and everyone else has done an amazing job of organizing everything. I'm getting a headache just trying to figure out where they stored all the fixings before they made things up.

There are six grills going with hamburgers, hot dogs and chicken near long picnic tables showcasing potato salad, baked beans, macaroni salad, tons of bread and buns, all sorts of vegetables and enough deviled eggs that a grocery store is probably out of stock for a few days. There must be 25 crockpots going full of baked beans. Another table is set up with cakes and pies, and 10 – yes 10 – ice cream makers are whirring full steam. At first I doubted that would be enough ice cream, but the temperatures are helping with that.

There's probably some of the approximately 20 bushels of green beans that I picked from these fields that's being served, too. I used to hate this place when I was growing up because I could never stand the heat. I'd bend over to pick the lovely, blasted beans and then I'd get light-headed. The other option was to get up early before the sun got too high to raise the temperatures, but I was never very good about that. Mom and Mrs. Knipstein would can green beans so we'd have fresh vegetables to eat all year. At least they'd eat them.

Anyway, there's an awesome amount of food being served, but we're expecting around 300 people. Thankfully, there's plenty of room to spread out.

My father thanks the Lord for the food by leading us in prayer.

"Dear Lord, thank You for this opportunity for fellowship with friends and family. Thank You for this bountiful food You have provided and all the blessings You have given us. Help us to always keep Your ways and Your path in our thoughts, and remind us that we represent You before our schools or our teams. Continue to use us as Your examples. In Your son's name. Amen."

Maybe because we're so spread out or because we're out in the middle of nowhere, the noise level seems fairly calm. Everyone is enjoying the food, and when Mom announces there's plenty for seconds, the players on the team all give a big cheer. Maybe the best thing about this trip so far has been the food.

Thanks to his ability to whistle, Jordan gets everyone's attention for a few seconds and somehow gets everyone to quiet down long enough so he can speak.

``Representing the team, I just want to thank everyone for everything you have done for us this week," he says, and every football player starts clapping. ``This has been amazing. When we started talking about this trip, I wondered, What in the world am I going to do in Indiana? I didn't know there was anything to do in Indiana, which is why I figured basketball was so big here.

``But this week has been an awful lot of fun for us, and the food has been outstanding. The Currys, the Prestons, the Blums and the Knipsteins and all of your friends have been amazing hosts and we thank you so much for making us all feel at home. The one thing I hope is that you can all come to California for the playoffs this year and we can return the hospitality a little bit. Thank you so much."

Everyone claps and cheers at that.

I'm extremely proud when everyone pitches in to help clean up after dinner. You'd think with that much food and that many people it would take at least an hour just to gather the trash, but most of it gets shoved into the bonfires. There's no need to refrigerate the leftovers because it's cold enough, and there really aren't that many. Industrial-sized urns are ready to plug in with hot chocolate, cider and coffee.

The Army would have been proud of this effort, and I quickly go around and hug all the moms and grandmas. I was very worried about my folks and how they would handle all of this, but as Dad always says, "The key to moving is having twice as many people to help out as you need. Then it's not such a big job for anyone." They certainly have plenty of help for this particular job.

"It wasn't too fancy," Mom says. "We couldn't do this all the time, but we had plenty of notice, and this has been kind of fun."

By the time the first few hayrides return after the meal, the barn has been converted into a dance hall, and Larry has things going full tilt. Mikala's dad likes to call square dances, and he's trying to teach 14 of the guys how to line dance. Thank goodness there are no children around to get stepped on. My biggest fear is one of my linemen turning an ankle, but within 20 minutes Mr. Blum has them organized enough that no one is getting hurt. It probably helps that some of the girls are there to guide the guys and show them how it's done.

CHAPTER 31

Because this is a private party, we finally don't have to worry about any IWU guys showing up to create trouble. I'm betting they wouldn't know how to find the place anyway, as it's 25 miles from Arlington, which means it's 25 miles in the middle of nowhere.

We can all just relax, maybe for the first time since we've been here. I'd like nothing better than to continue snuggling with Mikala, but I've got one more prank to pull, something Max, Gabe and I have been setting up for months.

Whenever we've had the chance in the locker room, at the training table or on the team bus, the three of us have talked about the joys of snipe hunting. We've even pulled a few other guys into it, telling tales about how much fun it is and how it's a lost craft that takes speed, cunning and aggressiveness – in other words, everything a Samoan prides themselves on, especially big Samoans who think they have the agility of cats. Yeah, maybe like Garfield.

After hearing these stories for a few weeks, our Samoan buddies have heard enough and Little Joe finally challenges us with, "What do you three know about hunting?"

"We're pretty good," I say. "Snipes are very hard to catch because you have to do it a certain way. They are very quick and exceptionally tricky. If they sense what you are up to, it can be a long chase. You have to be in pretty good shape."

"You must not be doing it right then," Big Joe says. "I can't believe you three could be any good at hunting."

The more we talked about snipe hunting, the more intrigued the Joes became.

Now, one key to the whole scam is that everyone knows Max rarely speaks and has absolutely no sense of humor. When he starts getting into it with the Samoans, we know we've got them!

"It's addicting," he tells the Joes one day at Hazeltine's Wings. "I never thought I'd like it either before Lars talked me into it, and now I can't get enough of it. I like to go out every chance we get. It's difficult, but there's almost something peaceful about it, getting out in the fields away from everything. When you finally catch one, you know you've accomplished something special."

In the weeks before we came home, every time we'd bring it up, Little Joe or Big Joe would ask if there would be any opportunity to go snipe hunting on this trip. I keep putting it off, telling them it's a very involved process that might take too much time.

"And it has to be done at night," Gabe said. "That evens out the odds a little and gives the snipes more of a chance. We were getting so good in the daytime that it wasn't much of a challenge."

This makes sense to the Joes, who nod in agreement. What fun is anything that is too easy, after all?

"What do they taste like," Big Joe asks.

"Oh, you don't eat them," I say. "They taste horrible, but the entire object of snipe hunting is catching the little buggers. They are very savvy and can change directions in a heartbeat. It takes some real skill to nail one."

"Catch them? You don't shoot them?" this from Little Joe.

"Where's the skill in that?" Max says. "It's more fun when you are both limited to the ground and you have to rely on your quick wits and hands."

Of course that only fires up the Samoans even more to try it. They figure they are the best athletes on the team anyway, and if we can catch individual snipes they can snare a whole flock.

Now the other critical part of this is making sure the Samoans ask for the chance to go snipe hunting. Alex, Randy and Gabe are sitting near one of the bonfires arguing whether snipes resemble quails or pheasants more.

"They are quicker than pheasants, but they are bigger than quails," Gabe says.

"They kind of remind me of seagulls that can't fly," Alex says.

The Samoans are sitting about 10 feet away taking in every word. Finally, Big Joe can't take it anymore.

"What can be so hard about catching a seagull that can't fly?" he demands. "I bet I could catch them with my bare hands!"

"Oh, you don't want to do that," Randy says. "They have mean beaks that can break skin so you have to wear some thick gloves and have some pretty sturdy cloth bags to catch them with. They'll fight you every second."

"You have to hang onto them until they wear out," Gabe says. "Only then can you release them because they'll get free and turn on you in a second. You better respect them because pound-for-pound, they are incredibly tough, maybe even tougher than you."

That's all Big Joe needs to hear and he pounds over to where Mikala and I are sitting on a blanket near one of the other bonfires.

"It's time for snipe hunting. I want to test myself against this skilled prey," he says formally, causing Mikala to bury her face in my coat so he can't tell she's laughing.

``Are you sure, Big Joe,'' I say. ``The odds won't be in your favor tonight. Because there are so many people here, I'm sure the snipes have moved deeper into the bean fields. It's also a moonless night which means they'll be even harder to see.''

``I don't want to hear any of your excuses. I can see great in darkness.''

``OK, then... ''

I swear Mikala is ready to laugh so hard she's about to double over, but somehow she holds it in.

``Is she OK?'' Big Joe asks.

``She's just having some trouble with gas from the baked beans,'' I say. ``I'll get the supplies. You get Little Joe and Max and Gabe together and I'll meet you guys 50 yards out into the grain field. We'll talk and plan there, but you should all be quiet to get ready. Don't tell anybody where you are going or they'll all want to come watch and that won't work. We'll make sure to tell everybody when this is over.

``I just want you to remember when this is over, if you fail it's because you pushed this and I warned you how tough it would be tonight. No excuses,'' I say, somehow still keeping a straight face.

``No excuses.''

As he walks away, I get first an elbow to the ribs and then a punch to the shoulder. Luckily, she doesn't go after my cheek which is very tender.

``Gas,'' she whispers. ``That's the best you could come up with? Gas?''

``I'm surprised he didn't turn and run away,'' I say.

``You're going to want to run away when I'm done with you.''

"Never," I say, and give her a kiss.

About 15 seconds later, she says, "You better go get your supplies before they get suspicious and start to reconsider."

"Yes, Ma'am. Keep my spot warm."

I've already prepared supplies that include a cloth bag, two stones, two pairs of gloves and three flashlights. By the time I walk out to the group in the field of green bean plants, I already know what I'm going to say.

"Have you two ever dug up worms after a rainy night for fishing?" I ask and both Joes nod. "OK, part of this is like that. Max, Gabe and I will use the flashlights to hunt for the snipes, but if we put the light directly on them, they'll take off and we'll never see them again. You have to look around the edges of the light just like you would when looking for worms. If we can't find any right away, we'll keep going deeper and wider until we do. We know they're out there, especially at this time of the season.

"Another thing you have to do is make sure to stay downwind, which means we'll have to go further away from the party because then the wind will be in your face the whole time. That's also good because it will carry the sound away along with your scent."

By this time, I'm really glad I'm wearing boots because man, is this getting deep! Somehow, the Samoans seem to be buying all of it.

"We'll start out in three lines with Gabe and I on the outside of Max who will try to get ahead of us to give us a broader area to work in. We'll try to push the snipes to the middle where you can snare them with the bags.

"The other thing is, one of you will have to tap these rocks together lightly while the other says 'Snipe! Snipe!' in a regular conversational tone. If you do either too loud, you'll startle them and they'll take off. You have to keep the right tone and pace to both of them. It should sound soothing and almost hypnotizing to the snipes."

At that, Max mouths, "Soothing? Hypnotizing?" to me and I just raise my arms out to the sides, palms up while the Samoans are putting on their gloves.

I make a big presentation of handing the rocks to Little Joe. Usually, this is where the gag breaks down, but the Joes are listening very intently. Gabe is so afraid he's going to crack a smile that he has to turn around and face away from us.

"Did you hear something, Gabe?" I whisper intensely. "Be careful not to scare them away."

Gabe just nods but doesn't turn around so he can continue to hide his face as his shoulders start to shake just a bit in the darkness.

"It is a little cold out here, Gabe. Head out wide, and I'll go this way," I say before turning back to the Joes. "If you lose sight of us don't panic. Be patient tonight because there's no moon and it will be tougher to catch sight of the snipes. If you can pull this off on a night like this, it will be quite an accomplishment."

"I wouldn't even try it tonight," Max says with perfect timing. "We've never been good enough to catch a snipe on a night like this. It might take a couple of hours."

It's a good thing Gabe is gone or he would have busted out laughing at that whopper.

"We'll make it work," a determined Big Joe says.

Crap, he's acting like this is some kind of test of manhood or something. That might be a good thing now, but later? He may kill me!

"OK, let us get about a five-minute head start, and then you two head straight up the middle following Max's path," I say. "Remember, once you start a chase, you can't stop until you finally track them down because they'll be doubly wary of you the next time. You'll be lucky to reacquire their track.

"Has one of you got a cell phone in case you get lost? Good. OK, well, then, good luck. This will be quite a test of your skill."

It's amazing how much blarney I can throw around when I'm inspired.

Max and I head out, and about four minutes later Max yells – yes, it has to be Max for this to work – "There's one! Get over here you guys!"

We can hear the Joes coming from 50 yards away. Water buffalo being chased by lions could be quieter but probably not nearly as enthusiastic. Or gullible.

"Where are they?" Big Joe whispers excitedly.

With perfect timing, Max tosses a clod of dirt behind his back about 25 yards toward the area where Gabe's flashlight can be seen about 100 yards away. Because it's pitch black, no one could see Max's arm move.

"They took off that way toward Gabe," I say in a tight whisper. "Run that way. We're getting close so they'll be making more noise."

Then Gabe tosses another rock which lands about 50 yards up the path between the rows of grain. That's all it takes for the Joes to take off... well, I was going to say sprinting, but it's more like a fast shuffle. Godzilla walking through Tokyo makes less commotion.

About 100 yards ahead, they finally catch up with Gabe who says,

``Dude, you almost stepped on one! Didn't you see it?''

``I must have missed it, but I swear I heard it,'' Little Joe says as Max and I run up.

``There they go!'' I yell, pointing my flashlight off to the right. ``Go get 'em!''

They put their heads down and stomp off in the general direction I'm pointing, and once in a while you can hear ``Snipe! Snipe!'' and the clicking of the rocks. I'm sure some helicopter flying over the next day is going to think there are crop circles in this field – huge crop circles.

With the Joes charging off to the North, Max and I start walking back to the party. Gabe circles around to join us on the way.

``They are going to be so ticked off,'' Gabe says with a laugh. ``They may strangle you, Lars.''

``Hey, they brought this on themselves. That's why it worked so well.''

We walk back to the party and warm up near the fire for a few minutes. Pretty soon the joke is making its way throughout the party and everybody can't wait for the Joes to turn up.

After an hour of eating smores and toasted marshmallows, I figure it's time to put them out of their misery and call Big Joe's cell phone.

``Have you caught one yet?'' I ask. ``Ready to come home?''

``We caught something, but we're not sure it's a snipe,'' Big Joe says. ``It's mean, though, and has a heck of a bite. Are they supposed to be this loud? It doesn't matter 'cause we're almost there.''

By then I can hear something howling, and as I put the phone down, I can hear it coming closer to the party. I can soon see them approaching, and something in Big Joe's bag is making all kinds of racket trying to claw its way out. The noise is horrible, a crying bark if there is such a thing. It sort of sounds like Big Bob's stomach in the morning before breakfast after closing the night before with sliders.

`Is that what a snipe sounds like?" Little Joe asks, holding the bag and his arm away from his body. `I think this might be a little bigger than a snipe, though. Good thing I had the gloves on because it tried to take a chunk out of me. Does a snipe have fur?"

As `Does a snipe have fur?" runs through my head, I wonder what in the world these two have caught, can it be contained and how do we do this so I don't end up getting killed by two angry Samoans?

Now the girls have all moved quietly behind the guys who have formed a semicircle around the Samoans. I'm beginning to fear the joke is going to be on us in a big, bad way.

`Don't you guys realize there really are no snipes?" I say. `It's a practical joke! And somehow you fell for it. Don't you get it?"

But what I'm really wondering is what's in the bag? Oh, man, what could that possibly be?

`It was too dark out there and we just assumed it was a snipe," Big Joe says. `Wait a minute – what do you mean there are no such things as snipes? Then what's this?"

Holding the bag away from his body, he turns it over and lets the opening drop. Whatever creature is fighting for its life inside sees a little bit of light from the bonfires at the bottom and dives through the hole. As some of the girls scream, the small, grey and quick as a hummingbird animal lands on its two back feet and makes a head-long dive for the fields. The grey blur is gone before anyone can draw another breath.

`Was that a coyote? Somehow you idiots trapped a coyote bare-handed!" I say in awe. "No wonder it tried to take a bite out of you. You didn't get bit, did you?"

Oh, man, now my heart is racing at the thought they might have been bitten.

"You might have to be tested for rabies. Please tell me you didn't get bit!"

For a split-second, I'm thinking 1.) how will I explain this one to Coach Schebig; 2.) who's going to play nose tackle in the game?

"No, we didn't get bit," Little Joe says. "Dang, too bad it got away because I wanted to mount it on a wall or something. Are you sure that wasn't a snipe? We figured it had to be a snipe the way it fought. It was every bit as tough to catch as you guys said it would be."

"You two are absolutely crazy. That was a coyote! Max, you tell them. Maybe they'll believe you."

"Guys, there are no such things as snipes in Indiana," he says. "It's a joke. Honest."

"Now you're just pulling our leg," Big Joe says. "We caught something! I told you I could see pretty good in the dark, but you didn't believe me."

"Somehow you caught a coyote," I say. "You're very lucky you still have a leg to pull! That animal is way tougher and meaner than any snipe could ever be, even if they were real.

"You win, OK? You guys are the best, toughest hunters here! You win the title."

I turn to walk away with Mikala toward the pole barn, saying, "I swear, last time I ever try to pull a joke on a Samoan."

As soon as the words finish coming from my mouth, a collective howl starts out in the fields. It must be a big group of coyotes, maybe 10 to 15 of them because they are making a lot of noise, sending shivers down everyone's backs. Somehow the Samoans must have intimidated all of them, but the pack came together to face a threat.

What a way to end a party. And it had been such a howling good time.

CHAPTER 32

The morning newspaper has a little bit of a surprise for me with the headline, "Preston's 'Me-First' Attitude galls teammates." The story says that the reason I left IWU was because none of my teammates could stand my selfishness.

"Everything was always all about him," one of the IWU players says. "Nothing could please the guy. If the coaches wanted him to do one thing, he always wanted to do the other. When he was running the scout team, our defense never got much preparation because he would always run his own plays instead of what our opponents were expected to run."

Of course, the sources are all anonymous, which is no surprise. I'm called a prima donna and one former teammate (wonder who that could be? Hmm.) calls me a cancer in the locker room. Coach Jackson's name is absent from the story, but his fingerprints sure aren't.

"When those guys left, some of us had a party to celebrate," one quote says. "The best thing I can say about them is that we get another chance to play against them, and for real this time."

The only good thing, as far as I'm concerned, is that none of my current teammates are quoted. No surprise there.

"Guess we should have expected that," I say to Max as we leave our hotel room for practice.

"Amazing how brave anonymous people are," Max says. "If they believe it, they should stand up for it."

"That would require too much character," I say. "I think it's interesting we didn't get a chance to respond to the story. I'm guessing Randy, Alex and Big Bob would love to have a crack at that. Not much we can do about it so let's not worry about it."

Sounds good, but my teammates are one ticked off group in the locker room. The story may have backfired. Instead of tearing us apart, it's bonding us even more.

``Those gutless wonders!" Big Bob roars. ``I'll be happy to put my thoughts into a story with my full name! Does the idiot who wrote that think I moved all the way I moved all the way to California because I hate Lars?"

``Tell it, Big Bob," Randy says. ``Ain't no way anybody is getting through our offensive line anywhere near him tomorrow because then they'll say we've set him up. That is NOT happening."

``Guys, it's OK really," I say. ``Just play tomorrow and everything will be fine. This is exactly what I expected."

``No, it's not OK," Jordan says. ``If I didn't want to run any more laps, I'd say exactly what I think about it, but frankly, Lars, I don't care enough for you to run that far."

Everybody laughs at that, which is why it's the perfect thing to say. I'm even laughing so hard I have to bend over.

``Now I really understand what playing in this game means to you guys," Jordan says. ``I understand the sacrifices you guys are making. I can't imagine all the bad memories this is stirring up."

``It doesn't matter," I tell everyone. ``As a favor to me, nobody respond to a reporter about this story. As long as everyone in this locker room is cool with what is going on and with me, that's all I care about. So please, if anybody has any problems with me or anything of concern, please bring it forward so we can talk about it. If I've done anything that has offended any of you, I apologize. Except for Jordan, who I'm very sure had it coming."

Everyone chuckles at that and it's time to head out.

When we arrive on the practice field, the Joes still don't believe us that they didn't catch a snipe. They. Just. Don't. Get. It. I need a 2X4 to smack them with, and then maybe some nails to put in it to go all Buford Pusser on them. Maybe then I could knock some sense into them, but I doubt it.

The joke, or lack thereof, finally hits them both during practice.

"What a minute..." Big Joes says as the offense approaches the line of scrimmage about 30 minutes into practice. "You really mean it that there are no such things as snipes?"

"The light finally dawns," I say as everyone else on both sides starts laughing. It's a wonder either of them is eligible to play.

"But we caught one!" Little Joe says.

"You caught a coyote, a wild dog, not a snipe. There are no snipes in Indiana except in the naive imagination of people being played for practical jokes. Honest. The only way this worked was because you two begged us to take you snipe hunting. You fell for the whole thing."

"I was just following his lead," Little Joe says, pointing at his partner.

"No, you weren't," Big Joe teases back. "You were the one who convinced me we should do it."

"Could I maybe convince you all to get back to the play," Coach Schebig says before blowing his whistle. "Is it true you guys really caught a coyote?"

So of course he starts calling the defenders his "Coyote Defense," which just cracks everyone up. It will be our inside joke for the rest of the season. It's also going to stick because of the special defense we have prepared to face IWU.

It's the fun part of what is really a boring practice as we just run through a few plays to make sure we are sharp. This is our last practice before the game, and if we don't have it all under control by now, it never will be.

The weather has brightened a bit, which is good for us. We'll need decent temperatures and little wind tomorrow if we're going to pull off a few of our special plays. Because we haven't had a ton of opportunity lately to work on their timing, the fewer complications the better.

"Everybody sure of what they're supposed to do on each play?" Coach Schebig asks as we gather up at the end. "Now is the time to ask any questions. Anybody got anything?" he asks, looking around to make sure he's not missing anything.

"OK, Lars, you're the next man up."

I'm the last player to give his speech on what this game means, and I'm not sure I've ever thought about something more in my life. Right now I'd trade with Max in a heartbeat for tonight's retirement ceremony talk.

"Guys, I hope you take this the right way, but right now I'm not sure I want to play tomorrow's game," which causes a few shocked grumbles. "Hear me out, please. I don't say that because I'm afraid we won't do well or because I'm worried that we'll lose, but because I have absolutely loved all the preparation we have done for this game, and I'm not sure I really want it to end.

"I used to hear my dad talk with some of his buddies about surviving boot camp and how much it meant to them and helped them grow as men, and I wondered if I'd ever have a similar experience. I know now that I have and we have.

"In a way, I'm almost sad that it's over because we have really had a lot of fun with this, and I'm very encouraged to see what we can do tomorrow. I think we've all grown up a bit as we've grown together and bonded. I think this is something we'll be talking about together and with our friends and kids for years to come, just like my dad and his buddies. I know I'll never ever forget what a `Coyote Defense' is, that's for sure.

"I'm proud of what we have accomplished, but I'm just a little sad that it is coming to an end."

I step back and lower my head to take a deep breath.

"I want to thank all of you for what you have done. Jordan, you have become a brother to me by joining with Max and me to help lead this team. Miguel, you, too. I have tremendous respect for you. I also have a tremendous appreciation for the defense, something that I probably didn't have as much as I should have before this. I truly understand now that we are an entire team and not just two units who dress in the same locker room. We are a team, a complete team.

"I also have a tremendous respect for the rest of you who have worked so hard who may get to play special teams tomorrow or may not even get to play at all. You worked so hard and I swear to you it wasn't for nothing because it helped make the rest of us better. If you don't get to play tomorrow, I hope you can use this experience to help make yourselves better players and better people. I hope you feel like you are a total part of this because you are. The future of this program depends on you believing that, and I thank you for pushing us to be the best we can. I'm talking about guys like Landon Reid, Case

Pallister, Jesse Davids, Alex Alesia, Owen Purinton, Luke Rennison and Ken Dutton who just give everything they have to be part of this team. Landon, you truly are a huge part of this.

"We have been through a lot this season, and tomorrow will be the toughest test of our discipline as Max said, our friendships as Jordan said and our passion as Randy said. We need to put it all together tomorrow, but I'm sure we will because we have grown into this chance. We have evolved to meet this challenge.

"No matter what happens tomorrow, I will always be thankful for what we have done together, and I know I will have these memories and friendships forever. I think we have proven that given enough preparation and the willingness to work, we can meet any challenge, and I can't wait to seize that opportunity with you guys tomorrow. I am convinced we are ready, and IWU has no clue how good we are. After tomorrow everyone will know. Everyone else may be surprised, but we won't be because we know how hard we have worked and how much we have come together.

"I don't think we should be nervous or apprehensive in any way heading into this game because we should remember that we'll be doing it together. I think we should be a little excited to see how all the hard work we have done will play out. To everyone in the world but those of us standing on this field, we're 30-point underdogs in this game. No one thinks we have any chance except the one we give ourselves.

"I kind of like those odds. How about you?"

Everyone claps and gathers around. Raising our right hands to point to the sky, we chant "No excuses! No excuses! No excuses!"

"Nice job, Lars," Coach says. "Now I have to go rewrite some of what I was going to say tomorrow. You stole my thunder."

``Then it must have been what needed to be said," I say before running off to the locker room.

After practice, Coach Schebig, Randy, Big Bob and I meet with The Sports Network broadcasters. Max begs off saying he has to go work on his speech for tonight's retirement ceremony, but he still has to go through the line with the other starters to give his name and hometown for the introductions.

Usually, this is a time to share some inside information with the guys who will call the game about the kind of plays we're going to run, what they can look for and maybe give some tips to make them look like they know what they are talking about. I don't have a problem with that most of the time, but we've all agreed we're going to hold most things back and let them be as surprised as everyone else when they see the real thing. We aren't going to give anything up on what kind of plays or what kind of defense we're going to use.

``I'll just say we've been working on this game since June, and we have specific plans for every situation," I tell them. ``We believe we are as prepared as we can be for this game. I've never had this much time to get ready for one opponent, and I think we've made the most of it."

The one question that surprises me is probably the one I should have expected the most.

``How personal is this game for you with Duncan Welker and Andrew Crow against you?"

``I could lie and tell you that it's just the business of the game, but it is personal for me. This entire trip has been personal. I've approached this game as being personal since we found out about it in June. I'm sure all the guys on my side who got kicked out of here are looking at this that way. We didn't do anything wrong, in fact, we performed very well for this school, and it meant nothing to anyone. They just used us.

``But the time for it being personal is over because we can't let that affect us during the game. Making it personal helped drive us to improve to be ready for this chance, but that doesn't mean I'm going to let it get out of control where I use the opportunity for a cheap shot on one of those guys. That's more their style. That's why I have his shiner on my eye. I would never embarrass Coach Schebig, my parents, my teammates or my school by getting that far out of control.

``Yeah, I want to do very well in this game and win, but not because of what it would show Coach Jackson or Welker or Crow. I want to win because of what it will mean to my parents, my teammates and my school. That's the only reason I agreed we should play this game, because of what it will mean to all of them."

One of the announcers comments, `` So you guys are looking at this like a grudge match, when we figured you'd look at it like just another regular-season game."

``There's no grudge for 95 of the players on my team, and that's why and who I'm playing for more than anyone."

The rest is all just clichés that will fit in the little sound-bite holes they need.

Does anyone ever wonder why athletes just talk in clichés? Because mostly that's all the electronic media wants, something that will fit into their little sound bites. Have you ever listened to what a coach says on his way off the field at halftime when he gets asked a question by the sideline reporter? It's all clichés and 90 percent of the time doesn't actually answer the question. It's all the network has time for. It's actually a waste of time.

If they had to deal with something in-depth or profound, they'd likely panic and not know what to do with it. Haven't you ever wondered why some of the supposedly better-educated people in the country – they are all attending college – all sound so inane and the same? That's exactly what TV wants from them.

When I'm finished with the interview, I quickly run through the introduction line and then head home. Even though we've been in Talbott most of the week, I haven't gotten to spend much time with Mom and Dad. One reason I wanted to come back was to see them, but it hasn't worked out that way.

"Looking forward to tonight?" Mom asks, handing me a bowl of vegetable soup. "It should be a lot of fun."

"I guess so," I say. "I'm really excited for Max and Mikala. I think it's wonderful that the school is making sure to include them. I kind of wish I could just stand back and watch this for them. This a great soup, Mom."

After Mom thanks me, Dad says, "Well, we're proud of you, too. I think this will be a lot of fun for us. I can't wait for you to see the senior quarterback at Talbott, Logan Carter. He's pretty good, and if he had any receivers, some of your records might be in jeopardy."

"Yeah, Coach Snuff wanted me to find some time to talk to him again sometime this week, but I just haven't found the time. I have to get that done. Maybe I'll head over to school after eating."

We continue eating, talking a little, telling a few jokes and hearing old stories. It's a very comfortable afternoon, even though I haven't lived here for three years and rarely get a chance to come back in the off-season. I don't know if I ever will, either. I'm going to graduate in May, but I don't really know what my plans are after that. Some of that probably depends on what Mikala figures out she wants to do. Maybe we'll come back here, but maybe we'll end up staying in

California.

"I'm thinking about asking Mikala to marry me at Christmas time," I say, causing Mom to halt her spoon halfway up. "I don't mean we'd get married at Christmas, but we'd start planning then."

"Are you sure?" Dad asks and then sees my dark glare. "Look, I have no doubt Mikala is the girl you will marry. What I mean is, are you sure this is the right time. You've got an awful lot on your mind and on your plate coming up in the next six months. That's all I'm asking. You know we love Mikala."

"I see what you mean, but to me, a lot of that other stuff can't start to shape up until we get this decided and under way. If I can get that settled down and we can set a date maybe for the summer after this one, we can start to figure out what happens next. Does she try out for the Olympic team, where do I look to get a job, do we come back here? All of that stuff can start to be figured out."

"You'll also have to start to save some money," Dad said. "Rings and weddings and honeymoons are not cheap, and I'm guessing you might not make a tremendous amount of money your first year or two."

"There's a lot to think about," I say. "She may not want to get married right away, either.

"Who knows, maybe I'll just take Mom's ring and ask her tonight during the ceremony.'"

This time Mom sputters her soup out, and believe me, her glare is 10 times more lethal than mine.

"Excuse me," she says. "You're not taking this ring anywhere. Now your grandmother's ring we could talk about – at Christmas. If you embarrass her like that tonight, she'd have every right to clobber you, and I would, too!"

"Don't worry, Mom, I was just saying that for your benefit. When I propose, it's going to be just the two of us and private. You'll be notified by text message in time to catch a plane to Las Vegas.

"Hah! Got you again."

"Just get out of here! Don't you come back here until you're ready to apologize!"

"Yes, ma'am!"

Five seconds later I stick my head back in the door.

"Love you two. See you tonight!"

They just laugh.

A few hours later Max and I meet up at Mikala's house. She's running late from a practice and is in the shower, so we take a little time to chat with her folks as they are ready to go to the game. We'll have to leave after the halftime ceremonies to ride back to the hotel for one last team curfew check before tomorrow's game.

At Mikala's suggestion, all our parents are going to join us on the field for the number retirement presentation. Max doesn't know it yet, but Natalie will be there for the game, too. She and Emma will arrive just before tonight's game with a few remaining athletic department staff, and then she and Emma will stay with Max's folks after the game.

"How's the speech coming?" I ask.

"Why, nervous?"

"Not at all," I say. "Are you?"

"You probably should be. Mikala helped me write it."

"Wait a minute, how come she got to help, but I didn't when I offered first?"

"Lars, there's a five-minute time limit on this thing. If you had written it, we'd need five hours."

"Fine, fine. The slings and arrows I take for being your friend, always sticking up for you when others disparage you. I just hope it's good, because I've heard plenty enough speeches this week. You'd think we were at a political convention and not getting ready for a ballgame."

"He'll do just fine," Mikala says from the stairs. I turn to see she's wearing a light blue cocktail dress that sets off her eyes and her hair and well, just her everything. She looks amazing. I'm feeling underdressed in my sport coat and slacks, but I'm used to feeling like that when we go out.

"Wow!" is all I can say for about the 5,483rd time since meeting her.

"See," she says, "You'd have trouble speaking anyway."

She's got that right.

Talbott's game is just about decided by halftime as the Broncos lead 28-0. Logan Carter has a great arm and he can run the ball better than I ever could. Harding's Hawks have no idea what to do against Carter, who has come a long way since I first talked to him as a sophomore.

The stands are packed. People are still coming in and trying to find seats throughout the first quarter. The Camarillo contingent is sitting in folding chairs down on the curve of the track. I would think most of the guys will be bored senseless, until I notice all the girls from last night's party are sitting with them.

Just before the half, Natalie and Emma arrive, which really helps in a way because Max isn't thinking too much about his speech. He's hugging and kissing Natalie, while his mom is doing the same with

Emma. It's really hard to say with member of the Curry family is more thrilled by their arrival.

As for the ceremony, Coach Snuff lists our accomplishments for about two minutes and unveils the banner which will hang from the scoreboard with the retired No. 4 for me, No. 2 for Mikala and No. 7 for Max. There will also be banners placed in the gym with our names on them.

As everyone in the stands and standing along the fences applauds, we nod and wave to them, throwing kisses to our family members. It takes about 45 seconds for the sound to ease away.

"You're up," I say to Max. "Don't blow it, or we'll make you do it again sometime. And don't forget, there are about 25 cameras recording every word."

"You're a lot of help,"

"Don't mention it," I say, but I know he's ready for this.

"First of all, Mikala and I would like to thank you all for including Lars Preston in this celebration tonight. It's been very difficult for us to carry him along for so many years, making his statistics look good and his prom dates look even better." This draws a loud round of applause and quite a few laughs. "He would have been crushed if he'd have been excluded tonight. Take a bow, Lars."

What can I say? They nailed me. I just wave and bow on command. Then I turn and shake my fist at Max, drawing a few more laughs.

"Just be glad he doesn't get the opportunity to speak tonight."

For some reason, this draws the loudest applause of the night. I just hang my head and laugh.

"There are two specific things we want to emphasize tonight. The first, is to thank our parents for everything they have done for us. All the sacrifices, all the encouragement, all the groundings even, all the trust they put in us, all the driving to and from games, and especially all the discipline to make us study and behave. We truly are first and foremost representatives of you and your hard work. Thank you.

"Second, we want to thank the community for all the opportunities you presented to us, from PAL football to Wildcat Baseball to the Little Boppers volleyball program, through elementary, middle and high school. We definitely could not be where we are today without you. We also thank you for providing us with such outstanding coaches, teachers and role models to follow. You never really know how good your teachers have been until you leave and measure yourself against others, and we've been very blessed to do well in that regard.

"The final thing we'd like to say is that we are proud to be from Talbott. We realize anything we accomplish only happens because of the help you gave us. We are proud to be graduates of Talbott High School. We will always be part of Talbott, and Talbott will always be a part of us. Talbott is our hometown no matter what. We are truly humbled by this honor. Thank you."

The speech was just like Max, short and sweet and always in the perfect spot.

"Great job, buddy!" I say as the three of us hug while the crowd cheers. Then we motion our parents over for an even bigger hug which draws even more cheers. Even Emma starts chanting, "Yeah, yeah, yeah."

That leaves the microphone free for me to grab.

"Thank you again," I say. "I apologize that we have to leave, but Max and I are under Coach's orders because there's something big we're supposed to do tomorrow if I can ever remember what it is. Good luck, Broncos, the rest of the game and the season. We'll see everybody tomorrow afternoon. Logan, keep it going buddy."

It takes us almost an hour to work our way through the crowd, shaking hands and signing autographs, until we can get to our cars. By then, Emma is asleep on Max's shoulder, and the rest of us are exhausted. As excited as I am for the game, I'll have no problem sleeping.

It's been an amazing week. I just hope the climax comes close to living up to our hopes.

CHAPTER 33

The locker room on game day is always unique. A lot of it depends on the mood you are in when you wake up that day, and a lot of it depends on the situation, the location and the opponent you are facing.

During the regular season, a locker room is often a lot looser than it will be for a playoff game when everyone is feeling more tense. Sometimes before a big game, there will be a line waiting for the bathroom to either let go from the top or the bottom for the last time before taking the field. Sometimes, it doesn't feel right to you unless a guy who usually chucks his breakfast has done so.

"C'mon, go get rid of it so we can get ready!"

And he'll trot off toward the john.

We're all superstitious. I like to get dressed the same way every time, all the way. Max will put everything on but his shoulder pads and jersey until we're just about ready to go out on the field.

A lot of it is about learning to channel the nerves. The looser the game, the louder the stereo which is controlled by the captains. Today, we've picked some heavy tempo hard rock but it's loud enough only to be heard in the background. Some of the guys have their headphones on. Miguel is fully dressed two hours before kickoff, leaning back in his stall with his eyes closed. We know he's not dozing; he's picturing what he thinks will happen during the game.

A few guys sit back in their stalls going over the scouting report one last time. Jordan sits in his trying to complete a crossword puzzle. Some guys like to read, and Alex always has his Bible with him.

I'm sitting next to Max taping up my socks and shoes. This is the one time where I'm as quiet as he normally is, and it's also the one time he likes to talk more. It's all nervous energy, and I just nod as if I'm hearing everything he's saying. He's not saying anything important, he's just talking.

And it's always 10 degrees hotter in the locker room than it needs to be, especially on the road, so we've got the doors open to the outside if we can get some air circulating. Messing with the thermostat is an old trick, but we are used to ignoring it.

Maybe because it's so much earlier than we are used to, everyone seems a little off-kilter so far. A few guys are still wiping the sleep from their eyes, there are some yawns and everyone seems to be mumbling a little bit more. There's a line to get ankles and wrists taped by the trainers, but no one is talking much.

The atmosphere is controlled and also chaotic, but everybody has their own routine and knows exactly what they are doing. The busiest area is around the coffee machine. The managers circulate, asking if anyone needs anything and passing out aspirin if asked.

A few of us head out to the field to test the footing and loosen up. This is something Max and I have done together for 12 years, tossing the ball back and forth. We're really just killing time, but it's part of our routine. Someday we'll do it with our kids, but we've only got a handful of opportunities remaining to do it with each other. Somewhere in the back of our minds we know that, but we quickly find our usual rhythm and stretch my arm and his legs. Sometimes I think that we have done this so often we could do it blindfolded.

"You feeling OK," he asks, re-starting a conversation we've had hundreds of times. "You loose enough, feeling confident?"

"Yep, I'm fine," I say, throwing the ball 20 yards back to him. "I feel good, I'm just focused in. There's a lot going on in my head today, a lot to remember and a lot to plan for. I'm trying to relax and take it all in. There's also a lot of memories here."

"Yeah, relax, that's the key. Never really thought we'd be back here inside this place. Never wanted to be, either, but now I'm glad we've got the chance. Today we get to show the doubters what we can really do."

I look him in the eye and nod, really hearing him for the first time today.

"You know, that's right," I say. "I've been so wrapped up in making sure everyone else is OK and ready to go, I haven't thought in a long time about what this can mean to me, to you and me. Maybe that's a good thing. It WILL be nice to come out here and just play like we always dreamed of. We never really did get that chance before, did we?"

"Nope, never did."

"Maybe that's the way we should really be approaching this, Alex, Randy, Big Bob and you and me. We finally get to play here the way we want to, do it how we know we can. The only people we have to impress is our parents, and they don't care as long as we don't get hurt. I really want to do well, though. I don't want any more regrets from this place to haunt me."

"Oh, I wouldn't mind looking good on national TV," Max says with a grin. "Natalie is taping the game so we can show Emma when she's older."

"That's cool! Maybe we'll have an annual party someday and watch the game so much the kids will all be sick of it," I say with a laugh. I'm feeling better by the second.

"Hey!" I ask, "Did you go check that spot on the 30? I wonder if they've gotten that fixed yet."

We walk that way to check it out. When we were playing here, there was an old sprinkler head that stuck out of the ground about an inch at the 10-yard line on the north end of the field, about two yards inside the sideline. I remembered it because Ken Sorenson tripped over it during a preseason scrimmage our freshman year and missed an easy touchdown pass. It's colored green so it's easy to miss unless you know it's there. There was even a call in the IWU playbook if the situation was right to take advantage of it.

"Yep, there it is," Max says when we're 10 yards away. "I can see it already."

"OK, let's turn back," I say. "Maybe that's something we can use later if nobody realizes we know it's still there. Let's go tell Miguel so he can let the DBs know about it."

As we turn to head back in, Coach Schebig sticks his head out of the tunnel and gives a little toot on his air horn to let us all know it's time to go back to the locker room.

Now it's time for the last speech before the game, and it's finally Coach's turn.

"Guys, I'm not going to tell you what this game means to me because I don't want that to be your focus or your motivation. I want you to all concentrate on what this means to you. I think you all know how much I hate them, but I truly love you guys more than that. This isn't about me, it's all about you today, and that's a good thing. I'm more excited for you than I am anxious for revenge against them.

"Like Lars said yesterday, I want to thank all of you for how hard you have worked and how disciplined you have been to help us all prepare you for this game. You ARE ready. I can't think of one thing that we should have spent more time on or something I wish we could tweak just a little. You are as prepared as this staff and I can make you.

"If we fall behind, we have a plan for that. If we get a lead and they start to come back on us, we have a plan for that. Whatever happens, we have a plan for that.

"The biggest thing I can ask you to do is to not worry. Trust yourselves and what we have worked so hard on. Trust our game plan and give it a chance to work. Trust us. I don't think they will come out and stomp us, but if they do, you betcha I've got a plan for that!"

That causes everyone to laugh.

"Good! Laugh and have fun out there. How many times in our lives will we ever get to go out for a game and just have fun? Let me tell you, there probably won't be too many times after this one because the rest of this season there will be pressure and expectations and consequences. Play smart today, but just go out and have fun. Listen to Lars and Max and Jordan and Miguel. Do what they tell you to do because they will lead you. Don't talk back or strike back at the IWU players because some of them will take cheap shots at you. Shoot, they've been doing it all year. Think how frustrated they will be when you don't respond!

"We're better than that, and today is the chance we get to show everyone how good we are. This is our opportunity, and we are ready for it in this moment. No excuses!"

"No excuses!" everyone chants back.

"Be loose!" he says and wiggles his arms out away from his body and then shakes his lower half, cracking everyone up again.

"That's what I'm talking about! If anyone tells my wife about this, you are off the team!"

That draws more laughter. Now we're getting into it.

"I want to tell you guys something that it took me 45 years to learn. When I was your age, I used to sweat tests something terrible. I'd be nervous three days beforehand worrying about how I was going to do, and it never got any better even if I knew I was perfectly prepared. I still got uptight and anxious all the time.

"Then one day I realized I couldn't remember what any of my grades were in college for an entire class, let alone a test. Then I realized that my grades in high school didn't matter a week into my college career, and my college grades didn't matter a week into my first job, so why was I getting stressed out all the time? It wasn't that I didn't want to do well in all those things, but I realized it wasn't worth the wasted energy I was using up being nervous. In the big picture of my life, the grade on some test wasn't that big a deal.

"That's how I'd like you guys to go out there and play today. Sure, it's a big game, but it's not the most important thing in your life. It's not like you are asking some girl to marry you, or making a health decision about one of your children. Keep it in perspective and go have fun playing. Today, let it be just a GAME!

"The other thing I want to talk to you guys about today is that we are going to play to win on every play of every series. How many times have we seen teams lose a game because they played a prevent defense, or they got too conservative on offense and played not to lose? We're not going to do that today. We will be as aggressive as possible to keep them constantly guessing what's coming next. We have nothing to lose in this game, so we're going to play to win. Period!

"You guys all know about the things we've been holding back this year for just this game. I can't wait to pull them out of the box and show them off to everyone. I hope we surprise those guys so much we knock them smack on their butts! That's another reason I want you to all have fun out there today. I want this game to be a positive experience for all of us, win or lose, and we can show that by having fun.

``No matter what happens today, I am very proud of you and what you have given me and each other. I will always remember what we've gone through and what we've meant to each other during this time. We are ready, so let's go have some fun!''

Everyone roars and it sounds three times louder than a jet taking off inside that little locker room with 120 people screaming. None of us care because we know this is our chance to prove everyone else wrong, play for each other and make history.

``No excuses! No excuses! No excuses!!''

``Gather up,'' Coach Schebig says one last time and we pray, ``Our Father, who art in heaven, hallowed be thy name; Thy kingdom come, Thy will be done on earth as it is in heaven. Give us this day our daily bread and forgive us our trespasses as we forgive those who trespass against us. And lead us not into temptation but deliver us from evil. For Thine is the kingdom and the power and the glory, forever and ever. Amen!''

``Amen!''

Finally, it's time to take the field.

CHAPTER 34

No one is yawning now as our adrenalin starts kicking up. I'm feeling anxious and not afraid to admit a little overwhelmed. This is not just any game for me or Max, my family and my team and I'm already breathing hard. I hope my second wind comes fast because the emotions are going to take my first one away in a hurry.

I can't afford to be too fired up. I have to be the one under control.

And I know if I'm reacting that way, everyone else is going to be feeling worse. If they see me acting nervous, they're going to freak out and we're going to get blown out. Just before we step onto the field, I turn away from everyone else in the tunnel and say a quick prayer to ask for calm and patience.

"Dear Lord, help me to be a positive influence today on my teammates and these fans and an example of your will. Please give me the strength, courage and integrity to follow the path you have for me. In Your Son's name, Amen."

With all the noise going on around me, I find a moment of peace and almost immediately feel better.

"Remember, calm and focus," Coach Schebig yells at us. "Let's head out!"

Just as we hope, Max's plan of marching out together works perfectly. We pace out to the 35-yard line and turn toward our parents and fans who are sitting in the northeast corner and bow and wave. They all stand and shout at us, waving back with their purple and white pom poms.

It seems a little strange, but I notice that Moord Stadium is reasonably quiet when we do this, as if the rest of the fans are staying calm out of respect for our gesture. Even the IWU band is silent. It was never this quiet during our worst games my freshman season.

But not for long as the IWU players come charging out of the tunnel, screaming and jumping around to encourage their fans to yell and applaud. After pointing and yelling at us on our sideline, they run to midfield and dance around their logo, jumping on one another as the band plays the school song for the first of 185 times today.

Then we all stand for The National Anthem. Some people never sing along, but I always do because I know what the song meant to my grandparents so I do it to honor them. Both of my Dad's folks lost family members in World War II, and my Mom lost an uncle. It's not just a song to our family or an obligation to stand through.

After the Anthem and the IWU school song, Max, Jordan, Miguel and I walk out as captains for the coin toss. I see Duncan Welker and Andrew Crow representing the IWU defense, but I also see old friends Mason Parker and Jim Wallace standing there.

"Jim, how the heck are you?" I ask, slapping hands with him before wrapping him in a hug.

"I'm doing OK, Lars," he says. "Max, it's good to see you, but I wish it was under different circumstances."

"Me, too, my friend," Max says before giving him a hug.

"Good luck, Mason, hope we have some fun out there," I say to the Sagamores' quarterback as we swap grips.

"I plan on it," Mason says before grinning and giving me a slap on the back. "You're still trying to stir it up, aren't you."

"All in good fun, buddy, you know that."

"Yeah, I do. Tell you what, even if no one else shakes your hand at the end of the game, I'll be there."

"Thank you, Mason. You're the best. When I get back this summer, we'll go out for a beer."

Andrew and Duncan shake hands with us but none of us look each other in the eye. I feel like I want to rub my hand against my pants.

We win the toss, but as much as I'm itching to get the ball, we elect to kick off. Though most of our surprises and trick plays have to do with our offense, we've got a big one to reveal on defense that we hope gives Mason and particularly B.J. Cowen a lot to worry about.

"See you out here," I yell to Duncan and Andrew as we turn to head back to our sideline.

"Oh, yeah, you'll see me in your nightmares," Duncan says.

"Wow, original," I say to Max as we trot toward Coach Schebig. "I think we've got them right where we want them."

"I just hope you know what you are doing," Max says.

"Do I ever?"

"That's what worries me. I hope to be your best man next year, not your pallbearer."

"Well, if you have to speak, at least it will be a short funeral."

"Not funny," he says as we get near the sideline, but then he grins.

"Let's go," I yell. "Let's have some fun out there! Offense, get over here and let's talk."

Maybe everyone is a little pumped up because Manuel Jimenez's kickoff flies high and long through the end zone. By the time it lands, our defense is already on the field waiting to line up and take on the Sagamores' defense.

The first tip-off to our defensive surprise comes when both Big Joe and Little Joe trot onto the field at the same time. Except for a few plays, we've been using them separately the entire season to replace each other on the defensive line. It's always best to keep a fresh nosetackle in whenever possible, but not many teams can do it. Now, we figure our best chance against a Midwest Conference offensive line is to use them together at the same time.

The real surprise comes when IWU breaks the huddle and Parker looks across the line. Instead of our traditional 4-3 defense with four down linemen and three linebackers, we're switching things up and going with a 3-4. That's because a 3-4 is usually better against the run. I know we've had lots of trouble going against it in practice, and that's with an experienced offensive line that knew what was coming.

So we've got Nate Higgins, Big Joe and Little Joe across the front. The Joes weigh around 300 pounds, and Nate comes in at 265. Their job is to tie up the five offensive linemen so the four linebackers can fill the holes before Cowen can get to them. The defensive linemen have a huge task today going against IWU's offensive line which is just as big, definitely taller, but maybe not quite as quick. The biggest concern is we don't have much depth behind them so the offense needs to be able to move the ball so we can keep them off the field as much as possible so they are fresh longer.

When Mason looks over his center and sees what we're doing, he stutters in his call, points across the line at our guys and gets so flustered he backs away from the center. You can almost see on his face that he's not sure what to do and finally takes a delay of game penalty instead of wasting a time out. That just fires up our guys even more.

"Yeah, we've got a few more surprises for you today, baby!" Jordan yells.

Coach Jackson counters by sending in an extra tight end to give IWU seven players up front, but that's OK with us because it allows our safety to sneak in and help more on the run. Basically, we're daring Mason to throw, and we're leaving Miguel against Wallace in single coverage as a tempting target. Do the Sagamores take the ball away from their best weapon in Cowen and attempt to throw it more?

Oh, no.

Cowen gets the first handoff and tries the middle but Jordan is there in the hole between the Joes to smack him for no gain.

Our guys are getting more fired up by the second, but Miguel snaps in the huddle, "Use the emotion, don't lose it! We've got a long way to go today!"

On the second play, IWU sends Cowen wide right on a sweep, and he gets two yards past the line of scrimmage when Miguel dives and takes his legs out with help from linebacker Nik Hoot. With the Sagamores facing a third-and-long, we send Cory Hoersten in to go with a four-man front and take out Jake Ryan and Hoot to add in Dyer Ball as an extra defensive back.

Because we've used basic, vanilla coverages and packages all season, Parker is seeing all of this for the first time. When he can't find anyone open, he finally throws the ball into the sidelines before Nate Higgins can run him down.

The first defensive series went perfectly for us as the Sagamores are forced to punt from their own 18-yard-line. After Trever Andrews fair catches the punt at our 35-yard line, now it's our offense's turn.

"Everybody feeling OK?" I ask in the huddle, but I can already see the nerves on some faces. "Everybody take a deep breath. Do it again. OK, we all know what we're supposed to do, so Anthony, you're going right with this handoff. On two!"

We've got plenty of time until the play clock goes off so I walk to the line and then take a step back to look around. There are 80,000 people in the stands, almost all wearing green and black. I can hear everyone yelling at me and I can see everything, including Mikala sitting with my parents past the far end zone.

This is everything we've been working for. I've wanted this moment so badly, it almost doesn't seem real now that we're finally here.

When I call for the snap with two seconds left on the play clock, Anthony Tomlinson cuts behind me for the pitch. He turns upfield quickly, but can only get back to the line of scrimmage before Duncan Welker and friends bury him.

"You're going to have to do better than that," Andrew Crow yells as his team celebrates.

I just shake my head on the way back to the huddle.

"OK, same play Anthony, same count. Everybody do the same thing. On two!"

And again, the same thing happens, this time with Crow making the tackle 1 yard past the line.

"That's it," Crow says. "Play it conservative and you might be able to keep the score close for a while. The point spread is only 30!" Then he laughs and slaps the shoulder pads of his defensive linemen.

Yeah, get cocky, I think to myself. Now, we're ready.

All fall we've played conservative, careful football. We have hidden half our playbook for this game, and it has killed me to play it safe all

244

the time. Now we get to play my game.

"All right, time to unwrap the present," I say in the huddle. "Let's show these jerks what we can really do. Everybody knows what to do, right? Max, blow them away."

It's third-and-9 on our 36 yard-line and everyone in the stadium is expecting me to throw, so we're going to run a play that looks like that's what's going to happen. When Anthony trots out of the backfield to line up in the slot, we've got an empty backfield behind me. We've also got Keaton Alexander in as an extra receiver on the left side with Trever, and Max is lined up wide on the right side.

As Big Bob's snap hits me in the hands, Keaton, Trever and Anthony all take off 25 yards downfield, spreading the defense wide. Max acts like he's tied up at the line of scrimmage with the cornerback like he can't get off his man as I start to roll out that way. The entire offensive line slides with me. I stop, plant my back foot and pump fake deep down the right sideline, then pull the ball back down to my waist where I flip it backward to Max as he runs behind me.

"Reverse! Reverse!" I hear Andrew yelling.

Not quite. Lined up at left tackle, Randy started off inside and then pushed his man wide and deep. Thinking I was going to pass, the defensive end went with it, figuring he could get wide enough on Randy to come around and hit me from behind. That left a wide-open hole on IWU's left side, which their weakside linebacker sees and rushes to fill.

Except Max isn't going that far. He hesitates for half a second to allow me to get a running start in front of him and we head right up the middle. Half of IWU's defense is on the ride side, and half is sprinting to the left, but Welker is the only one left in the middle. There's no way I'm big enough to take him out, but I don't have to. All I have to do is lower my head and stick my shoulder in his gut because he's not looking at me, he's looking at Max with the ball.

As Welker tries to throw me to the left, Max runs by him to the right and passes midfield before any of the defensive backs realize it's not going to be a pass after all. The middle is so wide open, Max doesn't even have to use a fake as his spikes just tear up the turf faster and faster. He gets all the way to the IWU 20-yard line before the safety manages to fight past Alexander's block and get a hand around Max's ankle enough to trip him up.

By the time Max is ready to get up, there are nine teammates there to pick him up, but we're not there to congratulate him. Instead of going back into the huddle, we immediately take position at the line of scrimmage so IWU can't have time to send any replacements in. As soon as the linesman places the ball when the chains are set, Big Bob snaps it to me and I follow him right up the middle again for 5 more yards.

When we line up right away to do it again, Coach Jackson calls time out to give his guys a breather. They are all breathing hard and must be freaking out, wondering what's happening because they haven't seen this on any film or in any scouting report. Even if they've had spies at our practices, they had no idea this was coming.

My heart is pumping, too, but it's all from excitement of seeing everything we've tried work so far. I don't even go to the sideline and our offense just stays in the huddle. We know exactly what we are doing and how we are going to run the next play. We've had the first 25 plays scripted since Coach Burgess came in August, and we've practiced them every Wednesday since. We're not changing a thing, except the snap count.

``Time to scare the crap out of them some more," I say. ``You ready, Alex?"

"Can't wait," Alex says. "I told Ruth I'd score a touchdown for her today."

That brings a few groans from some of the linemen, but I just say, "That's OK because here's your chance."

Once again, we're ready at the line as soon as the referee signals the time out is over, and one second later I'm dropping back with the ball. This time Max is spread out wide right with Keaton in the slot. They both cut across the middle on crossing routes, taking two defensive backs, a safety and the linebacker out of the play. Alex cuts inside off the line, but then drifts outside to the corner of the end zone where the ball lands in his hands just before he steps out of bounds right in front of all our parents.

Touchdown!

"Ruth will never believe this!" I yell to Alex after running to slap him on the helmet. "You'll be able to tell your kids about this someday."

And we just laugh and laugh on our way to the sidelines where everyone is screaming in joy at us. The stadium is so quiet you can hear all of us yelling and that's about it.

The surprises are just getting started. We know we can't slug it out with IWU. They are about two inches taller and 20, 25 pounds heavier per man. We must take advantage of our surprises. Coach and I figure if we can hit on half of them, we'll have a chance.

And maybe our biggest one is still coming up. When Coach Schebig said we were going to play for the win and be aggressive all the time, he wasn't kidding. We've decided to do anything we can to keep them off-balance.

With all of the offensive unit sitting on the bench so we don't give anything away, Manuel lines up like it's going to be a regular kick-off, but as he approaches the ball, he nicks the top of it so it rolls to the right. The IWU blockers are so surprised, a couple even turn to sprint back to set up their blocks so they are 15 yards away when sophomore Eric Miller dives on the ball for us at the 40-yard line in front of the IWU bench.

"He was offside! He was offside!" Coach Jackson is screaming, but none of the referees listen. They know we've just pulled off another unbelievable surprise.

"First down, UC-Camarillo," the referee announces.

Again, we line up right away with Andrews and Alexander split on opposite sides. They both take off on crossing patterns with one running right in front of Welker and the other right behind him in the middle of IWU's defense. He doesn't know what to do, but decides to go after Alexander who is running in front of him. Seeing that, I drill the ball into Andrews' stomach for a 15-yard gain to midfield.

"Wrong guess, Duncan," I say. "You keep trying and maybe you'll get one right."

He snaps back something unprintable but it's obvious the Sagamores' defensive players are totally frustrated and mad. Pretty soon we hope they are tired, too. They don't know what's coming next or what to do about it. They are ready to explode.

This time we huddle up, giving them more time to stew.

"OK, this is where you guys have to trust me," I say. "Randy, you and Gabe have to let Crow come on through. I'll take the hit because we're going to use this to set up the next play. Stick to the plan."

"You just be ready to duck," Randy says.

"I'll be OK, I promise."

With Anthony lined up to my right, I drop back as if I'm going to pass, but the plan is actually to let Crow cream me – just after I release the ball. I know he's coming and I don't even have to look to see him. A second after I throw the ball out of bounds, I bend at the waist and Andrew flies right over me. If I had been standing straight, his helmet would have drilled me in the back and I'd be waiting for a stretcher.

The entire crowd lets out an `Oh!'' as his legs and feet carry me to the ground. A few seconds later, as my linemen pick me up, Coach Schebig starts screaming for a roughing the passer call, but really, there's no call to be made, and Coach knows it. Crow just missed.

`Almost had you there, Lars!'' Crow growls at me.

`Ah, you missed like always,'' I say. `You won't touch me the rest of the game. Tell you what, we'll run the same play again, and you'll miss this time, too.''

`You're on!'' he says. `I'll be right back.''

Which is what I'm counting on. This time, instead of dropping back to pass, I pull up short and toss the ball forward to Anthony cutting in front of me and he pops directly through the hole Crow just left. I never see it because Crow spears me in the back with his helmet, driving me to the turf, but Anthony gets 10 yards before he's touched.

And this time the referee sees Crow's helmet hit me and he immediately throws the flag for a personal foul penalty. We just gained 25 yards because he can't control himself and have a first down at IWU's 20-yard line.

`Nice play, Andrew,'' I say, patting him on the helmet. `Thanks for the extra yards.''

Before he can respond, Duncan and a couple of his teammates pull him away or he might have gotten kicked out of the game. That's OK with me because I want to exploit him a few more times today.

After I miss Max on a post pattern and Alex across the middle, our drive stalls, but Manuel nails the 37-yard field goal to put us up 10-0 with less than five minutes left in the quarter.

When I sit down on the bench, half the guys congratulate me and the other half ask if I'm all right. I know I'll feel that hit for the next week, but right now it's not too bad, and the points were worth it. IWU has to be panicking, and we all know how Coach Jackson reacts when he's in a tight game, a game he expected to be an easy victory. The pain is worth it because he'll just keep screaming and making things worse for his own players.

Unfortunately, we've got plenty of time to sit as IWU's offense starts a long drive. This time our 3-4 "Coyote defense" strategy doesn't fool them, and they start pounding the ball outside with Cowen. The Sagamores are using Parker on an option and he pitches the ball or turns upfield depending on which way our linebacker chooses to go.

When the first quarter ends, IWU has driven to our 18-yard line.

"Come on, defense!" I yell. "You can stop them."

But they can't, and Cowen bulls over from 5 yards out for a touchdown.

"That's OK," I tell the Joes. "Take a breather. We'll try to keep you off the field a while."

"We could use a breather," Jordan says.

CHAPTER 35

Because we know our defense is tired after the long IWU drive, we start out a little more conservatively with our play calls this time. Anthony Tomlinson gains 7 yards on two carries and then I run a delayed sneak up the middle for 5 yards and a first down at their 32.

"Time to unleash the Beast!" I say in the huddle.

Everyone's heads pops up at that one.

"This early?" Randy asks.

"Why not? We need to give them an uppercut and get their attention again. Max, you ready?"

"Get your running shoes on."

"I'll be there if you can get it to me."

"No problem."

We line up like normal for the snap with Anthony behind me in the shotgun, Max on the left side and Keaton and Trever on the right, but then I start trotting toward the right sideline to leave Anthony as the only one in the backfield in the Wildcat formation. Just as I reach the sideline, Big Bob snaps the ball to Anthony who takes two steps to his right, stops and flings the ball back to Max who has dropped back behind the line of scrimmage on the left with Alex charging out to knock Max's defender aside.

With Keaton and Trever both racing across the field looking like they are waiting for a pass, everyone on the IWU defense scrambles to run over to Max's side of the field. Actually, Keaton and Trever are the real decoys on the play and both stop three-quarters of the way across and lining up like they are going to block for Max – except Max isn't running the ball. He took two steps forward and stopped, still well behind the line of scrimmage, and this time he's throwing the ball – to me! I stayed next to the sideline when the ball was snapped and everyone on the defense forgot about me. After counting two Mississippis, I took off running down the sideline.

I thought I had everyone fooled, but somehow Duncan Welker figured it out. Maybe it was because he was just watching me to see what would happen, but he ignored the other side of the field and started running after me. I still had enough time to catch Max's throw, but I had to slow up just a little to come back and get the ball. Thank goodness I didn't drop it, but Duncan had just enough time to drop me, nailing me in the left shoulder and driving my right one into the turf at the IWU 40-yard line.

If the pass had just been a hair stronger, I might have been able to make a move on Duncan and get away, but I've never been the fastest guy on the field. Right now I figure I'm one of the slowest as I try to recoup and find the rest of the sense that got knocked out of me.

"You OK?" Gabe yells as he runs up to me. I can tell by his face he's really wondering how bad I am.

"Yeah, my shoulder's banged up, but luckily it was not my throwing arm."

On the way back to our side, he has to help me pull the shoulder of my jersey back over my pad.

We try to line up again as quickly as possible. After hitting them with three big plays so far, they're jumpy as a cat at a daycare center. Because we run a bunch of motion before snapping the ball, they are reacting to everything we do, yelling at each other to make sure players are covered.

"You got that man, Duncan?" Crow yells over his shoulder.

"Just shut up and get to him, Andrew, and none this will matter!" Welker snaps back.

"Both of you shut up and concentrate on the play!" their safety comes up to yell.

They may think they have us, but they don't. Alex runs off the left side to turn and catch the ball 15 yards downfield for another first down. When we rush to the line of scrimmage again, Coach Jackson calls another time out. He's yelling so loud everyone in the lower deck on the far side doesn't need to be able to read lips to hear what he's saying, and it's definitely not for family consumption.

I almost feel sorry for Duncan and Andrew as they have to walk over to the sidelines to get chewed out again. .

With the way they are reacting whenever we keep running lots of motion, two dives by Anthony almost seem like more trick plays. On a third-and-2 at their 17, Crow finally slips his block to nail Anthony for a yard loss to force another field goal from Manuel.

We lead 13-7 with seven minutes left in the first half, which may be shocking to everyone watching at home on TV, but we're not feeling that great. We all know we could have done better so far and probably needed to.

"We should be leading by a lot more," Randy says. "We've got to find a way to punch it in and take pressure off our defense."

So far, we haven't thrown the ball to Max at all, but they are still paying so much attention to him that Alex has been wide open from tight end. Everything we've tried has worked, just not well enough to score. We've controlled the ball, kept them off-balance and we haven't given up any turnovers.

``Lars, we may go off script for the final drive of the half," Coach Schebig says. ``If they score here, we have to get at least a field goal to go in with the lead, and then we'll get the ball back to start the second half. We may need this to be a huge momentum swing."

It's obvious to me that our defense is not going to be able to hold IWU off the scoreboard. We can slow them down with some different formations and by guessing right on some plays, but they are just too big and strong all over the field for us to force them to punt. The best we can expect is to make them grind the ball down the field, but that only works as long as we maintain the lead. We might get lucky with a turnover, but that's probably unlikely as we can't slow down the Sagamores' running game enough to force them to take a chance with a pass. They are bulldozing us.

We're just not fast enough or big enough to match up with them, especially once they get past our defensive line. The longer they keep the ball, the quicker we're wearing out. Our guys are trying, but they just aren't big enough, and there's nothing that can change that.

They push us down the field until they get to the 23-yard line, tearing off 8-to-10 yard plays. The defense is pulling Miguel within 5 yards of the line of scrimmage to help with the run, but he guesses the wrong side on one play and Cowen takes a counter, bounces outside the other way and sprints to the corner for a touchdown with 1:17 remaining in the half. The extra point gives them the lead.

Though we've out-played them most of the half, we're trailing 14-13.

``Offense, huddle up over there," Coach yells before the kickoff. ``OK, here's where we trust you guys. Our plan here was to go with the script and use Anthony to control the ball, but we don't have enough time for that if we're going to score. Trust Lars out there and listen up because he's going to call the plays at the line. Go get us some points!"

As we walk onto the field with only 1:05 left, I tell my team what the first play is, and a few of them look at me like I'm crazy. I definitely am, but in a good way.

Considering we're deep in our own territory and this is the best defense we've ever played against, this might be the riskiest play I've ever run. We've got Keaton and Trever lined up on the left side next to Alex at tight end. Anthony is behind me in the backfield, leaving Max alone on the right side. I take the shotgun snap from Bob, and toss it to Anthony who is charging hard for the left side where everyone is locked up blocking on their man.

It looks like a normal start-of-a-drive sweep is coming until Anthony shifts the ball to his right hand and tosses it 10 yards back to me like I'm the trailer on an option – just before he gets smacked in the legs by a diving Duncan. Here comes the risky part because I have to turn my back to the defense now. Using my shortstop motion, I tip the ball with my left hand to my right hand before whirling 360 degrees to plant my right foot and heave the ball as hard as I can. I can't take the time to look where Max is running to aim much, but I'm hoping he can run the ball down.

Because the play started like a run, the IWU safeties came running in which should leave Max with a single defender. To sell the fake, he stopped 20 yards downfield for half an instant to mimic throwing a block at the defensive back trying to cover him like it was a running play and then took off sprinting again.

For the first time all day, I don't get knocked on my backside so I get to see the whole thing develop standing up. The ball is high enough to fly about 60 yards. I put a lot of air under it, thinking he might need some more time to run under it and because I didn't have a chance to see where Max was before I let it go. My biggest worry is keeping it inbounds on his side of the field so he has a chance. After I follow through, I look up to see that he's got a 5-yard lead on his man, but I immediately wonder if I've thrown the ball too far.

Sometimes I wonder how fast Max is, and I'm not sure even he knows. He's run a 4.3 in the 40-yard dash before during workouts, but I swear he's even faster when going after the football – like this time. It's like his cleats are barely touching the grass.

Knowing he's beaten, the Sagamores' defensive back dives at Max's legs, probably hoping to knock him off-balance and just take an interference call, but he misses by 2 yards and lands chest-first before rocking onto his face. As Max glides under the ball, he grabs it in stride with both arms extended, making it look like we've run this play a 100 times before.

This is actually the first time we've ever tried it.

When Max catches the ball at their 20-yard line he's free by 10 yards and no one is going to catch him. Knowing he's got time to kill, Max slows up and trots slowly into the end zone, taking a little bit of an angle to kill more time. He doesn't just stop and walk in which would have taken even more time off the clock because that might be seen as showing up the Sagamores, but I'm betting he'd love to. He's got too much class for that. Instead he just hands the ball to the official who catches up first.

Thunderbolts 20, Sagamores 14.

The entire stadium is quiet except for the small Camarillo section over my left shoulder, which is screaming so loud a few people won't have any voices left for the second half. You just know every Sagamore fan is saying to themselves, "Why couldn't they have stayed and done that here?"

The other people who are making a lot of noise are my teammates who all seem to be screaming in my ears while they are pounding me on the back. The beating gets worse as we get closer to the sideline, including a bear hug from Coach Schebig.

``When I said go off the script, I didn't mean you could re-write the whole dang thing!" he yells in my ear.

``I just wanted to make sure we had the momentum," I mumble out when I can breathe again.

After Miguel boots his kickoff out of the end zone, the Sagamores know they can't go 80 yards in 40 seconds so Mason just kneels to end the half. The IWU crowd is still too stunned to even boo such a conservative play call.

They'll have plenty to boo about later.

CHAPTER 36

Well, we think we've got all the momentum until we get to the locker room and watch Anthony limp in, his arms hanging over the shoulders of managers Tabitha Cohn and Roxanne Bentley.

``He's done, Coach,'' Roxanne says. ``I think it's broken.''

Anthony had been running toward our sideline when he got hit by Duncan, so he was able to drag himself off the field, but I never saw him after that and didn't even know he had been hurt.

Crap! Without him out there, this exposes our biggest weakness on offense. Our back-up is a true freshman named Tucker McClure who has only taken a few snaps this year, mostly because he thinks a running back should only run the ball. He's lousy at picking up the blocking scheme, meaning my life is going to be a lot more difficult in the second half. Anthony is great at picking up the blitz, and I can always count on him in case anybody from the defense breaks through.

The worst part is that there's no way we can run the ball any more. Anthony is a very good Division II back and he was adequate to keep the Sagamores' defense honest with a sweep here or a dive there, but there's no way the rookie can run anywhere against these guys. They'll know within two third-quarter plays that we're going to have to throw on every down. Without the running game to make them hesitate, I'll be a piñata out there for their defensive linemen. I just hope my guts don't spill out.

``We'll think of something,'' Coach says, patting me on my good shoulder. He can tell which one because the other has an ice bag strapped to it.

"I have an idea," I say. "What if we put Alex in the backfield? We can use him in a double tight end formation with David Beier or use him as a blocking fullback. He's sharp enough to nail some of the blitzers, and we might even be able to use him to run the ball once or twice."

"I'll think about it, but you get with him and prepare him before we go back out."

"We can always use Big Joe if we get close to the goal line. That might give the defense a boost, too."

He nods his head, looks up into my eyes and says, "Hey, I told you and Max that we'd have a chance to win, not that it would be easy."

"I'm OK. So we have to get a little creative. I'm all about creative."

We're probably going to need a lot of creativity. As I look around the locker room, I see about half the starters have ice bags strapped on, and a few guys need help getting their shoulder pads off. We're beat up, and it looks like the end of a big game rather than only halftime.

Everyone is sucking down energy drinks as they try to catch their breaths. We've only got 10 minutes so I look for Alex and find him near the offensive linemen who are sitting in a corner. They look worse than I feel. Gabe has a red splotch on his cheek where he got tagged. Randy is flexing his hand that got stepped on and Big Bob is trying to stretch out his sore back, which is not a good sign for a center.

We need some extra help, and we're not going to get any.

"Anthony is out for the second half," I say approaching their corner.

"Aw, man!" Randy says, leaning back to bounce his head off a locker as a couple of other heads drop.

"Now, c'mon, we're the team that's ahead here," I say. "We've surprised everybody so far because we're right in this. I've still got a couple of ideas that might work. We just have to be a little more selective in what we try."

"What are we going to do?" Gabe asks as I pull up a chair to sit down.

"That depends on you guys," I say, leaning forward so I can look them all in the eyes. "What are you ready to let me try? Are you guys physically OK to do what I need you to do so I can have some time back there? Are you too beat up to do the job?"

"Oh, heck, no!" Big Bob says, scrunching down and trying to look around to see if any of the coaches heard him swear. "We didn't work this hard to fall apart now. We've got them right where we want them. For one thing, they have to be scared spitless, and the longer we hold onto the lead, the worse it will get on that sideline. We all know that."

"Without a running game, all we have to do is get in the way and stay there," Randy says. "I can do that as well as anybody."

Speaking of which, I see Alex a few rows over and wave him in. His smile is still beaming from scoring the touchdown until I tell him Anthony is hurt.

"Well, hero, you're my new and only fullback," I say. "We're not going to ask you to do something you can't, but we need you to be ready to get in the way and pick up the blitz every once in a while. We're going to try to run some roll-outs to avoid most of the rush, but there will be some times when I need you to watch my back. Can you do that?"

His eyes show everything Alex is thinking as he panics for one second, starts to shake his head no, and then clams down.

"Sure, I guess," he says with a sheepish grin. "What have we got to lose?"

"Exactly," I say, slapping him on the shoulder. "That's my guy.

"Now let's get the receivers in here because I know what I want to do on the first series."

Except I never get the chance to try anything.

CHAPTER 37

"We're close," Coach tells us all before we take the field again. "Nobody believed we could do this but us, so don't leave anything in reserve this half. We can do this! We are doing this! The longer we go, the more scared they are going to get, the more pressure they are going to feel and the more mistakes they'll make. No excuses!"

"No excuses!" we all roar.

After getting chewed out for the entire halftime, the Sagamores finally get a little smarter. Instead of kicking off to Max and giving him another chance to make them look foolish, they boot the ball short and on the sideline where Tucker McClure fields it at the 35. Instead of just dropping down and covering the ball for good field position, he tries to get cute, pick it up and take off.

Unfortunately, his blockers aren't expecting that, and he makes it 5 yards before getting massively smacked by about three Sagamores. The first thing that gets hit is the ball by an opposing helmet, and the fumble rolls 3 yards before an Indiana Western player falls on it.

Now we have no momentum, the crowd is back into it and IWU's offense can't wait to get onto the field.

Sensing a big chance, Mason Parker drops back to pass on the first play and throws a line drive to Jim Wallace who leaps at the goal line. His five extra inches in height are just enough of an advantage over Miguel Perez to snag the ball away from Miguel's outstretched right hand.

Sagamores 21, Thunderbolts 20

"I thought I had him," Miguel says when he trots to the sideline. "I was right there!"

"Don't worry about it," I say, swatting him on the backside. "We'll get it right back."

This time a thoroughly embarrassed McClure just falls on the kickoff at the 30-yard line, drawing a big derisive cheer from the crowd. We all pick him up and dust him off as we take the field.

"Keep your chin up, Tucker," I say. "We're going to need you."

As soon as we line up at the line of scrimmage, the Sagamores' defense starts chattering when they notice Anthony isn't in the backfield.

"I told you I knocked him out, Andrew," Duncan yells. "I told you!"

"Yeah, I didn't believe you," Andrew says. "Now it's my turn!"

Knowing I've got time on the play clock, and that we need to shut both of them up, I look over the line and say, "Hey, Duncan, remember what happened the last time you took out one of my guys?"

Gabe, Bob, Randy and Alex all laugh at that loud enough for Duncan to hear, and he barks, "I oughta..." as he charges toward the line. As he comes charging up close enough I can smell his breath, I yell, "Snap it!" and Big Bob brings the ball up into my hands.

Just as I'd hoped, the side judges both throw their flags because they see that Duncan is offsides, meaning I've got a free play. Instead of going for another home run to Max, I look to the other side where Keaton Alexander is cutting over the middle just into the spot where Duncan should be standing if he wasn't so fired up to kill me. Keaton doesn't even need to extend his arms to catch the ball and turns upfield to run for another 17 yards and a first down at the 47-yard line.

"Way to keep your cool, Duncan," I say after declining the penalty. "Just remember, though, I never forget and always stick up for my guys. You better keep watching."

"You're all talk, Preston!" he yells back. "I'll get you yet. You're done, you just don't know it yet!"

"Sir," I say innocently, turning to the head referee, "would that be taunting, or unsportsmanlike conduct or something like that, possibly?"

"Both of you shut up and play!" he tells both of us.

"Yes, sir," I say, but by then my entire offense is laughing and the tension is broken. We've got our mojo back, and my guys are fired up again and pushing back.

"Thank you, Duncan," I say under my breath. "I can always count on you."

On the next play, we surprise them by running Alex up the middle. He gains maybe two yards but stays on his feet and upright long enough that it gives all the rest of us a chance to run to the pile and jump on top of Duncan at the bottom. It's a perfectly legal play, but by the time the officials pull us all off him, Duncan is barely breathing and has to come out for a couple of plays.

"Funny, he's not talking much now," I say once we get back in the huddle.

Since we can't run the ball much, we need to work on short passes so we can keep our defense off the field at least a little bit. We're confident we can score, but we've got to use some clock.

They are giving Max plenty of room on the outside now, so I drill him with a short buttonhook pass for 8 yards and another first down.

"Wish we could figure a way to suck them in again," Max says.

``Maybe, but I'll take that pass all day and we'll dink them to death,'' I say. ``They're too afraid of you getting deep on them again. Trever, you're up! On two.''

Trever cuts inside Max's block for a receiver screen and he cuts across their 40. We need 10 more yards to get into field goal range, and I gain six of them on a bootleg around the left side. This time I sense Duncan coming and slide down just as he flies over the top of me.

``Whew, I just about had you there baby!'' Duncan yells. ``You better be ducking!''

I'd have some sort of snappy reply, but my left ankle got caught in the turf as I was sliding and I twisted it pretty badly. I'm sure the replays on TV are making some folks watching at home a little sick to their stomachs. Just what I need! At first the shock of the pain about makes me want to barf, but I immediately know I have to get to my feet and start walking it off. The longer I stay on the ground, the more my ankle is going to tighten up.

``Are you OK, Lars?'' Randy asks.

``Aw, crap!'' I mutter as Randy and Big Bob help me up. ``Not really, but it's going to be a lot worse tomorrow.''

Thank goodness it's my left foot and not my right which I push off with to throw. I can still lean back and throw, but this means I can't move out of the pocket much at all. I'm a sitting target with a beat-up line in front of me and a tight end trying to learn how to stop the blitzing defense which knows I have to throw on almost every pass.

This day just keeps getting tougher.

I limp back into the shotgun, and we try the screen again, this time to Max, but Andrew Crow figures out what's coming and drops him for a 2-yard loss. After I miss Keaton on a slant, on third down Alex slips out of the backfield against the blitz to catch a short lollipop pass for 5 yards. Right now, that's the best throw I can make. We're short of the first down, but Manuel has it going today and I bend down to hold the snap as he kicks a 48-yard field goal to give us back the lead.

Thunderbolts 23, Sagamores 21

I need to get to the bench and get my ankle taped up before it swells any more. I lean on Randy as we walk, or rather he walks and I hop a little bit, to the sideline. I can forget about the injury during a play, but now that I'm just sitting on the sideline, it starts to throb.

"Don't take my shoe off," I tell trainer Dave Kuhn. "The minute it comes off, my day is over because it's going balloon up."

"Then you should sit," Dave says.

"No way. We have the lead and a shot to win this game. I'm not coming out and letting everybody else down! This is our chance! As long as I can walk, I'll find a way to throw. Just tape it up for me, Dave. Please?

"I can't hurt it any worse, right? And don't tell Coach!"

Dave shakes his head at me, but he tapes me up. So right now I can only use half of my body because my left shoulder and left ankle are messed up. I know Dave has a responsibility to tell Coach and would never let a player talk him into something that wasn't right, but that means I have get on my feet again and keep moving. If I let on how bad I'm hurting, I know Coach will yank me from the game, taking care of our chances to win. I'm not going to let that happen.

Instead of looking around for Coach, I gather the offense again. By the way the Sagamores are pushing our defense down the field, we've got a little time to talk.

"Who's got something they want to try?" I say. "Max, you got anything?"

"Can you take one more hit?" he asks.

"What? I'm good, just tell me the play."

"Seriously, can you take another hit? Tell the truth. If you can't, I don't think this play will work."

I'm standing next to the bench rocking back and forth on my left foot to keep it loosened up. Right now, the pain isn't too terrible. It will be really bad tomorrow, and I'll probably even need crutches, but I don't care.

"Yeah, I'm good. Tell me the play."

Before he can answer, the stadium explodes as Cowen pushes over from 5 yards out for another touchdown. It's the last play of the third quarter, so we've got a little extra time to talk before the television network comes back from commercial.

Sagamores 28, Thunderbolts 23.

Max tells me the play and now I understand why he needs to know if I can take a hit. It's a really risky call, but haven't they all been today?

"We'll have to set this up with another play first. Are you guys good with that?"

Everyone nods and we walk to the sideline to watch the kickoff. That's when Coach grabs me.

"No B.S., how are you?" he asks.

"I'm hurting, but I can do this," I reply. "We'll never be this close again, and I think our slogan all along has been 'No excuses,' right?

This will not be an excuse."

"What if it costs the national championship?"

"I can't answer that right now. It won't. I know that means a lot to you and to the school, but this is bigger than that. I think we'll all regret this, this right here, forever if we don't take every chance we have. I can still do that.

"We've still got a chance. The moment we don't, you can yank me. You said we could have a chance to win the game, and I still want that chance."

"I did, didn't I?" he says. "OK, you've got it.".

We all know that none of us are going to play in the NFL. We're all going to be accountants, advertising executives, teachers and engineers after we're done playing, but right now we are football players. We won't be that forever, but they have to let us be that with everything it means as long as we can hold onto it.

This whole thing has been about getting a chance, and we've got 15 minutes left to see if we can make the most of it. I'm not giving up yet.

CHAPTER 38

As I limp onto the field, the crowd quiets as if they aren't sure what they are looking at. I must look like a zombie Halloween costume because I'm limping, my left shoulder is drooping a little, and my uniform is covered in dirt and a little blood. I've also got my right elbow taped up because of a cut I suffered earlier. The only thing I'm not doing is moaning. My mom is probably cringing right now just looking at me.

``All right, everybody know what to do on this? Let them come. Keaton, you make sure you're within 5 yards of the pass because I don't want an intentional grounding call.''

He nods, and I call ``On three!'' and we break the huddle.

Alex is lined up to my right with Max and Trever on the right and Keaton on the left. I look across the line and I can see Duncan knows I can't move. He's got their strong safety lined up next to him like an extra linebacker because he knows Alex isn't coming out of the backfield to catch a pass. They are all coming after little 'ol me.

I catch the snap and look right, but no one's open. I know I have to get rid of the ball so I turn and loft a little push pass to the left side just as Alex steps in front of me to knock down the blitzing safety. Duncan gets his arm up too late, but there's no energy on my throw. A 6-year-old could toss a Nerf ball harder. The ball is headed in Keaton's direction but it lands a good 10 yards short of his position as Duncan pushes me to the ground.

When Alex helps me to my feet, I start rubbing my right arm and trying to shake it like I'm feeling a stinger or something. I want everyone in the place to think I can't throw any more.

``I don't know what happened,'' I tell Alex. ``I couldn't get anything on it.''

As he's walking back to his side of the line, Duncan hears all of this -- as he's supposed to. He runs to their huddle, anticipating telling his teammates I can't throw and then pointing back toward me once he has their attention.

As we huddle up, Gabe asks, ``Think he fell for it?'

``He fell hard because he wants to believe it so badly,'' I say. ``This is where we throw them an uppercut. You guys ready?''

We line up in the same formation, except this time when the snap comes, Max races into the backfield behind me from the right where I pitch him the ball for a reverse to the left. The Sagamores know it's not a pass because none of our receivers have run downfield and there's no one further than seven yards away from the line of scrimmage. Even Alex has come out of the backfield to block the right side linebacker who is the last player on that side of the field. All of them are blocking their man as like they would be if it was a run.

But it's not.

Just as Max gets to the left end, he plants his left foot, turns and tosses the ball 20 yards back to me with a lateral. I'm standing all alone about 15 yards behind the line of scrimmage where no one is paying any attention to me for the first time all day. Surprise!

By now, Alex has slipped away from his linebacker, who is still concentrating on Max, and started running for open field. There's no one within 10 yards of him as he crosses the 50. My throw hits him in stride at the IWU 40, and he's gone! The closest Sagamore to him is still the linebacker, and he's got no prayer of catching Alex and stops once he gets to midfield and is still 15 yards behind.

With 14:12 remaining in the game we lead once again as Alex crosses the goal line. The only sounds in the stadium are the whooping and yelling in joy coming from our sideline and from our offensive players as they race the length of the field to congratulate Alex again.

Thunderbolts 30, Sagamores 28

I just walk down the middle of the field, dragging my leg a little, to get ready to hold the extra point. I look up and see Mom and Dad and Mikala standing and cheering in their section with the rest of our fans. I can also see that the IWU fans are all in shock, shaking their heads and wondering how this could be happening. They can't believe what they are seeing and aren't quite sure how to react.

That's when I get creamed from behind throwing me face-forward into the turf, grass and limbs flying.

`You cheating piece of garbage," Duncan yells at my back. `I ought to beat the crap out of you!"

I can hear the crowd booing which is getting louder. For once, I don't think they are booing me. It takes me a few seconds before I find the energy to turn over.

`You've done a pretty good job so far, Duncan," I say, gasping. `Besides, we both know you'd be exhausted before you finished."

I finally sit up, shake my head to clear the numbness and then start the slow process of standing up as one of the officials jumps in.

`We didn't cheat, we fooled you, and there's a big difference. You fell for it, Duncan, and that's your problem, not mine. Now you've got a bigger one."

I figure for sure he's going to be kicked out of the game for this one, except this time I'm shocked because there's no penalty flag on the field! Somehow every official on the field missed me getting tagged from behind. No matter how much Coach Schebig screams from the sideline, nothing is going to happen to Duncan.

"I'd rather you stayed in the game anyway so I can keep exploiting you," I say as I turn and continue to limp down the field. This time everyone leaves me alone until I finally catch up.

"What happened back there?" Big Bob asks.

"I just needed a breather," I say.

Because we scored so quickly, we probably are hurting our defense which has to come back out on the field pretty quickly with little rest, but we needed to push back some and prove we weren't giving up yet. We also need the IWU defense to start thinking some more about what might happen on each play so they give me a little time to breathe in the pocket. We need them to be a little jumpy. We need to be able to dictate to them a little.

"C'mon, defense!" I say as they pass us on the field. "You make one stop and we'll win this game! Give me a turnover!"

And that's about as much energy as I have left right now. My entire body is sore, and what I really need is about two hours soaking in a hot tub. This time I fall back upon the bench and I don't care who sees it. I need a minute to try getting my head to convince my body it doesn't hurt so bad.

Maybe later on in the hot tub. Now I'm hoping Indiana Western's offense leaves us enough time to have one more chance.

There's about eight minutes left in the game, and I know the Sagamores plan is to use at least 7:59 of that pushing our defense back about four yards per play toward the game-winning touchdown. Outside of a fluke turnover, I really don't think there's anything our guys can do to stop them. Our best chance is for a fumble or an interception, except Cowen never fumbles and Parker isn't going to throw the ball unless he absolutely has to.

IWU is pounding on our guys. The Joes and Nate are fighting back as much as they can, but they must be exhausted, trying to find handholds and leverage against players who are taller and weigh just as much as they do if not more. They're getting overwhelmed as the Sagamores pull everyone into the offensive line and just pound away inside. You can hear the grunts going on and slaps of flesh from the sidelines, but after each play we walk five yards further down the field for the next one.

Cowen has already rushed for more than 200 yards, and he's not slowing down. He tearing off 5- and 6-yard chunks on every play as the Sagamores cross midfield and start pushing deep into our territory. There's only 4:00 left. We're running out of room on the field and most importantly time.

``Coach Schebig!" I yell as I lurch to my feet. ``Call time out! Call a time out!''

He turns and looks at me like I've finally lost all my marbles. ``Are you serious?''

``Totally. I've got another idea, maybe the biggest one yet. Please call the time out.''

Now everyone on the sidelines is looking at me and wondering if I've got a concussion. Dave Kuhn rushes up, looks in my eyes and asks, ``How are you feeling?''

``I'm fine, Dave, honest," I say, looking around. ``You guys have to trust me again on this one.''

I walk over to Coach Schebig where Jordan Eichorn is trotting toward us.

"This is going to sound really crazy, and Jordan, don't get too ticked off, but I think I know what we need to do," I start. "We can't stop them. You guys are totally whipped, and it's because you have played so hard and tried everything you can think of. They are just too big and strong, and they are going to take the ball the rest of the way, run the clock out and score a touchdown or kick a field goal to win the game.

"What I'm going to suggest is really nuts, but it will give us a chance to win. They want to end the game with their offense, their best unit, on the field. For us to win, we have to get our best unit, our offense, back on the field. The only way to do that is to get the ball back."

"Of course, that's what we're trying to do," Jordan says, exasperated.

"But while you are doing it, we're running out of time... So we have to let them score."

Shifting his head back and forth between Coach and I, an incredulous Jordan asks, "Are you serious?"

Coach just looks at the clock and then tilts his head down, hopefully considering what I'm suggesting.

"Right now our only chance to win is if we get the ball back with enough time for us to work on offense," I say. "We can't do that unless we get the ball back very soon. They are not going to turn it over, so we have to let them score. They'll lead 35-30, but we can still win it with a touchdown, and we'll have the time to do it. They are already within field goal range so no matter what happens, they are going to lead. If we hope they get a field goal, it's going to take too much time to stop them and we'll have less time to try getting back down the field. I'm sorry, Jordan, but they are going to score anyway, and this

274

gives us our best chance to come back because we'll need at least two minutes to do it."

We're also running out of time during the time out. We need a decision.

"He's right," Coach says, nodding his head. "He's absolutely right. I know you don't like this, Jordan, but it's the right thing to do. It's the only thing we CAN do to give us a chance. This is one more sacrifice the defense has to make.

"You want us to give up the lead?" Jordan asks.

"They haven't been able to stop us all game, but we haven't been able to stop them, either," Coach says. "This is our best choice, Jordan, and you need to tell everybody out there to let Cowen through the line and nobody tackles him. Bring all 11 men up like we know it's going to be a run, and let him through, but then you all have to chase him all the way so he doesn't just drop down to kill the play. He has to think this is him just finding a big hole and getting lucky. If he stops for a first down, then we have to start using the rest of our time outs."

The last thing we need is for Cowen to run out of bounds or get half a second to realize that IWU can run out the clock and still win the game with a field goal. The only thing we have going for us is we still have two time outs left.

"Jordan, you have to make this happen," Coach says.

"I don't like it!" Jordan says before poking me in the chest. "But I'll do it. You just better win this game!"

"We will," I say, "as long as you give us enough time."

"Well, we're probably going to get hit with a delay of game penalty as I try to explain this to those guys," Jordan says. "They're not going to like it."

When he trots back to the huddle, we can tell by the gestures and arm waving that not everybody agrees with this order. Several players look over at Coach who just nods his head emphatically, and yes, the referees throw a flag for a delay of game penalty, pushing the ball to our 25-yard line.

Jordan wants to call another time out, but Coach shakes his head, and Jordan goes back into the huddle. We can see him yelling in the middle, and then Miguel adds his opinion and everyone settles down. Jordan points to the sideline and holds up his index finger.

"What's that mean?" I ask Coach.

"I'm guessing they want one more play to come up with a turnover or something."

Coach nods his head and we line up for the play. All 11 guys are creeping in near the line of scrimmage, but they can't stop Cowen when he goes right up the middle for eight yards, mostly because our guys are all trying to strip the ball from him instead of making the tackle. When the officials finally blow their whistles, B.J. is still holding onto the ball inside our 20-yard line, but his arms are all scratched up.

The defensive players head back to their huddle, heads down, maybe finally admitting our plan is the only chance. They just can't stop the Sagamores. All we can see is Jordan talking in the huddle and eventually everyone nods agreement.

I know this is killing them because they have played so hard all day, and they have dedicated just as much time and training to this game as the offense has. But we're running out of time. Even if this play works, we'll still only have about 3:00 left once we get the ball, and we'll have to drive the length of the field for a touchdown, not just a field goal.

IWU is at our 17-yard line when Mason turns to hand the ball to Cowen again, his 40th carry of the day. He sprints between center and right guard where Little Joe throws a hand out to hit him on the shoulder. Nik Hoot lets the tackle jump out and block him while the center somehow ``pushes'' Big Joe back into Jordan at middle linebacker.

Maybe the Sagamores should figure out that it's a hoax because for the first time all day the blocking is easy, but by then Cowen is charging ahead at the 10 and the crowd is screaming. It's the perfect surprise play on our part, but just in case Cowen gets smart at the last second, Jordan is sprinting right behind him and makes sure to shove him into the end zone with 3:10 remaining.

Sagamores 35, Thunderbolts 30

IWU thinks they have won the game and is ready to start celebrating, but the Sagamores have made a big mistake.

This is everything I've ever dreamed of, I've got the ball and now they have to try to stop me.

CHAPTER 39

With all of their 79,500 fans screaming, Indiana Western kicker again boots the ball away from Max on the kickoff, this time to the far sideline where Trever Andrews catches it at the 20 and gets to the 27-yard line before being shoved out of bounds.

We've got 73 yards to go in 2:57 with two time outs left.

Just like me, my guys are beat up, tired and a little worried, but they are still all of my guys.

"You guys remember how we used to dream of moments like this when we were on the scout team here?" I say in the huddle, looking around at all the faces. "What do you say let's give them a nightmare? How much fun will this be? We've still got nothing to lose, so let's relax and go have some fun, OK? They think they hate us now, well, just wait until after this game!"

Everybody laughs at that and I say, "Snap on two!" and we clap and break the huddle to approach the line.

I can tell immediately that IWU is sticking with their regular formation. There's no way Coach Jackson will let them sit back in a prevent defense so I can pick them apart. He may not like me, but he does respect me, though he'll never admit it.

"Hut, hut!" I bark just before Big Bob's snap smacks my hands and I look left toward Max and fire on another buttonhook for 7 yards. Max almost slips away for more and to get out of bounds, but he gets buried.

Second-and-3 at our 34-yard line, 2:38 remaining and clock running.

We line up quickly and snap it so I can throw a rope to Trever on the sideline. He catches it 4 yards downfield and stops out of bounds.

First-and-10 at our 38-yard line, 2:30 remaining and clock stopped.

``OK, now we're moving," I say in the huddle. ``Alex, I've got a hunch you can get us some yards up the middle right now. What do you guys think?"

``Oh, yeah," Randy says. ``This will be fun."

``We'll call time out as soon as he gets tackled," I say. ``On one!"

The way their linebackers immediately turn and ran away from the line of scrimmage, the Sagamores are not expecting our tight-end-turned-fullback to be carrying the ball this time, and Alex pops past the line of scrimmage, head down and shoulders squared charging ahead. He finally gets knocked down 10 yards ahead.

``Time out! Time out!" I limp up to the pile and yell so the referee blows his whistle.

First-and-10 at our 49-yard line, 2:11 remaining and clock stopped.

``OK, we're moving and they don't seem to know what's coming," Coach Schebig says. ``You want to try for another buttonhook to Max?"

I lower the water bottle to say, ``Actually, I want to fake one and let him go and see what happens. We've hit him for three or four buttonhooks in a row and maybe their guy will try to jump the route and let Max get free. We might surprise them again."

``OK, then after that, let's hit them with another crossing route with Keaton and Trever. Call them both at once in the huddle."

``Will do," I say and turn to head back out.

I can sense the tension in the crowd which means the Sagamores on the field can, too. Good. It's always harder to focus on doing something right when you are trying to ignore something else.

After calling the plays in the huddle, I pull Max aside for a quick second to tell him I'm going to pump fake him on the button so he can try to beat his man and take off.

When I see the safety sneaking over to Max's side, I should change out of the play but I'm too stubborn and it costs me. As soon as I pump fake, the cornerback runs up on Max, which frees him up for half a second. That's not long enough to take the chance, and by the time I can look up again, their safety is right there.

Now I'm in trouble because it's too late to find another receiver. Somehow Andrew Crow has moved inside to push past Big Bob and Gabe and he's bearing down on me. Luckily, I see him coming so I can throw the ball toward Max and out of bounds, but that leaves me wide open to Andrew plowing his right shoulder pad into my exposed ribs. Then he drives me back into the turf to knock the breath out of my lungs.

Though I know my lungs will recover in a few seconds, my heart is still racing with panic. It's such a helpless feeling, hoping your body responds and the pain goes away, but it hurts bad enough you're not exactly sure it will. Worse, I still can't move because Andrew remains on top of me.

"Got you this time, you jerk!" he yells.

I, of course, can't breathe let alone respond. Not sure what I'd say anyway because he's right. He sure got me. It's the biggest hit I've taken all day.

"Get off of him!" Randy yells and drags Andrew off me. That leads to more shoving among the linemen, but I still can't breathe and could care less. I'm trying to gasp in little breaths.

I've never been this beat up from a game before, but I know I have to save the time out so I motion to Gabe and Bob to pick me up. They lift me slowly, but it helps me drag in some air.

"Huddle up,'" are my first gasped words.

Second-and-10 at our 49-yard line, 1:54 remaining and clock stopped.

"Alex, this one's yours," I say in a low voice. "I need a play to recoup. Bob, snap it to Alex, OK?"

"Sure," Bob says. "Shouldn't you...?"

"I'm not coming out, I just need a play. We have time."

We line up and I lean over in the shotgun, hands on my legs holding me up with Alex standing beside me, but I can barely talk let alone shout out the signals. As soon as Big Bob snaps the ball, I hobble a couple feet to the left away from the play, and Alex catches it and rushes up the middle. He pounds only 2 yards before his momentum stops, but we're on their side of the field, and I can finally breathe.

Third-and-8 at their 49-yard line, 1:42 remaining and the clock is running.

We skip the huddle this time and line up right away because time is flying by. I can finally take a deep breath and call out the play. Trever and Keaton both attack the middle from separate sides. As soon as they get to a spot right behind Duncan, he has to make a decision which way to go. He goes left, and I throw right to Keaton who catches it and gets tackled at their 40-yard-line for another first down.

First-and-10 at their 40-yard line, 1:25 remaining and the clock is running.

From the moment the snap hits me in the hands, I can tell this play is not going to work. I am supposed to dump it off to Alex for a little screen after the other receivers take off downfield, but the outside linebacker figures it out and covers Alex. I have to move.

I hear Randy yell, "Duck!" and I know Andrew has gotten free to come after me again. I try to run, but my left leg won't support it. I've got no speed, just adrenalin-based fear pushing me toward the sideline. Just before stepping out of bounds, I look up and see Max has come back on his route, and I flip the ball toward him just as Crow smacks into my back, driving me into their sideline where I flop into three players standing there.

I actually feel my back crack from the hit and everything else. I have no idea if Max caught the pass or what happened after because I can't get up with Andrew lying on my back and legs with my head and shoulders pinned against the midsections of his teammates. All I can do is groan until I hear the referee yelling at Andrew to get off me.

By the time I get to stretch out and roll over, I'm surrounded by players from both teams shoving and arguing. I'd yell at my guys to stop but simply don't have the energy. Finally, one of the officials pulls his flag and that starts a rain of three or four others and it seems six whistles are sounding at the same time.

Everyone takes a step back then, and I'm able to stand up with a hand from Jim Wallace and one of the IWU trainers I remember, Anna Grace.

"I'm OK," I say somehow. "At least I think I am. Let me take a step or two."

Back on the field, I can see one official marking the ball at the IWU 25 so Max must have caught the pass somehow.

"After the play, we've got off-setting penalties," the referee says. "Personal fouls on both teams so the play stands. First down!"

First-and-10 at their 25-yard line, 1:08 remaining and the clock is stopped.

"What happened?" I ask when we get back into the huddle.

"Max dove sideways and caught the ball one-handed," Alex says. "It was his best catch ever! I'm surprised any of the officials saw it because everybody was watching you get drilled."

"All right, we need a play. Max, you up to trying a reverse? They won't expect that."

"Sure," is all he says, as if he expected the call all along.

With Alex lined up to my left, I fake a handoff to him as he runs to the right behind the offensive line. When Max runs behind us, I toss the ball to him heading left. It could have been a good idea, but we're not fooling them this time as Andrew stays home on his end and Max can't get to the sideline after he gains 2 yards.

Second-and-8 at their 23-yard line, :55 remaining and the clock is running.

We line up right away, ready to run another one of our set plays during this situation. We can all feel the pressure shift a little because now we're running out of time. If they can stop us on this play, we could be in real trouble.

That's why it's great to have such an experienced team which is used to high-pressure moments. Trever starts out from the slot and cuts outside at the same time as Keaton takes off from the outside and cuts inside. That gives Trever about a six-inch window to beat his man to the sideline where I drill the ball into his hands a split-second before he gets shoved out of bounds. The clocks stops because he went out of bounds, but did he get a foot down? The officials signals for a catch but not for the first down.

We also get some extra time because the officials want to measure if it's a first down.

"Did you make it," I ask Trever.

"I made it. I knew exactly where the line was," he says. "I made it."

He did, by a toenail.

First-and-10 at their 15-yard line, :48 remaining and the clock is stopped.

"Whew, that was close, but we're still alive," I say in the huddle. "Who wants the ball next? Think it's time to see if we can use that sprinkler hole, yet, Max?

"Sure," he says again.

Is even Max starting to feel the pressure?

"Hey, c'mon, guys, isn't this fun? This is what we've always dreamed of! We've got them pinned deep and we've got the ball. Just give me a little bit more, and let's go finish them off. On two!"

Max lines up in the slot this time, and if I didn't know better, I'd swear he was moving before the snap. Somehow, he gets off to a great jump, and within two strides he's got his defender pinned to the outside of the field. He's open!

I wind up and let the ball fly when he's a yard from the hole at the 10, and the throw is perfect. So is the coverage as the IWU defender sidesteps the hole to stay stride-for-stride with Max. The Sagamores' defender dives at the last second to tip the ball away.

"You guys think you're the only ones who know about that old hole?" he says to Max as they trot back toward the huddles.

"Guess not," Max says.

"You'll have to do better than that."

Second-and-10 their 15-yard-line, :40 remaining and the clock is stopped.

We need something good here, but I don't want to use our last time out. Without a real running back, we're limited in what we can try, and IWU has seen everything else we've got. I'm trying to think of something outside-the-box when a hand taps me on the shoulder and I look up to find Big Joe in the offensive huddle. I'm not sure how I didn't hear him rumbling up.

"Coach says run the three-receiver set on the right side and then throw me a screen pass behind it," he says. He's got a maniacal look on his face that says he's ready to run some people over.

"You sure?"

"Oh, yeah, it's my turn to hit some of them," he says and lets loose the biggest belly laugh I've ever seen or heard. "Just let me get moving downfield and I'll have the momentum."

He'd be like a boulder rolling downhill, but I'm just wondering if he can actually catch a pass. He's not known for having the softest set of hands.

Well, he did catch a snipe once.

It's a good call because they'll never expect it, but we'll have to hustle up to the line after he gets tackled or use our last time out.

The crowd is already buzzing because we've got Big Joe on offense.

Unless they've been to Africa, the fans have probably never considered seeing anything this big before, and definitely not in the backfield when he lines up behind me.

When the snap comes, I realize the first problem is it's going to take a little extra time for Big Joe to get in position to catch the screen. Usually, I just count "One Mississippi, two Mississippi, three Mississippi" and let the toss go, but Big Joe will barely be up to the right tackle position by then. There's no sense in looking left because there are no receivers on that side of the field, and Trever, Keaton and Max are all heading for the end zone. Luckily, they've taken all five IWU defensive backs with them, meaning Big Joe only has to get by Duncan and he might be able to score.

I loop the pass so Big Joe has time to reach up with his hands to grab it, but he still bobbles it once before tucking it into his belly. I swear the ball almost disappears. Then he turns toward the defense and starts "running." I've seen lines at the Bureau of Motor Vehicles move faster, especially since Big Joe has the idea that he's supposed to aim at defenders, not try to avoid them.

Maybe that's the right idea as he goes shoulder to shoulder with Duncan. Somehow Duncan manages to grab hold of Big Joe's left leg, but he's still getting dragged down the field. Big Joe is lunging ahead with his right leg, stopping to pull his left and Duncan forward and then lunging again. I swear you can feel the ground vibrate and hear the "thump" each time he plants his right foot on the field. It looks just like a 6-year-old boy trying to slow his father down.

Big Joe is inside the 10-yard-line before another Sagamore linebacker sprints up to wallop him from the left. That just causes Big Joe's right leg to drift a little to the side on his next step. When he pulls his left leg forward, he's effectively using Duncan's body to block any Sagamores from getting around to his right leg.

Two more Sagamores finally jump on Big Joe's back from behind, and one flips over Big Joe's head and shoulders to land in front of his right leg. The defender latches onto the leg with both hands so Big Joe can't go any further. Pulling him down takes two more players before the whistle finally blows the play dead.

First-and-goal at their 5-yard line, 27 seconds remaining and the clock is running.

The only thing I can hear under the pile is Big Joe laughing.

"Let's do that again!" he says when everyone finally gets off him.

The IWU defenders all groan at the suggestion.

It takes a few seconds to get Big Joe back on his feet and pointed back to our side of the line of scrimmage. When we finally line up and snap the ball, I spike it to stop the clock.

Second-and-goal at their 5-yard line, 20 seconds remaining and the clock is stopped.

"Everybody take a couple of deep breaths," I say. "I guarantee you they aren't breathing too easily in that huddle. Big Joe, you really want to try another one?"

"Oh, yeah! Give me the ball," he says, clapping his hands.

"OK, this time we're running it right up the gut. You go right behind Big Bob and you follow his butt into the end zone. Bob, Randy and Gabe, this is your moment right here. You keep pushing them back until we're in and nobody in football history will ever forget you."

"We're ready," Big Bob says. "We've been waiting for this chance."

Maybe the Sagamores sense what's coming because their defensive linemen all dive at the feet of our linemen and never give them anything to push back. Big Joe takes the ball, sees the carnage up front and tries to jump over the line. There's no way a 350-pound man can clear the pile. If the timing wasn't so critical, it would almost be funny enough to bring tears to my eyes.

Big Joe lands on the back of Big Bob and Gabe and then tries to roll toward the goal line. With the wall of bodies in front of them, the Sagamores' linebackers all hit Big Joe mid-roll, and he stops at their 3-yard line. Well, his momentum stops, causing the officials to blow the whistle, but Big Joe is still kicking his legs, trying to regain his forward progress.

``Time out! Time out!'' I yell, but no one can hear me at first. I finally turn and run up to the official in the backfield with my hands in a ``T'' formation before I can get him to notice.

Third-and-goal at their 3-yard line, 10 seconds remaining and the clock is stopped.

We've got time for two more plays.

``We almost surprised them there,'' I say to Coach at the sideline.

``What do you want to run?'' he asks.

``I know what I want to run on our last play, but I'm open to suggestions on this one.''

``How about another Keaton and Trever crossing pattern with Max heading for the corner,'' he says. ``Throw it to whichever is open.''

``Wish it was that easy.''

``Maybe it will be. Won't know until you try it.''

``Yes, sir.''

Just then, Big Joe finally finishes it trotting to the sideline beside us.

"I know I can get it in if you give me one more try," he says.

"I would give you that chance, but we're down to too little time, Big Joe. It's in Lars' hands now. Go make something good happen."

"Yes, sir."

Love how that man has such confidence and faith in me. I'd play anywhere for him against anyone, and I'd like our chances. That's the kind of man I want to be.

When I get back to the huddle, everyone's eyes are a little big. They are feeling the moment, realizing we are running out of time and options on plays with the short field.

"Relax, guys, we've still got this. Remember, they have to stop us, and this is where we're the best at anything we do. Am I right?"

"Yeah, sure," Randy says.

"Am I RIGHT?"

"Right!" everyone yells.

"OK, here's what we're going to run. It's nothing fancy but I'll need a little time back here. If nothing is open, I'm going to fire the ball into the stands so everybody hustle back to the huddle for the last play."

I call the play and then yell "Snap on one!" and everyone claps their hands.

I know the play is dead before I get the snap because they've got their two biggest defensive backs on Max, and all three linebackers are bunched over the middle. It's almost like they had someone in the huddle with us. Because of my little pep talk in the huddle, the play clock is down to three seconds so I can't even change the play. I just have to try making something work.

As small as he is, Max fights like a werewolf to get off the line, but he gets shoved out of bounds to take him out of the play. I look back over the middle and neither Trever or Keaton is open and neither has seen that the linebackers are waiting for them.

Then I hear Randy yelling, "He's coming!" and I know Andrew is charging from my backside. A sack will end the game because we don't have any more time outs so I take a step toward Max and whip the ball into the sideline. Max is smart enough to know he can't touch it because he hasn't had time to re-establish position back inbounds. That would be a penalty.

I swear I can feel all three heartbeats it takes an official to whistle the play dead.

Fourth-and-goal at their 3-yard line, 2 seconds remaining and the clock is stopped.

"Huddle up!" I yell.

We've got a chance on one more play, and I know exactly what I want to call. This isn't the time or place for a trick play, we've got to go with something we are supremely confident in and know will work.

I sure can't fool them with the "Don't touch the cheese play." Besides, I can't lift my left arm, let alone throw with it right now.

"Here's what we're doing...," I start in the huddle.

When I finish describing what I want to happen, I tell them I want to snap it on three.

Looking back later, I'll think that was a mistake.

We line up with Keaton and Trever on the right side facing three defenders. Max is far to the left with two defenders, but one of them has to keep an eye on Alex who is lining up at tight end and has already killed them a couple of times today.

``Hut one!" I yell.

``Hut two!"

And then the whistles blow. I'm hoping one of their linemen jumped offsides, but when I look around and can't see a penalty flag, I'm not sure what happened. I turn to find the head linesman waving his arms and signaling a time out to IWU.

The whole stadium lets out a collective sigh. While we've been having fun on the field, I forgot how much tension must be building in the stands. I'm so zoned in right now, in all honesty, I forgot that there were even fans in the stadium.

``Why you think they did that?" I ask Coach when I get to the sidelines.

``I'm not sure. What were you going to run?"

I describe for him what I had called.

``That's a solid play, and we haven't run it yet today." he says. ``That's as good as anything I've got for you. Go make it happen."

``Yes, sir."

Enough said.

As I walk back to the huddle, I try to look across and see what, if any, personnel substitutions they have made, but there's nothing obvious I can spot. So, if they didn't change up players, maybe Coach Jackson thinks he knows what play we're going to use.

No, that can't be it because we haven't used this play all year. He'd have nothing to go off of unless he's just got a hunch.

"OK, guys, same play," I say in the huddle. "Let's win this and start partying. Everybody sure on what they're supposed to do?"

Everybody nods yes so I say, "This time on two!'

When we walk to the line of scrimmage, there are still 15 seconds left on the play clock so I've got time to look over the defense. I still don't see any personnel changes, but I also don't see them set up in any way to indicate they know what play is coming, which allows me to relax a little bit.

"Hut," I yell and nobody on the defense shifts.

"Hut," and I'm already taking a step back as Big Bob's snap pops into my hands. I can't hear anything as I take a couple of steps to the right and watch the offensive and defensive lines shift that way, along with two of the IWU linebackers.

As I plant my right foot, Max races into the middle of the field along the goal line and starts his slide. Because the lines started moving to the right, I've got an open throwing lane to him. My arm is already cocked and I whip a rope to where his knees would be if he was standing up, but now he's sliding on his backside right on the line with the defensive back a full stride behind him. He's open!

The ball is thrown perfectly, and Max does his job perfectly, but I never see Duncan ducking down behind the line of scrimmage.

Coach Jackson's hunch is right.

Duncan jumps to his right to dive in front of Max and knock the ball away. Incomplete.

The game is over.

Sagamores 35, Thunderbolts 30.

We lost.

CHAPTER 40

I'm betting I'm always going to wonder what would have happened if I had used a two count instead of the three count when we first went to the line of scrimmage for the last play. That extra count allowed IWU to call the time out, and Coach Jackson could set up his defense for the play.

I think that's the only thing I may ever wonder about with this game. My teammates performed brilliantly, we fought as hard as we possibly could and I feel like we played the best we could. We just made one mistake.

No, that's not true. They made one great play.

As everyone in an IWU uniform celebrates around me, I limp over to Max and help him up before wrapping him in a hug.

"We did everything right," I say in his ear. "But so did they."

By the time I'm done, we're both getting hugged by everyone else on our offense.

"Heck of a game," Max says.

"I'm still proud of what we did today and how we did it," I tell everyone. "Each of you keep your head up. They may have won, but they didn't beat us down, so don't act like they did. I'm proud of all of you so show some pride here!"

Now I've got to go shake some hands.

I turn and limp toward midfield. I know tomorrow I'm going to need some help getting out of bed because I'll be so sore, but I'm hurting more because we wanted to win the game so badly. Both types of hurts will heal.

"We beat your butts!" I hear from behind and turn to find Andrew there.

"You won the game, congratulations," I say and offer my hand. He ignores it and just keeps yelling, so I turn and resume heading to the 50. I dodge through some people from both teams, which isn't easy because they are all moving faster than I can. When I finally get there, Coach Schebig and Coach Jackson have just finished shaking hands.

"Congratulations, Coach," I say to Coach Jackson.

He looks me in the eye and nods his head before smiling and turning away without taking my hand.

"Fair enough," I say to myself before reaching up to take my helmet off.

The coach won't shake my hand, but just like he promised before the game, Mason Parker is trotting out to me, hand extended.

"Congratulations, Mason, that was a great game."

"You played the great game," he says. "You guys surprised us in so many ways. I'm glad this is over."

"Your team deserved to win because you made the play at the end."

"You're a great player, Lars, no matter where you play or who you play for. Never let them take that away from you."

"Thank you, Mason, I appreciate that."

He turns and starts jogging toward his locker room, leaving me standing there alone. I look around to see if anyone else wants to shake, but no one appears right away. What I do see is Max and the rest of my teammates gathering 15 yards behind me, maybe making sure I don't take any more cheap shots today.

I still stand there for about 20 seconds, looking for Mom and Dad and Mikala in the end zone. I wave to them and start to mouth that I'm OK, when I begin to hear some boos coming from the crowd. Thinking there may be a fight going on or something, I whip my head around to see if I can figure out what they are booing, but there's nothing else going on.

Are they booing me?

I put my helmet on the ground, and stand back up to clap my hands at the crowd, nod my head in a thank you and then give them a thumbs up. Then they start to cheer.

So what were they booing.

Then I start to hear a chant, "Shake his hand! Shake his hand!"

I can't believe this. They were booing their own team for not shaking my hand!

The majority of the IWU players are still on the field, heading into their locker room entrance in the southeast corner. Some of them stop and hear the fans, but of a few wave the fans off when they hear the chanting. That just makes the fans add some more boos in with the chants, but the players continue heading off the field.

I'm not sure what to do next, but Coach Schebig comes beside me and says, "Let's go in. If they won't act with class, at least we will."

I put my hand on his shoulder and start limping toward our locker room. The chanting turns to cheers but we just keep walking. It's not our stadium, not our fans and I'm really confused about how we're supposed to react.

Then I figure it out. I call Max, Alex, Bob and Randy over to me as we get to the end zone. With the rest of our teammates standing behind us, the five of us start clapping and we bow toward the fans. Then we wave for a few seconds.

As each of our teammates pass, the five of us shake each of their hands and thank them for their efforts today. When Jordan gets to me, I finally lose it and start crying as we hug. I swear I've never cried on a football field before, but I've never played this hard or wanted a game this badly, either.

When I look over, I see Big Joe and Max hugging and Randy and Little Joe grabbing each other and Alex and Miguel hugging. More than anything, this is probably the moment I'll always remember from this day.

And the crowd keeps cheering.

When everyone finally makes it inside, the locker room is quiet except for a few slamming lockers, the sound of cleats on cement and heavy breathing. We're all just spent, emotionally and physically. Nobody is saying anything. No one knows what to say even if they felt like it.

We just can't believe we've lost because now it's starting to really hit us like an uppercut to the gut – or maybe even a little lower.

No one's even looking around. We're all just... numb.

"Listen up!" Coach Schebig says. We're so quiet, he doesn't even need to yell or say it twice.

"I know right now you are hurting, and you should be," he said. "I've never seen a team fight so hard as you guys did today. Right now they think they've proven that they are better than us, but we're not the ones their fans were booing at the end. They weren't the visiting team. They weren't the 30-point underdogs.

"We may have lost on the scoreboard, but we won everywhere else. I'm proud of you and you should be proud of yourselves. We accomplished some things with this game that will never be forgotten. Someday you'll look back at all of this and be very proud. That's OK, and I'm giving you permission... I'm encouraging you to feel good about this game. You have earned every bit of respect and honor you are going to receive because of your play today.

"I know we lost, but it's going to be OK, and I'm telling you it's OK to feel good about today. I can't imagine any one of you playing any better than you did today. How many times do you think you'll ever get to think that about a game, even one you win? Be proud, be strong and most of all be encouraged! You've earned that right. You may have won a lot more today besides the game."

Then he starts clapping.

At first no one knows what to do, so I start clapping and then Max and pretty soon everyone in the room is clapping. The noise keeps building as a few players start to yell, and then everyone is yelling until someone starts chanting, "No excuses!"

That's when I fully understand Coach is right. We don't have any excuses because we don't need them. We played our hearts out! Isn't that the only thing any of us can really control?

We're all chanting "No excuses!" for what seems like about a minute when Coach puts his fingers to his mouth and whistles to regain everyone's attention.

"As far as I'm concerned, 'No excuses,' still holds," he says. "We've still got some goals to accomplish this year, and I won't accept any excuses from anyone if we don't get them done. No excuses!"

That sets off another round of chanting and clapping and yelling until

Coach comes over to me to wrap his arms around me in another hug. Dang it! I'm getting misty-eyed again.

"You did everything right today," he says. "If Anthony hadn't gotten hurt, we'd have had a lot more options. You gave us a chance to win, which is remarkable. You can't believe how proud I am of you and how happy I am for you that you played so well today."

Everyone is hugging everyone else in the locker room. You'd think we just won the national championship instead of losing a game. It's unbelievable. This whole trip has been.

By the time things settle down, Randy James is standing near to tell me it's my turn in the press conference. He's sending Max and Jordan along with me. I really don't want to go. I just want to sit here and sulk for a few minutes, but if I know if I sit down for long I'll never get back up.

Inside a mid-sized room, there's a table sitting on a riser about 18 inches off the floor with three chairs behind it facing the small crowd of reporters. A microphone, three bottles of water and our name tags are placed on the table, with Max on my right, Jordan on my left and me in the middle – of course. I lean on Max until I can get my right foot up on the platform and then hobble over to sit down. Randy stands off to the side and when I nod at him, he calls on Win to ask the first question.

"What happened on the last play?"

"We ran it perfectly, but they defensed it perfectly," I say. "I don't think we've run that more than twice since we've left here, but Coach Jackson obviously remembered it or he wouldn't have called time out. Give him all the credit on that one. I never saw Duncan, but that was by design."

Randy points to Rich Griffis.

"I know we're never supposed to ask this, but it's what we all want to know: How do you feel right now? Do you have any regrets about this entire week?"

I look at Max first, and he simply says, "None."

"Maybe I will later," Jordan says, "but right now I'm just really proud of my team. We came in here as huge underdogs and we played as hard as we possibly could and almost beat a Top 10 team on their field without our best running back. I take tremendous pride in that, and if any of them say they don't respect us now, they are lying. We earned that respect."

"Lars?" Rich asks.

"How do I feel?" I say, blowing a slow breath out and leaning back in my chair. "I'm sore, I'm beat up and I'm heartbroken, but I am not defeated. One of the reasons we wanted to come back here was to prove that we are all just as good as anyone else on that field if we'd only had a fair chance to show that. We did that, and no one can take that away from us. We now have proven we can play with anybody in the country under the toughest circumstances. Now the IWU fans got to see what they missed out on."

Randy points at Pete DiPrimio.

"Do you still feel bitter at Coach Jackson?"

"No way," I say, "because that means I would not have gotten to play with Coach Schebig for three more years, and I would have really missed that because I love that man and I love playing for him. I also would not have gotten to know my brother Jordan here or the rest of my teammates. I have no problem saying I love being at UC-Camarillo.

"For a couple of years I always wondered what I was missing here, but now I realize I'm not missing a thing. I am humbled to represent the Thunderbolts and all that they stand for. I have made lifetime friends there, who have stood by me through this entire process and those people are every bit as loyal and honest and respectful as the people in Talbott and Arlington. If I can't come home again, I'll be very happy building a new home there."

"How do you feel about Andrew Crow and Duncan Welker," Wendy Bartle asks.

"If they play that hard all the time, they're going to make a lot of money in the NFL," I say. "So will B.J. Cowen, Jim Wallace and maybe even Mason Parker. You guys have no idea how good Mason is because he's never been allowed to show it. I hope some NFL team gives him a chance. They'll be surprised."

"What have you learned from this process?" Win asks.

"If you want it bad enough, you can do it," Max says. "If you don't, that's your fault."

"That everything Lars says, he believes he can back it up," Jordan says. "I'd follow him anywhere."

Hearing that, I need to take a couple of swallows of water to slow things down a bit.

"For me, it all comes back to something Coach Snuff always taught us and drilled into us," I say. "It's not about what the other guy is doing, it's all about what you are doing. Did you prepare enough? Are you willing to commit enough and be disciplined enough so that it only matters what you are doing and not what the other guy is trying to do? Are we smart enough to make the adjustments with what we are presented? Everything Coach Snuff taught us is still true. We could have won today, but we didn't. We have no excuses, and, frankly, we don't need any.

``Thank you for having us back, everyone. It was fun talking to you, but I've got a very pretty lady who's been waiting long enough for me."

CHAPTER 41

Despite wanting to hurry so I can go out and see Mom, Dad and Mikala, it takes me more than an hour to shower, then get my ankle and shoulder taped up and finally get dressed with the help of a manager. The hot water rolling down my back felt so good I feared falling asleep.

Except for the managers and trainers, I'm the last one to leave. As I look around the locker room, I remember all those times as a kid when I would have done anything to get dressed here every week, when I thought I would live and die with how the Sagamores did that day.

It's not the same anymore, but neither am I, thank goodness. I realize now that wasn't really my dream. My dream was to find teammates like I have to play with and build with and grow with. I am so blessed.

I'm just so happy that I truly have no regrets on this game. We truly left everything we had out on the field, because there's nothing left but to move ahead. I grab my crutches and start hobbling toward he door. Even that's more of a struggle than normal because of my left shoulder. Maybe I am getting old.

I'm halfway toward the door when I look up and see my dad standing there.

"They send you in as the search party?" I ask.

"Pretty much," he says.

Then he grabs my left crutch and sticks his shoulder under mine.

"I'm very proud of you," he says. "You stood up for your teammates and yourself today and showed the kind of man you really are."

"Aw, Dad," I say because for once in my life I don't know what else to say.

"You're going to hear a lot of praise for the things you did today. You earned it. Just remember that tomorrow that won't mean anything so temper it. Just remember who you are, and who you represent"

"Always," I say somehow. "I just wish we didn't have to go back tomorrow. I'd like to spend a few more days here with you guys and Mikala. Coach would let me, but I don't think that's the right thing to do now."

"No, it's not."

And then Mikala comes running into my arms, and she's crying and shaking.

"I was so worried about you," she bawls into my good shoulder. "And I'm so proud of you. You did everything you said you would."

"It's over, Baby," I say and then I shut up and just hold her.

Then Mom comes in and joins our hug, and finally, Dad, and we stay that way for what seems like five minutes. I don't want to let go, and, in a way, I realize I won't ever have to.

Then I feel Mom slip a small box into my jacket pocket, and I look over at her and she nods.

"You can look at that later, but I made up my mind that you can have it," she says and then whispers into my ear, "Grandma would be very pleased."

I'm so shocked at that statement, that I have no reply so we all hold on a little longer.

``Let's go get something to eat, and then I've got a long appointment with a hot tub," I say, and everybody laughs.

CHAPTER 42

Maybe I shouldn't have been surprised, but so many things about this entire process knocks me on my butt. The hardest part of Sunday isn't getting out of bed, though that takes a while, or saying goodbye to Mom, Dad and Mikala at the airport, though that takes a little longer. At least we know we'll see each other soon, and Mom has made sure this Christmas will be very special.

The hardest part comes after the plane ride home when the busses pull up back at the school. Though we left Arlington at noon, Indiana time, it's 4 p.m., local time, when we arrive in front of the Krieg Family Athletic Complex.

When the busses stop, there are hundreds of fans waiting for us like we are the conquering heroes. I see the Hazeltines, fellow students and a ton of the kids from last summer's football camp, including Isabelle Miller and her family, the Sosenheimer boys, Cole Foreman and Kenny Wiegmann and just all kinds of recognizable faces, including President Stein sitting on a lawn chair as if she owns the place, which basically, she does. Lots of fans are tailgating in the parking lot, and there are a few signs saying things like ``We Love You Bolts!'' and ``You made us proud!''

I just want to go home and crawl into bed and forget about this week. We've still got practice tomorrow because there's another game coming up Saturday. Right now, this has to be the priority, though. I also know talking to these kids is going to be the hardest part because as much as we wanted to win, they wanted it 10 times more for us. The Sosenheimer boys in particular sent me weekly letters of encouragement during the season. Time to put on my happy face.

The kids are playing some sort of football game on the grass next to the building, but they stop and come running when they see us unload off the bus. Though I'm on crutches, I almost get gang-tackled by the three Sosenheimer boys as they all try to wrap around my waist.

"Whoa, guys!" I say, raising my voice a little. "I'm injured here so please be gentle."

"You're hurt?" Kedrick says, looking up at me. "I'll bet it was that rotten Crow player! I hate him, and I hate Welker!"

"Yeah, he did his share, but I'm OK and you shouldn't hate them. They just did what they were supposed to. I'm just a little sore and need to take it easy if I want to be able to play next week."

"We cheered so hard for you," Hunter says. "We got up early even though it wasn't a school day, and we yelled and screamed the whole game."

"And then he cried at the end," Kedrick says.

"Did not!"

"Yeah, you did, so don't lie about it!"

"Well, at least I wasn't the only one. You guys were, too!"

"That's OK, Hunter," I say, reaching down to put a hand on his shoulder. "Thank you, guys. It means a lot to me to hear that. Really, thank you."

"But why did you lose?" Drake asks, lip quivering.

What do you say to that? I think my lip is starting to quiver the more I look at them and see their disappointment.

"Aw, I don't know, buddy," I start. "You know we tried real hard and sometimes that's just not enough so you have to learn from games like this so you can do better next time."

"But you always told us we can do anything if we want it bad enough," Hunter says. "Didn't you want it bad enough?"

"Oh, we wanted it bad enough," I say. "Let me sit down, OK?"

I hobble over to a nearby lawn chair and flop into it. I can finally put these blasted crutches aside for at least a minute.

"Come over here, guys," I say, pulling them close. "Sometimes, when you want something so badly, it can change the thing that you want so much. I think that's what happened here. We wanted this game so much that we missed how it was changing us and making us better because of it. We focused so much on the game that we missed what was really important about it. I think in the long run the things we received from this are more important than the win we didn't get. Does that make sense?"

"Kinda," Kedrick says.

"Does that mean you're not going to lose again?" Drake asks.

"I sure hope so, but the most important thing is do you guys still believe you can do anything you want if you want it bad enough and if you work hard enough at it?"

"Yes," they all three say.

"Even though we lost?"

"Yes."

"That's good, because that means we succeeded more than any win can mean. Sometimes all you need is a little perspective to see what you've really won. You may not understand that now, but someday you will, and I think I finally do. I won so much more from this whole experience than just a football game.

"Maybe someday when you guys come to play for the Thunderbolts, I'll coach you and we can go back there and beat the Sagamores next time. Wouldn't that be fun?"

"You bet!" Hunter says. "We'll starting working to get ready right now!"

Yes, it really would be fun.

"Have you guys ever heard of snipe hunting?"

ABOUT THE AUTHOR

Blake Sebring is the author of eight books including the novels "The Lake Effect," "Homecoming Game" and "Lethal Ghost." He has worked for The News-Sentinel in Fort Wayne for more than 30 years, winning national awards for his coverage of hockey, tennis and volleyball and in 2015 was the youngest-ever inductee into the Indiana Sportswriters and Sportscasters Hall of Fame. More of his work can be found at blakesebring.com and at news-sentinel